Leah Chishugi grew up in eastern Congo before moving to Rwanda. In 1994 she was caught up in the conflict but managed to escape to Uganda, and later South Africa and the UK where she was granted asylum and trained as a nurse. She has set up a charity called Everything is a Benefit to support women and children in eastern Congo.

A LONG WAY FROM PARADISE

Surviving the Rwandan Genocide

LEAH CHISHUGI

virago

VIRAGO

This edition first published in 2010 by Virago Press

A CIP catalogue record for this book
is available from the British Library

ISBN 978-1-84408-657-3

Typeset in Bembo by M Rules
Printed and bound in Great Britain by
Clays Ltd, St Ives plc

Papers used by Virago are natural, renewable and
recyclable products sourced from well-managed forests and certified
in accordance with the rules of the Forest Stewardship Council.

Mixed Sources
Product group from well-managed
forests and other controlled sources
www.fsc.org Cert no. SGS-COC-004081
© 1996 Forest Stewardship Council
FSC

Virago Press
An imprint of
Little, Brown Book Group
100 Victoria Embankment
London EC4Y 0DY

An Hachette UK Company
www.hachette.co.uk

www.virago.co.uk

A SHORT HISTORY OF RWANDA AND DEMOCRATIC REPUBLIC OF CONGO

Zaire/Democratic Republic of Congo

Established as a Belgian colony in 1908, the Republic of Congo became independent in 1960.

Colonel Joseph Mobutu seized power and declared himself president in a November 1965 coup. He subsequently changed his name to Mobutu Sese Seko and the name of the country to Zaire. Mobutu held on to power for thirty-two years. He was a brutal and corrupt leader.

When Mobutu was driven out of government, the country became Democratic Republic of Congo.

Rwanda

In 1959, three years before the creation of Rwanda (formerly part of the Belgian colony of Ruanda-Urundi), the majority ethnic group, the Hutus, overthrew the ruling Tutsi king. Over the next few years, thousands of Tutsis were killed, and approximately

150,000 driven into exile in neighbouring countries. The children of these exiles later formed a rebel group, the Rwandan Patriotic Front (RPF), and began a civil war in 1990.

Paul Kagame, who went into exile in Uganda with his family at the age of two, became leader of the RPF.

The war, along with several political and economic upheavals, exacerbated ethnic tensions, culminating in April 1994 in the genocide of roughly 800,000 Tutsis and moderate Hutus. The genocide was triggered by the shooting-down of Rwandan President Habyarimana's plane on 6 April 1994, as it came in to land in Kigali Airport. Extremist Hutus are thought to be behind the attack.

A resolution by the UN Security Council condemned the mass killings but did not use the word 'genocide'. If this term had been used, UN troops would have been legally obliged to 'prevent and punish' the perpetrators. Instead they stood by.

Rwanda/Democratic Republic of Congo (formerly Zaire)

The Tutsi rebels defeated the Hutu regime and ended the killing in July 1994, setting up an interim government of national unity, but approximately two million Hutu refugees – many fearing Tutsi retribution – fled to neighbouring Burundi, Tanzania, Uganda and Zaire.

Many have returned to Rwanda, but several thousand remained in refugee camps in Zaire and formed an extremist group, determined to win back power in Rwanda. In 1996 Rwanda moved against the camps and invaded Zaire, eventually taking the capital, Kinshasa. This led to the toppling of the Mobutu regime and Laurent Kabila took power. He renamed the country the Democratic Republic of Congo (DRC).

In August 1998 Kabila's regime was challenged by a second

Rwandan invasion, backed by Uganda. Angola, Zimbabwe, Chad, Namibia and Sudan all supported the DRC. A ceasefire was signed in July 1999 by the DRC, Congolese armed rebel groups, Angola, Namibia, Rwanda, Uganda and Zimbabwe, but sporadic fighting continued.

Laurent Kabila was assassinated in January 2001 and his son Joseph succeeded him as President of the DRC. A transitional government was set up in July 2003, with Joseph Kabila continuing as President and four vice-presidents representing the former government, former rebel groups, the political opposition and civil society.

Kabila was successful in negotiating the withdrawal of Rwandan forces occupying eastern Congo, although rebel groups allied to the Rwandan government remained there. Hutu extremists then launched a new armed group, the Democratic Forces for the Liberation of Rwanda (FDLR), many of whose leaders had overseen the Rwandan genocide. Laurent Nkunda, leader of a Tutsi-controlled rebel faction, the National Congress for the Defence of the People, said it was protecting Tutsis in eastern Congo. But the Congolese government viewed Nkunda, who has been accused of war crimes, as a tool used by Rwanda to continue to destabilise eastern Congo.

In 2009 Kabila and the Rwandan President Paul Kagame overcame their past enmity to launch a joint military operation to destroy the FDLR. This initiative was backed by the UN force in Congo, MONUC.

PROLOGUE

I held my breath: almost at the border now. I had crossed this part of the border from Rwanda into Zaire so many times before without any problem. Just a couple of years ago, when I was still a carefree child, I clambered up the brilliant green hill behind my uncle's house in Gisenyi and skipped from one country into another, nodded through by smiling border guards. But that was before the killing started.

Slaughtered bodies, some without heads or limbs, were strewn around us. Their blood had pooled and crusted on the rich earth beneath them. The expressions of horror as the machetes rained down on them were frozen for ever on to their faces.

And the smell was everywhere. After three weeks of hell I had not managed to accustom myself to this terrible, acrid smell of rotting corpses. Where was the beautiful Gisenyi I knew, with its fragrant flowers and cooling trees? I glanced at the carnage all around me, certain that my Gisenyi would never return.

Just keep going, just keep going, not much further, almost there, I kept repeating to myself, over and over again, trying to brainwash myself that we were going to make it. I wasn't sure why I wanted to survive after all this but somehow I did. Everybody told us that we'd never make it as far as Gisenyi alive, but miraculously we had. Ten minutes more and we would be safe. Our plan was to cross the border from behind Gisenyi's St Fidel's University.

I knew the Interahamwe could not be far away. They were like human landmines that we were desperately trying not to step on. If fear had a smell they would have been able to sniff out our bedraggled little group from ten kilometres away: Donata, my son's loyal nanny, who was just a couple of years older than me; Jean-Luc, my precious baby, who was just six months old; a small group of abandoned children and babies we had collected on our journey through hell; and my Uncle Jean, an important member of the Tutsi-led Rwandan Patriotic Front, whom I had just pulled out from under a bed in his home where he'd been hiding. He was too weak to lift the heavy bed off himself and would have slowly died there had we not arrived and discovered him. If only I had left him to die under that bed.

We crept along the path, desperately trying not to draw attention to ourselves. We had barely eaten or drunk since the killing began on 6 April, and had not been able to wash our bodies or our clothes. But now I knew that the stink of unwashed living bodies is infinitely pleasanter than the smell of the dead.

All of us were suffering from a depth of mental and physical shock and exhaustion that we had never experienced before.

Then we saw them, a collection of dark, glaring shapes moving slowly and deliberately towards us. I was sure that all of our hearts momentarily stopped beating. They weren't wearing their uniforms but we knew immediately who they were. They were brandishing clubs studded with nails and smiled terrible smiles when they saw my uncle, whom they recognised immediately. Because he was an important figure in the RPF he was a great prize for the Interahamwe.

Their smiles broadened into grins as they surrounded their prey. We stood frozen and helpless as they started beating him all over with their clubs until his skin was so punctured by the nails that he changed from a black person to a red one. Again and again they battered him. I was horrified to see that my poor uncle was still alive. He was dying in agony and his eyes were still open, aware of everything that was happening to him.

'Please, please just shoot him. Hasn't he suffered enough?' I yelled at the Interahamwe.

'No, we can't do that, we can't waste a bullet on a cockroach like him,' said one of them, smirking at the suffering he was causing. Then he pulled something out of my uncle's opened chest; I don't know which organ it was. I looked away, covering my eyes and screaming.

'Please let me shoot him myself then, if you won't do it yourselves,' I begged. Even slitting his throat would have been kinder.

The man slowly shook his head and walked towards me as my uncle's massacred body finally fell into a useless heap on the ground. I prayed that his soul had flown somewhere peaceful.

I had seen many terrible things in the last three weeks but I had remained silent, partly to keep Jean-Luc calm and partly so that we could avoid detection as we ran from one place to the next. Jean-Luc and the other babies Donata and I had collected along the way all knew instinctively that to make a noise was dangerous and miraculously none of them had so much as whimpered.

But what I had just witnessed was too much. This was the first time I'd seen the slaughter of my own flesh and blood. All my last shreds of composure shrivelled and I screamed louder than I had ever heard myself scream before. The children and babies followed my lead and started screaming too. Donata collapsed and vomited. There was no food in her stomach; only blood and bile came up as she retched.

The man who had taken the lead in battering my uncle came closer; the odour of sweat and killing overwhelmed me. I looked into his dark eyes, shining with adrenalin and dead to any of the emotions I recognised as human. I smelled alcohol on his sour breath. With one deft slash he cut my stomach open. I felt sticky blood running down my thighs but was too shocked to feel pain. I kept saying to myself, I must pick up Jean-Luc, I can't be separated from him.

I fell to the ground, too weak to move. I felt arms lift me and knew from the putrid smell and the feel of soft flesh and hard bones that I had been thrown on to a pile of dead bodies. Then everything went black.

CHAPTER ONE

The sun always shone on my childhood. I was born in Rwanda but at the age of two we moved next door to eastern Zaire, a lush, green place blessed with trees heavy with mangoes and papayas and dense forests of scented trees. It was also the place with the best schools in this part of Africa, built by the Belgians who had colonised us.

I grew up with my parents and my nine brothers and sisters in a state of more or less perfect happiness. We had comfortable homes in Goma and Bukavu, the two largest towns in the region. My parents were both Tutsis. They loved each other very deeply and made a good team. Both worked very hard, began their adult lives as teachers and then became wealthy, successful coffee farmers.

I was born in 1976, during the reign of the dictator Mobutu Sese Seko, fourteen years after Zaire proclaimed independence from the Belgians, who had treated so much of the population cruelly and plundered so many of the country's mineral riches. I was blissfully unaware of the politics of my country, both past and present, and lived in a happy bubble, protected by my parents' wealth and love. Maman was a very intelligent woman and like Papa she had a real eye for business. Her mother died giving birth to her and she was raised by Belgian nuns in eastern Zaire. As a result she had a different perspective on life from many other people in the area. The nuns instructed her in the ways of well-bred Europeans, teaching her how to write in a precise, flowery script, how to do dainty needlepoint and how to cook traditional European dishes like omelettes and spaghetti bolognese. She sang the Latin mass in the sweetest voice and the nuns taught her how to sing opera too. Her surrogate mothers were unable to import statues of the Virgin Mary into their Zairian church and instead chose my mother when she was a young girl to be a living, breathing, walking representation of her. She was paraded up and down in a flowing robe and worshippers threw flowers at her as a mark of respect.

When Papa came across Maman as a beautiful, accomplished teenager he was too shy to approach her. His older brother was forced to play matchmaker and introduced them to each other. Maman was her poor mother's first- and last-born and she had always longed for a big family, something she managed to achieve with the ten of us. My oldest sister Brigitte was born nine years before me, followed at regular intervals by the rest of us – Micheline, Christine, Pauline, Timotei, me, Jean-Claude, Henri, Sans Souci and Alice.

Many Belgians remained in eastern Zaire, pursuing their businesses extracting and exporting Zaire's minerals. Some of these Belgian businessmen came to our home in the evenings to drink, smoke cigars and do business deals with Papa. Maman and I both hated having them in the house. I begged Papa to stop smoking the cigars because I couldn't bear the smell of them on him.

At one time Maman ran a European-style bar in Goma that was very popular with businesspeople and foreigners. Mobutu, who liked to vacation in the temperate climes of eastern Zaire, was a regular visitor. She was the first to import beer from Belgium. Most people in the area drank the bitter local beer, so the European variety was a real novelty for them.

Papa had studied to be an accountant in Belgium and Germany before he became a coffee farmer. It was thanks to this training that he handled the financial side of his coffee business so skilfully. He told us that the Germans had treated dark-skinned Africans like him very badly. I didn't really understand what he was saying to me. I was used to seeing people from many different backgrounds with a variety of different skin colours in our home. Racism was beyond my experience.

Maman was equally at ease as a refined woman of sophisticated European tastes and as an African village woman. I remember she used an expensive cream in a lilac bottle called Ladies Day Cream that Papa bought for her on his regular business trips to Europe, along with all the latest fashionable clothes for us children. But Maman also visited women in the nearby villages, sometimes spending a week or more with them, arriving laden with the traditional Tutsi gift of milk or sometimes banana wine.

I loved living in Goma as a child. The town rolls away from the shore of Lake Kivu and you can see many beautiful birds nesting and swooping around the lake. If you walk past the big Roman Catholic church, there are many elegant houses on both sides. At the roundabout is the post office, which once so efficiently delivered letters. Now it is silent, without post or postmen. The streets were once lined with cooling trees and cacti, and roads were made of smooth, white concrete. Now everything is broken and spoiled, as if a giant gorilla has marched through the streets, trampling everything underfoot.

Everybody loved Goma because it never got too hot. We enjoyed the rain and unlike in so many other parts of Zaire we never got the thick red dust which the earth spat up lodging in our hair and our clothes and up our nostrils.

Children played football freely in the street, and rode their bicycles near the town's pavilion. Every house had a beautiful garden. Ours was full of roses and lilies; Papa was very good with his hands and he loved gardening. Whenever you walked into our compound the heady scent of lilies greeted you. Papa built a pond on which floated yellow and white water lilies; flowers were one of his passions in life. He never worked at weekends and liked nothing better than pottering around in the garden, working alongside our gardeners, teaching us all the different flower names. We had big trees in our garden with small yellow flowers that had a powerful perfume, as well as beautiful papaya and mango trees. Not everyone had papaya trees and ours were famous for their juicy fruit. We also grew strawberries, bananas, passionfruit and avocados as big as your head.

Although we children were many we never had to crowd together, as our house was a large villa with eight bedrooms. My four older sisters were often closeted together, whispering about things like periods and nail varnish that I was too young to understand. I was a tomboy and played mostly with my brother Jean-Claude, who was two years younger than me. Together we got ourselves into all sorts of scrapes. One Saturday morning when I was six we woke up while the rest of the household was still sleeping. Feeling hungry, we tiptoed into the kitchen and decided to make ourselves an omelette the way we had seen Maman do it. We got out the heavy frying pan, poured some oil in and then broke every single egg we found in the fridge into the pan. Then we waited and waited but nothing happened. We didn't realise that the stove needed to be switched on before the eggs would transform themselves into an omelette! Worried that we would get into trouble for using up all the eggs for nothing, we crept into the henhouse to get some more eggs. But one of the hens attacked my brother and we fled screaming. After that Jean-Claude completely went off omelettes.

The house was full of pets and I adored our dog, Max, and three cats. My favourite cat was called Irma. She was unusual-looking, a beautiful grey and white with flashes of ginger on her forehead. She particularly loved the local fish, tilapia, fresh milk and sweet potato.

As well as the dog and cats we had a monkey with a pale face called Kiki. 'Close the doors, close the doors,' Maman was always calling, because Kiki liked nothing better than to sneak into the kitchen and steal bananas from the bowl.

Those times, long gone, are imprinted on my memory for ever: the heady perfume of the roses mixed with the aroma of meat – from one of our cows, goats or sheep – grilling on the barbecue, and the piercing calls of the many birds that perched in our trees, the sounds of children laughing and Papa's deep-throated chuckle as he listened to our stories about school.

Although I wasn't the youngest I was called Bébé from an early age and the name stuck. Friends and family cooed over me when I was little, calling me '*joli bébé*', and even after the younger children were born I was determined to hang on to this flattering pet name. Whenever my parents referred to the little ones as Bébé I defended the title as mine and mine alone.

'I'm the one to be called Bébé, not the others,' I protested.

The children who came after Jean-Claude were much younger than me and I didn't have a lot to do with them when we were growing up. As children we more or less divided into three groups: the older girls, the tomboys in the middle, and the little ones.

Maman used to tell me that I was different from the other children in the family because from an early age I was interested in adult matters. She sometimes invited her female friends round to sew and chat together, and I always liked to creep into this circle of lively women and absorb their conversations about the births, marriages, deaths and other life-cycle events in the neighbourhood. Whenever there was bad news to report about somebody my eyes welled up with tears. None of the other children showed this interest or concern, and Maman often commented on it.

'Leah, you have a big heart. You should look after it,' she said. 'Don't ever let any obstacle get in the way of who you are.'

From the age of four I was also given the nickname

Mukecheru, which means 'old person', because I loved spending time with old people and listening to their words of wisdom.
I wondered how I could be Bébé and Mukecheru at the same
time, but was just happy to have two pet names rather than one.

I started my education at a kindergarten run by nuns in Goma,
followed by Chipuko primary school. Papa had a long, yellow
Volkswagen imported from Germany and I and my cousins who
lived near by piled into it every morning so that he could drive
us to school. We were always laughing and chattering together.
My older sisters either attended a different school or had finished
school, and my younger siblings also attended a different school;
so apart from Jean-Claude I didn't see much of the others during
the week.

I was always trying to find ways to spend more time with my
beloved Maman, and sometimes I used to hide in her little red
Mini and beg her to take me to school instead of Papa. Now and
again she relented and took me herself, but at other times she was
too busy and sternly told me to climb into the Volkswagen and
to stop making a fuss. 'Bébé, you must do as you are told. Get
into the car with Papa now and stop being such a silly girl.'
Morning school was from 7.30 a.m. until 12 noon. Maman
always came home at lunchtime to cook for us. We ate vegetable
soup, meat, cassava leaves, rice and potatoes, slept for half an hour
and then went back to school. My parents were very hard-work-
ing but they always made time for their large brood of children.

After primary school, I attended one of the best schools in the
country, College Al Fajire. Most of the teachers were Belgian or
Belgian-trained and standards were high. Papa was passionately
committed to ensuring we got the very best education. My parents were very keen that I spoke good French and arrangements
were made at school for us to have French pen friends so that we
could improve our use of the language. For many years I corre-
sponded with a boy called Philippe, who lived in Paris. He was
a similar age to me and we exchanged stories about our school

lives and our families. Teachers at the school commented on my flair for languages. I picked up French much more quickly than the other students and they noticed that I could move effortlessly and accurately between Swahili, Lingala and Kinyarwandan, while some of the other children struggled to do this. 'She'll have to get a job as a translator at the United Nations,' one teacher joked to my parents.

Maman paid regular visits to sick people in the local hospital. When I was seven I begged her to take me with her in the hope that I could cheer them up with jokes and funny stories from school. But she always refused to let me go with her.

'No Bébé, you're too young,' she would reply firmly.

But I was a stubborn child and one day when Maman set off for the hospital I hid behind a tree and followed her from a distance, only announcing my presence when she had almost reached the hospital and I was too far from home to be sent back.

'Bébé, you really are the limit,' said Maman, half laughing, half cross. After that she let me accompany her, or sometimes she allowed me to go with one of her female friends. I could see that some of the patients didn't have many visitors to talk to them and bring them food and I felt sad for them. (Our hospitals did not provide food or drink for the patients, and they relied on family and friends to bring in whatever they needed.)

When I visited the hospital with Maman's friend I raced home to give Maman a report about the condition of the patients. I remember one young girl of eighteen had an ectopic pregnancy. She was screaming in agony and didn't know what was going on. Maman was very surprised when I relayed her problem in precise detail and managed to remember and pronounce the word 'Fallopian' properly.

'Leah, you should be a doctor when you grow up,' she smiled.

'Yes, Maman,' I replied. 'That's exactly what I want to be.'

She cooked vegetable soup for the young girl in the hospital, and I also took milk and sugar for her from our kitchen so she could have hot tea in the morning.

Maman was very generous and was always giving food to children who were hungry. She often told people who didn't have much to eat to come to the house and pick up any surplus food. 'The food you don't share with your neighbour becomes poison,' she always said. We had lots of fat, sleek cows and they produced large quantities of milk. Maman made sure this was distributed widely. We used bamboo containers called *ingongoro* to give gifts of milk to friends and neighbours. In our culture to give somebody milk is to show them courtesy. In Tutsi culture cows and the milk they produce are greatly respected.

Our parents encouraged us to study, to be good children and to respect everyone. The golden rule was to treat everyone equally, no matter what background they came from or how rich or poor they were. Maman was a very humble person and she would sit and talk to anyone. It didn't matter who they were or where they came from.

The first thing Papa said to the children when he got home from work was 'Have you eaten, taken a bath and studied?'

We always nodded dutifully in response to all three questions. Even if we had been playing rather than doing our homework we all raced to the long table in the dining room and buried our heads in our books as soon as Papa walked through the door. Although there were a lot of us our parents always wanted to hear from every one of us what had happened that day at school.

Maman always tried to teach me that while we were lucky to be wealthy, money was ultimately a useless commodity. One day she said, 'Do you know what, Leah? You can wear a watch or bracelet and it can leave a mark on your wrist, but you mustn't go to people and say you used to have it because it doesn't matter any more if you don't have it now. You have to live with just what you have at the time and make the best of it.'

Maman had had a beautiful red Mini. But she had an accident

in it and it couldn't be repaired. I used to love that car and for years afterwards I said, 'Do you remember that car of yours?'

'What you don't have any more you shouldn't talk about,' Maman said firmly. I knew the subject was closed.

Maman was always full of fun. Sometimes I shortened her name to Ma. There was a popular song called '*Ma ta ra*', and whenever I called out, 'Ma' to her she slapped her hip and sang 'Ta ra.'

As far as I was concerned Maman was the cleverest and most talented woman in the world. She was wonderful at sewing anything, from dresses to curtains, taught me the way to cook chicken perfectly and showed me how to bake bread. Even though Maman worked hard she always found time to bake bread every evening so it would be fresh and ready for our breakfast the following morning. I always drifted off to sleep with the delicious scent of baking bread filling my nostrils.

I grew up without seeing people falling ill with malaria and illnesses from bad water. Everyone had electricity, even in the small dwellings, and a good sewage system. I really did have a very lucky childhood.

Most of our servants lived with us during the week, going home to visit their families at the weekends. Maman loved to clean our house when the servants had gone – she was particularly fond of polishing the windows. While she was cleaning I used to trail round after her, chattering about what had happened at school.

We tried our best to keep up to date with European culture, which we considered much more fashionable than our home-grown Zairian equivalent. I had a Walkman in the mid-1980s that one of my friends who grew up in Belgium brought for me. Whitney Houston and Madonna were my favourite singers and my friends and I made up dances to all their songs. We couldn't speak English so we adapted the words of Michael Jackson's songs into Swahili, Lingala and French. Some of the lyrics we reinvented in a mix of the languages we did know went something like this:

'Be careful of what is in front of you before you put your foot in shit.'

I'm sure Michael Jackson never sang of any such thing, but at least the words we invented fitted in with the tune.

I was always trying to run out of the house to avoid the house rules of a siesta and the after-lunch milk because I hated both. I wanted to play, not sleep. I used to sneak out to my friends' houses and came back covered in dust. I was constantly grounded for running off during the siesta. When my big sister Pauline was sent to bed she didn't want to sleep either and in the end my parents gave up and let her play in the compound.

As well as my little brother and partner in crime, Jean-Claude, I spent a lot of time with a group of friends from my school and neighbourhood. Often one of my friends would come over and say, 'Let's go and buy some bread and sausages on the street and go up into the hills for a picnic.'

I always jumped at this suggestion. 'Bravo,' I cried. 'What are we waiting for? Let's go right now.'

We had to keep these purchases a secret from our parents, who banned us from eating street food, which they declared unhygienic. We were instructed to eat only at home or at the homes of friends that our parents approved of. Of course we ignored them and continued buying street food whenever we could get away with it. My favourite dish was rice and delicately spiced beans. Sometimes this dish was made for us at home but it never tasted quite as good as the street version.

Our home in Goma was very close to the airport, and one of our games was creeping through the perimeter fence. In those innocent days there was almost no security at this tiny African airport. Plastic cutlery from the flights was a big novelty for us. We fished the used cutlery out of the bins and then used it to furnish our pretend houses. We had to make sure our parents didn't find out what we were up to but often they were very busy at work and didn't see us.

I developed a passion for tennis and spent many happy Saturdays and Sundays playing tennis at Hotel Karibu, built during the colonial period with beautifully landscaped rolling lawns overlooking Lake Kivu. I started playing at the age of eight, after I got chatting to a student who played and successfully begged him to teach me.

One of my favourite outings was to the beautiful Parc de la Rwindi. There we saw monkeys jumping freely along the paths and swinging through the trees without a care in the world. Later, when war blighted Rwanda and Zaire, some of the Interahamwe killed the monkeys and ate them. There were big lions and tigers roaming the park and you could see elephants, antelopes, giraffes and zebras passing. It was very exciting for me to have such magnificent creatures on our doorstep. I never tired of seeing them.

The keepers looked after them very well and loved them as much as members of their own family. Sometimes we went there during our summer holidays. Mobutu loved to stay in the park when he holidayed in eastern Zaire.

There was great excitement in my primary school when the teacher announced that Mobutu would be visiting in a couple of weeks. A collective gasp of anticipation went round the classroom when the teacher added that the two best-behaved students would be chosen to be flower girls for our president.

All of us wanted to be chosen and for the next two weeks nobody uttered a cross word to another child or teacher, everybody showed kindness to others and nobody handed their homework in late.

I was overjoyed when I was chosen with another girl and for the next few days was too excited to eat or sleep. I was just six years old and it was a thrilling moment for me. I was shaking with nerves in the special white dress that Maman had bought for me and warned me sternly must be kept clean at all costs. My older sister Pauline was very good at styling hair and she put my hair into two bunches which swung behind me every time I moved my head.

I trembled with awe and excitement when Mobutu stepped out of his fancy car. He looked like a giant to me, especially his hands. I had never seen such huge hands before. Nervously I handed over my bunch of flowers to him. All he said to me was 'Merci beaucoup,' and smiled. I felt very proud that I had given flowers to the President and that he had said two words to me. He watched a display of dancing, applauded politely and then got into his car and went off. I never saw him again.

Yes, Mobutu was a dictator and did many terrible things. But when I was growing up everyone I knew, whether they were rich or poor, had water and electricity, and every child went to school. Zaire used to be one of the best places to study medicine and the treatment at the hospitals used to be of a very high standard. Now our country, which has had its name changed to Democratic Republic of Congo, is in a terrible mess and the gap between the rich and the poor seems to have grown much wider.

My parents purchased part of Lake Vichumbi in Rutshuru. This purchase conferred the right to fish there for tilapia and catfish. I was too young to fish but enjoyed eating whatever was caught and freshly grilled.

Sometimes we visited the volcano Nyiragongo. In the years before its devastating eruption in January 2002, which ripped deep, angry channels into the earth and spluttered toxic ash for miles, it was a lovely, tranquil spot. Now the earth around it is charred and barren and they say that if you cut your flesh on a piece of volcanic rock the cut never heals. When I was a child the land around the volcano was lush and green and peaceful.

Although tennis was my favourite sport I was happy to join in with any sport or physical exercise that was on offer. One day we had come from Lake Tanganyika on the border of Burundi and Congo, where we often swam. You can stand up in parts of the water and I was used to being able to take a swimming break and stand up whenever I wanted to catch my breath. We moved on to Lake Kivu and I forgot that it was much deeper than Tanganyika. When I tried to stand up I was disorientated to feel nothing underneath my feet and almost drowned. I went down twice and came up again and started to cry out, realising that if somebody didn't rescue me soon I would die. At that point my friends realised that I wasn't just messing around and dived in to save me.

Everything happened too fast for me to feel fear. I gasped and gulped as they pulled me out. My belly was swollen with lake water. I vomited it up and started to feel better. I made my friends swear not to tell my parents or my swimming days would have been over for ever.

That was the first time that I almost died.

CHAPTER TWO

Many Tutsis in eastern Zaire were involved in coffee-farming, other agricultural businesses or mining the country's valuable minerals. Even as a little girl I was aware of undercurrents of bad feeling towards us Tutsis from Hutus, but nothing ever happened to threaten my sense of happiness and security. I knew that Hutus and Tutsis spoke the same language, shared the same customs, ate the same food and intermarried. The main difference between us was in appearance. Tutsis were generally taller and lighter-skinned than Hutus, with longer, thinner necks and noses.

At school some of the Zairian children sang horrible songs in Swahili about Tutsis, saying, '*Banya Rwanda bote barudiye kwabe*' – 'Go back to your country Rwanda.'

I used to go crying to Maman saying, 'They called me a Tutsi again.'

'Well you are a Tutsi and you should be proud of that,' Maman replied.

One of my big sisters was always trying to widen and flatten my nose with her fingers, saying, 'I don't want you to be bullied at school because you have such a Tutsi nose, Bébé.'

Sometimes we slept with plugs of cotton wool up our nostrils in the hope of widening our noses. Now and again people in the local markets shouted, 'Tutsi get out.' But we didn't have too many problems and because life was so much fun I managed to push any unpleasant thoughts to the back of my mind.

Unlike my sisters and brothers I didn't have a maid to look after me when my parents were working because I had formed a very close bond with my cousin Euphrasie, who came to live with us before I was born because her parents were killed in a fire. When I arrived Maman asked her to care for me and we became inseparable. She was a kind, gentle young woman, always well dressed and with her soft hair tied up in a ponytail. From the day I was born she became my second mother. She fed me, bathed me, sang me lullabies and taught me so many things throughout my childhood.

We grew pineapples and I was always eager to pick them as soon as they looked ready. 'No, no, Bébé, you have to learn what they smell like when they are ripe. Until you smell that ripe smell you must not pick them,' she warned me.

She got married when I was three and when I was five she and her husband moved to Masisi and got jobs as teachers at the school there. I missed her but we visited each other regularly.

When I was ten Maman and Papa announced that they were moving to Uvira, another town in the area, to continue with their coffee-farming. Uvira was much hotter than Goma and Bukavu and because I was prone to nosebleeds if I went anywhere too hot Maman and Papa thought it would be better for me to go and stay with Euphrasie in Masisi, which was much cooler.

Although I begged Maman to let me stay with the rest of the family I was also excited to be going back to Euphrasie because I loved her so much. Masisi is a beautiful, green, fertile area. It's a bit like Scotland, with mountains and small, crystal-clear rivers. But unlike Scotland it has crocodiles and hippos and brightly coloured parrots flitting from tree to tree.

I loved being in Masisi and settled in well there. Euphrasie and her husband owned twenty goats and gave all of them biblical names.

I was sent to Lycée Kilimani, a school with a very strong ethos of discipline. It was a fine building in the countryside run by Belgians. We drank milk straight from the cows and grew our own beans. I learned how to be a country girl, fetching wood and building chicken houses. I also learned how to ride a horse and felt proud to be the only person in my family able to do this. We had to carry any water we needed from the stream. I was used to getting water out of a tap and at first I spilled it everywhere, but gradually I learned how to carry as much as fifteen litres of water on my head. I didn't have such ready access to chocolate and biscuits there, the way I did at home, but after a while I found I no longer wanted to eat those things. We ate very fresh, natural food. It was organic long before people talked of such things.

When it was full moon we danced to Kinyarwandan music and sang traditional songs. This was a Tutsi area and people said it was the place where you could find all the tall, beautiful girls.

Euphrasie was still devoted to me. Sadly, she hadn't been able to have children as she suffered from fibroids that made her womb as swollen as if she was eight months pregnant. I was her surrogate daughter and she lavished endless love and affection on me. One day at school I fell ill with a fever and terrible sore throat. Although I was ten years old and quite tall for my age Euphrasie carried me all the way home on her back and nursed me devotedly with bitter-tasting herb potions until I was better.

I had a lot of independence in Masisi and, no longer surrounded by all my family, I got used to making my own decisions, something that, although I didn't realise it at the time, would stand me in good stead later on.

Masisi was a very safe area in those days and I was allowed to roam freely. One day I lost my way when I was walking in the hills and came upon a village of lepers. The roads around the village were well maintained and there were beautiful flowers and gardens everywhere. I had heard of leprosy but knew very little about it. I was startled by what I saw – people with no noses, ears or hands – and initially recoiled. At first I thought they had chopped their hands and noses off and was terrified they would do the same to me. But they approached me so gently that I soon realised they meant me no harm.

I was curious about their condition and, encouraged by their friendly attitude, began asking them questions. 'How can you do farming with no arms?' I asked.

They explained that those of them whose hands had been taken by leprosy had learned how to plant seeds with their mouths. 'It is not only people with leprosy who plant seeds this way,' one of them said. 'It is the traditional African way of farming to spit the seeds into the earth. That way you don't break your back from bending down all day.'

Soon we were laughing and chatting like old friends and I promised to return and visit them again. It seemed that they had very little contact with the outside world apart from the nuns, priests and nurses who looked after them. I asked one of the nuns, Thérèse, to teach me how to clean their sores. She told me to put surgical gloves on and showed me what to do.

They grew the best yams, cassava and sugarcane in the area and their produce was sold at the local market. I became friendly with one girl of my age whose parents had leprosy. She showed no sign of having the disease and I begged Euphrasie to let her come and stay with us for a while. To my delight she agreed. We shared a room with bunk beds; she slept on the bottom and I slept on the top.

I felt happy when I spent time with the community of lepers. They were good, kind people who had adjusted to their imperfect circumstances with grace. I learned a lot from them about how life can be lived.

When I was twelve my parents returned to Bukavu and I went

back home. One day Maman came home from work to make
our lunch. Her lovely leather purse which had a zebra design on
it was full of money. She had planned to go to the bank in the
afternoon to pay in the money, but was exhausted and decided
to rest first. While she was sleeping I saw Pauline and Timotei
covertly taking money out of the purse. I was horrified because
it had been drummed into us by my parents that we must never
steal. I felt very protective towards Maman and hid near by,
watching what they were doing. They crept outside and buried
some money in the garden. I was too scared to challenge them
but when they had gone I dug the money up and put it back in
Maman's purse. She rubbed her eyes sleepily as I was stealthily
putting the money back in her purse.

'What are you doing?' she cried.

'I'm putting it back in,' I whispered.

'Putting what back in?' she asked, puzzled, her brow furrow-
ing.

I explained to her what I'd witnessed. Maman called Pauline
and Timotei and smacked their hands. 'Don't you ever do that
again,' she said crossly. 'If I catch you stealing one more time I'll
be marching you straight down to the police station.'

My brother and sister were furious with me for ruining their
little enterprise. I prayed they'd forget about it and wouldn't punish
me for telling tales about them. My prayer wasn't answered.

That evening the servants were grilling fish from the lake and
sweetcorn on the barbecue outside for us. I was still feeling on
edge in case my brother and sister planned revenge. They called
me over to where they were sitting under a shady tree in another
part of the garden and accused me of taking the money from
Maman. My eyes widened. They knew that it was they, not me,
who had taken the money.

'You are so stupid,' said my sister. 'Maman only beat us instead
of you because she feels sorry for you because you have no
parents.'

'What are you talking about?' I said, aghast. 'My parents are the same as yours.'

My skin had always been lighter than my parents' and suddenly I started to wonder about my origins.

'Why do you think they sent you to Masisi? It's because you're not from our family. They found you in a bad home and brought you here out of pity.'

I couldn't believe what I was hearing. In a state of total shock I ran into my bedroom in floods of tears, grabbed a few clothes and some shoes and crept out of the house.

I can't stay there any longer and keep taking things from those people if they're not my parents, I said to myself, sobbing loudly. I wandered aimlessly down the street, stopping people and asking if they knew where I could find my parents. People looked at me as if I was mad, shrugged and walked on.

Eventually I saw one of Papa's friends. 'Where are you going, Bébé? Your home is in the other direction.'

'No, that's not my home,' I said, shaking my head sadly and wiping away my tears.

'Don't be silly. What sort of nonsense are you talking? I'm going to take you home right now,' he said. He put his arm around my shoulders, swivelled me round so I was facing the other direction and led me back home.

Maman and Papa were surprised to see me walk through the front door.

'Oh, Bébé, we thought you were in your bedroom. Where have you been? Why did you leave the house without saying anything?'

'See, that proves I'm not your child. You don't even know or care whether or not I'm in the house!' I cried.

'What on earth are you talking about? Don't ever say things like that again.'

I blurted out what my sister and brother told me. Maman gave me a big hug and she and Papa assured me that I did belong to them. I breathed a big sigh of relief and my sobs subsided.

I was keen to show the rest of the family how much I'd matured while I was away in Masisi, so one Sunday morning when most of the family were at church I decided I would kill a chicken and cook it for lunch. I wasn't sure exactly how to kill a chicken but knew it involved cutting the neck. I called on Jean-Claude to help me and after a big tussle I somehow managed to cut off the chicken's head. To my horror it continued running around after its head was severed. The rest of the family returned home to a trail of blood and thought a murder had been committed. I guiltily confessed to bungling the job of killing a chicken.

'I think that next time you should leave this job to the cook,' said Maman. 'Poor Bébé, you've had a shock. Have you not heard the expression "running around like a headless chicken"?' She was trying to look serious but I could see that part of her wanted to burst out laughing at my naïvety.

My first experience of a human death was when my older sister Brigitte died from breast cancer when I was just fourteen years old. I wasn't told much about what was going on but I caught sight of her once in the shower and was shocked to see she had just one breast. Nobody told me the truth about how seriously ill she was, fobbing me off with a story that she was suffering from malaria. She already had two young children, Vicki and Alida, when she became sick. My parents were very sad but they kept it to themselves. There was little talk at home of topics like sex or terminal illness. After Brigitte's tragic death many people came to our house to offer their condolences.

'Why are all these people here? Why did God call Brigitte to heaven?' I asked Maman. She did not give me an answer.

I kept on asking myself questions: How can God call someone who has children who need her? It just wasn't fair. I wouldn't be happy if someone took Maman away from me. As I tried to make sense of the loss of Brigitte, I had no idea how much more acquainted with death I would become and how many more unanswered questions there would be about why God allowed His children to suffer so much. My parents were devout Roman Catholics, and church played a central role in our lives. My favourite day of the week was Sunday. We always went to mass at the local church and afterwards friends and family came to visit us. The big people went in the first mass and the children went to the second mass. We killed a goat or chickens, were allowed to eat as much meat as we wanted that day, and to my delight could play outside until late.

One thing I loathed though was Bible study. It was a condition of getting confirmed that we had to attend Bible study classes for several months before the big day. I got sick of repeating the 'Our Father' a hundred times, and one day when I couldn't take the repetition any more I shouted out in the class, 'No more, no more, I already know it so well.' I got a severe telling-off from the nun who was teaching us.

We weren't supposed to have breakfast until after church on Sunday. 'The body of Christ must be in you first,' said Maman.

For church we had special dresses and shoes, always white or light pink. Maman and Papa were always very smartly dressed too. The women from the villages relaxed their hair by laying a hot brick and oil on it on Saturday nights so that they looked their best for church. I had soft hair and I just tied it back.

Maman's grandpa, Nyadera, had a big influence on my childhood. He never wore trousers in his life, instead favouring traditional clothes, the kind the Masai wore. He would put a beautiful coat on top of his wrapper for formal occasions, but never trousers. He was too tall to pass through an ordinary doorway but he never leaned over, always remaining elegantly upright. The only language he knew was Kinyarwanda. 'Don't ever forget your language,' he often said to me.

He was known as a wise leader of Tutsis. He had no official status but was accepted by everyone in the neighbourhood as a highly regarded community leader on account of his great wisdom and even-handed approach to solving people's grievances.

He had the gift of telling the future and lots of Tutsis trusted him to dream the truth of their lives for them. He used to tell me I was going to have a long, long life, that I would pass through difficult times but that afterwards my life would be clean. He said I was *nfura*, which means 'beautiful life inside and out' in Kinyarwanda.

'Take care of your little heart, Bébé,' he often said to me. He loved me very much. Papa was so strict that I sometimes ran from him to my great-grandfather so that he could cuddle and comfort me. He had many beautiful pipes and I used to clean them for him. He predicted that he would die in Rwanda and he did – in 2002, at the ripe old age of 102. An extra-long coffin had to be made to bury him in.

One day when I was sitting at his feet he started talking once again of the future. He looked at me intently and said quietly, 'Mukecheru. In a few years' time there will be a new Rwanda coming. But before that happens there will be a lot of blood.'

CHAPTER THREE

By the end of the 1980s, Tutsis were beginning to feel increasingly uncomfortable in Rwanda. But still many of those who were living in exile longed to return to their homeland. My parents sometimes said longingly of Rwanda when we were living in eastern Congo, '*Tura taha*,' 'We're going home.' Throughout my childhood we visited Rwanda regularly, to see friends and relatives. I never liked it as much as Zaire, which was livelier with much better food.

Although the Belgian colonists had highlighted divisions between the taller, lighter-skinned Tutsis and the shorter, darker Hutus, there was a remarkably strong sense of shared Rwandan identity between the different ethnic groups before the attacks on Tutsis by Hutus between 1959 and 1962. It was during this period that my parents fled the country and settled in eastern Zaire. Even after these attacks there was still considerable harmony, with intermarriage, shared food, language and customs.

I was blissfully unaware of any tensions. My parents never discussed such things with us. Although they had made successful lives for themselves, both were Rwandan rather than Zairian and were conscious that they were not living in their own country. This, coupled with their knowledge that Mobutu was a dictator, made them cautious of voicing opinions, even within their own four walls. As a result we grew up in blissful ignorance. Everything about my life was carefree and I had only ever known love, peace and privilege. No human being had ever done anything bad to me and as a result I harboured no bad thoughts towards any other person.

My parents once told me that they had been chased out of their own country, but it was clear they didn't want to talk too much about it. Zaire was a good place for them to do business and our whole family thrived there.

All the Tutsis who had left Rwanda seemed to be doing so well. My parents often told me they had left their country because they liked to travel, not because they had fled any sort of danger, and I preferred this explanation.

Our family had a television and others in the neighbourhood who didn't have one gathered around ours at every available opportunity. We eagerly watched cartoons like *Asterix* and imported pop shows featuring stars like Madonna. We did our best to commit her dance steps to memory. The word we all used to describe fashionable people, places and music was 'happening'. The shows we watched were always the most happening ones we had access to.

On Sundays after church we sometimes visited the home of the priest, who lived in our neighbourhood, and performed both traditional and more modern dances for him. Our parents were pleased to see we were doing something constructive on the Sabbath day and applauded our efforts. I was in a big group of children and young people aged ten to seventeen. I was fourteen when I started dancing and we had to restrict it to the school holidays. Papa would have killed me if I had spent time away from my studies doing something like that during school time.

We had two months off during the summer and were able to practise our steps every day. We gave our group the name Commandores. We weren't dancing in the hope of achieving fame and fortune like Michael Jackson or Madonna; the whole thing was just for fun.

Around this time my friendship with a boy in the neighbourhood called Christian deepened. I liked his kindness and quietness and thought he was very handsome. We used to sit on a rock on the edge of Lake Kivu, throwing small stones into the clear, aquamarine water and watching the way the sun lit up the ripples we made. We talked about everything under the sun. I'd never been able to talk so easily to anyone before and I felt very safe and comfortable with him.

He told me he'd watched me going to school with my friends and had heard how good I was at tennis, a game that few people played at that time because it was expensive and there were very few courts in the area. It was known as a colonial game and one that only the élite had access to. I usually played with people much older than me, and Christian was impressed when he saw me going off for lessons with racquets under my arm. I had become well known in the area because I was sport-mad. Christian was too shy to join in with the dance team but he was always interested in hearing my stories about our dancing expeditions too. 'I'm just happy to watch, you can do all the hard work,' he often said to me in his quiet, soft voice.

Our reputation as dancers began to grow and we started to cross the border from Zaire into Changugu in Rwanda. We were invited to perform at Centre Culturel Français, a big arts centre in the heart of Kigali. There was a big library of French books there and many French plays were performed. My parents were happy for me to be involved with the dance group. They knew and trusted the older members to look after the younger ones like me.

One time when we were performing at Centre Culturel I noticed that modelling shoots were going on in another part of the building. I loved experimenting with make-up and boldly walked up to the models and asked if I could help them with their make-up. To my amazement they agreed and I began help-ing out whenever we performed at Centre Culturel Français. The models were working on publicity shots for a large beer company in Rwanda.

A few weeks later I was bent over one of the models, carefully outlining her lips with a beautiful tawny lipstick, when the pho-tographer on the shoot called across the room to me, 'Please stay exactly where you are and turn to look at me.' Before I'd realised what was going on he'd taken my photo. 'You've got a great face, Bébé. Instead of helping out behind the camera you should be in front of it,' he laughed.

I blushed. 'Don't be silly. I'm just here to dance, and you know I love putting make-up on the models.'

'No, I'm serious,' he said. 'I'm going to get these photos developed and show them to the boss. I'm sure he'll want you to do some modelling.'

The next thing I knew a photo shoot had been organised by the brewery and I was featured in their promotional calendar holding a glass of beer. Modelling wasn't something I chose, I just fell into it.

Christian knew about this development but I was scared to tell my parents because I was sure they would disapprove. I thought they'd never get to see a beer company calendar and that my secret would be safe. So I was amazed and horrified when the brewery plastered my photo all over billboards in Kigali to adver-tise the new calendar.

Because Papa travelled there regularly on business I knew I wouldn't be able to keep my glamorous new sideline a secret for long, but I decided I'd wait for him to find out rather than make a formal confession to him. It wasn't long before Papa confronted me with the evidence, but his first question surprised me. Instead of shouting at me for secretly getting involved in modelling he asked accusingly, 'Do you drink beer?'

'No, of course not,' I replied. 'I've never tasted the stuff in my life and I'm certainly not drinking the beer in the picture. Do you know they put soap in it to make it look frothy? How can I drink soap?'

I realised that although Papa was strict he was not stupid. He believed me and seemed relieved that his teenage daughter hadn't turned into a raging alcoholic. Maman went along with what Papa said and accepted my work. I never once tasted the beer that I became well known for promoting.

'Don't worry, Papa, I'm only doing this modelling at weekends so I can still concentrate on my studies during the week. It's just a hobby for me. And they said to me that if you and Maman want it, they'll give you lots of free beer.'

Later on, when killing was all around me, my modelling work and the fact that I was known and liked in Hutu circles was one of the things that helped to keep me alive. There were many Hutus involved in modelling and I got to know lots of them in the course of my work.

When I was fifteen my parents left Bukavu and returned to Goma. Wealthy families in the area often moved around and liked to have bases in more than one town, especially those involved in business. I attended Lycée Chamcham and studied French literature. I also learned practical skills like dressmaking and woodwork. Maman helped me with the sewing. With her sharp eyes and quiet, nimble fingers she could work magic with any piece of cloth put into her hands. Her thoughts were always for others and sometimes she made school uniforms for families who couldn't afford to buy them.

My parents began to plan my future. There were no good universities in Goma and Kinshasa was too hot for me and would bring back my nosebleeds. So my parents offered me the choice of going to Kenya or to Europe to study.

We had had lovely family holidays in Mombasa, where the sea was a dazzling shade of blue, the sand was soft and the people were warm and friendly. In contrast I'd found Belgium, the only country in Europe I'd visited, dull and grey.

'I'd like to study in Kenya,' I declared. To me the decision seemed an obvious one.

'Kenya it is then.' Papa smiled and squeezed my hand. I had made no decision about what I wanted to study but I still dreamed of doing medicine since visiting sick people at the local hospital as a child. I saw how much people suffered when they were sick and envied the doctors who knew how to make them better.

My friend Christian, who was a couple of years older than me, was planning to study economics in Butari, Rwanda, where there was a good university. When I was fourteen, he had dropped a bombshell.

'Leah, I've wanted you to be my girlfriend for a long time but I thought you were too young,' he said, smiling shyly. 'I'm completely in love with you.'

I was shocked because I hadn't had any thoughts of romance and had never had a boyfriend before. But I liked the idea of being Christian's girlfriend and we began a very innocent relationship, kissing and cuddling and declaring our love for each other.

I was spending a lot of my weekends in Kigali now, doing modelling assignments for the beer company. During these trips I stayed in Christian's family compound. My parents assumed that Christian's family were there too but often they weren't. There was a small house in the grounds of the big family home and we moved in there. We vowed not to have sex, though, as both of us were devout Catholics and planned to wait until we were married. For a while we just kissed and cuddled but then we forgot our religious scruples. We were young and we got carried away.

As far as I was concerned I had a perfect life. I continued to work hard at my studies, was very happy living in Goma with the family I adored and looked forward to crossing the border at weekends for my modelling work and Christian.

During the first few months of 1993 I carried on as usual, playing tennis, swimming regularly and studying hard. But by May I was starting to feel unwell, and was overwhelmed by waves of exhaustion and nausea. I was very close to a cousin called Beatrice who was a few years older than me and I confided to her that I wasn't feeling good. I didn't want to worry Maman by mentioning it to her.

'Maybe you have malaria, Bébé,' she said. 'Do you have a fever?'

'No, not at all. I've never had malaria in my life. The mosquitoes don't seem to like me.'

'I'll take you to the doctor and he can check things up,' she said. Beatrice suspected the real cause of my illness but kept her thoughts to herself, waiting for confirmation from the doctor.

The doctor ran a few tests and took a blood and urine sample.

'Bébé, I have some news for you. You're pregnant!'

I gasped and no words came out. The shock of the news had made my blood freeze in my veins. I was engulfed in panic. Frantic thoughts tumbled over each other. What would my parents say? What would Christian say? Would I have to stop school and modelling? I was still only a child myself. How could I be having a baby? I couldn't think clearly and nothing at all made sense. The bottom had fallen out of my perfect world.

'We've done a test. You're probably five months along,' the doctor said.

'But how can that be?' I cried. I burst into tears and the only words I could get out were 'I want Maman, I want Maman.'

Until that moment my entire life had been lived in innocence. Instinctively I knew that all that was over now. I began sobbing for what I had lost and the terrible trouble I was sure I would get into with my family.

The doctor asked me if I had experienced cravings for certain foods.

'No,' I replied without thinking, then remembered that I had inexplicably gone off meat a few months ago and had developed a craving for lemons and guava, mangoes and passionfruit.

'Those cravings are your body's way of letting you know what your baby needs,' he said.

'We have to tell Maman what's happened to you,' said Beatrice matter-of-factly. 'But first you must tell Christian.'

I nodded my head silently. I was still in a state of complete shock. With each passing moment I was becoming more nervous about what my devout Catholic parents would say when they found out.

Breaking into my thoughts and offering me no comfort at all, Beatrice said, 'Your family will kill you. None of your older sisters has ever had a baby without being married.'

I started crying again, thinking about all the shame I was going to bring on Maman and Papa.

I told Maman I was going to stay with Beatrice for a while and started trying to work out what I was going to do. I was no longer a carefree girl, running to play outside with other young people of my age. Abruptly that life had ended, and I wasn't sure that I'd be able to cope with the very different life that stretched ahead of me. I felt as if I was standing somewhere outside my own body, watching my life crumble in front of me.

Christian was as shocked as me. 'I haven't finished studying yet, how can I be a dad?' he said. Over and over again he asked if I was absolutely sure that I was pregnant. Finally I convinced him that somewhere underneath my flat belly, the belly that could still fit snugly into my usual jeans, lay our child. He agreed to stand by me. 'We'll stay together and we're going to have this child, Bébé,' he said decisively.

Christian and I were so much in love that after the initial shock had subsided, excitement took over and we started discussing names. Christian liked the name Steve, but it was a name I had never been keen on and we settled on Jean-Luc for a boy, Christelle if the baby turned out to be a girl.

To my enormous relief Beatrice had prepared Maman for the news and she took it very calmly. She came over to Beatrice's house and questioned me very gently. She knew that I was scared. I begged her to break the news to Papa so that I wouldn't have to. I was sure he'd kill me when he found out what was going on.

'Relax, Bébé, I'll smooth things over with Papa.' She smiled and gave me a big hug. 'You and Christian are in love, you didn't realise you were doing anything wrong, and sooner or later I'm sure you would have had a baby together anyway. You've just done it a bit more quickly than we all expected. These things happen. It's not the end of the world.'

Maman's words reassured me but I felt terribly ashamed of what I'd done. I had never heard of any girl in our neighbourhood getting pregnant at such a young age without being married. I was relieved that the pregnancy barely showed and vowed to conceal it from all my friends.

Christian was doing his exams for the end of secondary school. When he had finished school he was going to start at university in Butari. His family had a house there. It was a beautiful part of Rwanda and because of the university was a place where many intellectuals gathered. At weekends he was training to be a pilot to fly small, local planes.

His family found it hard to believe that I was pregnant because the pregnancy hardly showed. When we told her the news, Christian's mother said, 'Leah, where is the pregnancy?' Like Maman she accepted the situation and promised that she and the rest of the family would do everything they could to support us.

Maman explained to Papa that the pregnancy was a genuine mistake that had occurred as a result of our ignorance. He listened carefully to Maman's explanation and then nodded his smooth, dark head softly, a sure sign that I'd been forgiven.

'It's OK, Bébé, but you must learn from your mistakes.'

I nodded earnestly. 'I will, Papa, I promise you that. I'm so sorry about everything but I'll finish the term at school, I've only got a couple more weeks to go, and I'll make sure I pass my exams and make you proud of me.'

I continued with my studies. Most of the students had no idea that I was having a baby because I barely had a bump. In fact, the shock of being pregnant made me lose weight. My appetite had vanished as soon as the doctor gave me the news and two weeks later it hadn't returned.

I worked harder than I had ever worked in my life, and to my enormous relief I passed my exams with a good grade – sixty-seven per cent, one of the top marks in the class. I promised Papa that even though I was going to have a baby it wouldn't stop me from going to university.

Christian and I told our parents that we would live together for now and get married later on when we were ready. They accepted our decision, agreeing that marriage was something that could wait until we had finished our studies. We held a traditional, informal ceremony. Both families sat together and drank a toast to our future, then everyone hugged us and congratulated us.

I whispered to the baby kicking in my womb, 'Don't worry, Jean-Luc or Christelle. Everything is going to turn out just fine.'

I didn't tell the beer company that I was pregnant. I simply said I was taking a break so that I could focus on my studies. They were very flexible and accepted my explanation, inviting me to return when I was ready.

By now my parents had made Kigali their main base, as an increasing amount of their work was there. My younger siblings and I continued to live in Goma with the servants looking after us so that we could complete our studies. My parents were always coming backwards and forwards between Zaire and Rwanda so we saw them all the time.

Papa gave me a car when I was sixteen and a friend taught me how to drive. The laws about driving tests were very lax in those days and the police rarely asked to see people's licences, especially if they were driving expensive cars.

Christian passed his flying exams. He was thrilled because he was now able to fly a small plane, an air taxi that ferried those who could afford it between the different towns in the region. He was just eighteen and I was very proud of him. He worked from Thursday to Sunday so that he could concentrate on his studies the rest of the time.

I left Goma at the end of the school term because I wanted to be near Maman in Kigali before the baby was born. People kept on paying me compliments, saying that my skin and hair and nails all looked great, but they didn't realise that the reason for this was that I was pregnant.

Papa was very patient with me and very protective once he had got used to the idea that I was going to have a baby. He encouraged me to eat lots of nourishing foods so the baby could grow well. Maman cosseted me, understanding better than I that this was my last chance to be treated like a little girl.

One Sunday in October 1993 I woke up feeling distinctly unwell. I had a dull pain in my lower abdomen and felt sick. I went into Maman's bedroom and whimpered, 'Maman, something isn't feeling right.'

She was fast asleep and said drowsily, 'Have a cup of tea and go back to bed, Bébé.'

An hour later I still hadn't managed to settle back to sleep. Maman came into my bedroom and put on surgical gloves. She understood the basics of childbirth and had delivered several babies in the neighbourhood over the years.

'Open your legs, Bébé,' she said. 'Let's see what's happening in there. Is this baby of yours ready to come out?' She felt for my cervix and declared that I was two centimetres dilated. 'The baby will come soon, but not too soon,' she said. 'I'm going to go to early-morning mass. Have a bath and drink some black tea, but don't put any milk in it or it will interfere with your labour.'

I drifted into an uneasy sleep while she was out. The sky was grey and a miserable sort of rain was falling from the sky. An hour later, I stirred when I heard her soft, soothing voice.

'Did you drink the black tea, Bébé? Has it helped you?'

'Yes, Maman, thank you,' I said.

'Here, drink another one.'

'I just want to sleep, Maman.'

She left the tea by my bed and I slept for fifteen minutes then was woken by a sharp pain.

Maman checked me again and informed me that I was now three centimetres dilated.

'I'll drive you to the hospital at seven-thirty. Let's take a walk first. It will help you, Bébé.'

I reluctantly agreed and she took me for a gentle stroll around the garden. The rain had stopped and everything was coated with a damp, glistening sheen. I wasn't in the mood to admire the beautiful flowers and trees. The garden looked very green after the rain. There were lots of birds nesting in our garden and we had a little house for the pigeons and a swinging garden chair which Papa had bought in Kenya.

Christian was in Nairobi doing more pilot training. I was quite relieved that he was away for a week as the only person I really wanted to be with at this moment was my beloved Maman.

'Shouldn't the baby have come by now, Maman?' I asked her innocently.

'Often first babies take their time. This baby will arrive when it's good and ready,' she smiled. She was so calm about the whole thing that my own anxieties about giving birth subsided.

At 11 a.m. she checked me again.

'OK, I'll take you to the hospital now, Bébé,' she said.

We arrived at a small, local hospital called Clinique Catholique de Rwanda. The nurse examined me and pronounced, 'You'll give birth in ten minutes.'

Sadly her diagnosis was not correct. Suddenly my cervix closed up and my labour ground to a halt. But the pain continued. It wasn't until two days later that my waters finally broke – but still no baby came out.

I sobbed with pain and exhaustion and said to Maman, 'Maybe you're not praying enough.'

Then Papa arrived, took one look at me writhing in agony and announced, 'I'm taking my baby to the big hospital.'

I was in too much pain to say anything. I was taken to the big hospital in Kigali by ambulance. All I could hear were other women in labour screaming.

'Maman, tell them to do a Caesarean. This labour has gone on too long and I don't want to lose the baby.'

Maman hadn't left my side for three days. Friends brought her food but she had no appetite: she was totally focused on praying for the baby and me. She closed her eyes, clutching her cross and her rosary beads, her lips moving fervently.

On Thursday morning my contractions suddenly became much more violent.

'Maman, I need to go to the toilet,' I cried.

'No, let me have a look,' said the nurse. 'Ahh, I can see the baby's head, just push now.'

I realised then that I didn't want to go to the toilet. A baby boy popped out. I had never felt such enormous relief and joy in my entire life. Our little Jean-Luc was healthy and cried immediately. It was 31 October 1993.

I was too exhausted even to look at him properly. Once I'd made sure he was healthy I fell into a deep sleep, leaving him in Maman's capable hands. She dressed him in beautiful white clothes that she had crocheted for him. I wasn't surprised that he was a boy; I had sensed that from the moment I discovered I was pregnant.

I slept deeply for a few hours. In the afternoon Maman woke me, saying, 'Bébé, you need to eat so you can feed your baby.' She gave me some warm milk and some vegetable soup.

Afterwards I felt stronger and took the baby in my arms, examining every bit of him. He was perfect in every way. His skin was white and he had lots of soft, dark hair. I was amazed to see that his eyes were blue. He weighed almost four kilos. I couldn't understand how a baby who looked almost as if he wasn't there when he was lying in my womb could weigh so much.

After the initial rapture had subsided I started to panic about Jean-Luc's skin. I couldn't understand why a child belonging to Christian and me could be so white. I turned to Maman and burst into tears.

'I swear I never slept with a white man, this is Christian's baby.'

'Calm down,' Maman said. 'What nonsense are you speaking about white men? You were born very light, I'm light-skinned myself. This is normal for babies in our family.'

After a couple of days my breasts were flooded with milk. I had far too much for Jean-Luc.

'Would you like to feed some more babies to get rid of your pain?' one of the nurses asked. 'Some of these poor creatures, their mothers died giving birth to them, so they have no *maman* to suckle from.'

I nodded eagerly, and she showed me how to feed some of the motherless little babies. By the time I left the hospital I had become very attached to them. My milk was spurting out in powerful jets and I thanked God that unlike some of the women whose poor babies I was feeding, I had survived to look after Jean-Luc.

He was a lovely baby and rarely cried. Mama showered me with advice. 'You mustn't carry the baby when he's sleeping. Wake him at six a.m., change him, wash his towelling nappies as soon as you take them off him.'

When I left the hospital I went home to my parents' place as Christian was away a lot while he was training.

'Oh, he's so beautiful,' he said when he first saw Jean-Luc.

'Come on, hold your baby,' Maman urged him.

'I'm scared of breaking him. I'll just look,' he said timidly.

Eventually he got over his fear and would pick up Jean-Luc with his long, elegant hands, with Maman showing him the right way to hold him.

Maman invited one of her distant cousins, Donata, to look after Jean-Luc. Donata came to our house often and Maman taught her how to sew and clean. She was two years older than me and had never learned how to read and write, so Maman was teaching her that too. Donata adored Jean-Luc and I felt very comfortable leaving him with her when I had to run errands or wanted to rest for a while.

CHAPTER FOUR

When Jean-Luc was two months old I resumed my work as a model and moved with Christian to the little house in his parents' compound. I could have continued quite happily living under my parents' roof – they would have welcomed Christian – but we wanted to prove to both sets of parents that although we were young we were grown-up and responsible enough to manage by ourselves. I had agreed with my parents that I would take a year off my studies and resume my education in September 1994.

Jean-Luc was such a sweet baby. When he was three months old he started smiling. We both spent hours tickling him under the chin and parading soft toys in front of his gradually focusing eyes, anything to elicit his magical smile. He loved water and I used to put him in the bath with me, delighting in his grins when I splashed him gently with water and bubbles.

We were lucky not to be short of money. I had my earnings from my modelling and Christian had his pilot's wages. Our parents also helped to support us financially. We loved to indulge Jean-Luc with all the latest fashions. There was a shop in the centre of Kigali that sold second-hand European designer clothes for children. Almost from birth Jean-Luc was decked out in the latest jeans and T-shirts, the kind of outfits the best dressed babies in Paris and New York were wearing.

Christian had started university and travelled from Kigali to Butari every day. I took my precious baby to work with me, putting him in Donata's capable hands while the photo shoots took place. Every day my love for him deepened. I was reluctant to let him out of my sight for even a moment.

Maman was a constant support to me. She was very involved with Jean-Luc and offered wise advice while at the same time never interfering with Christian's and my decisions.

My relationship with Christian deepened. I know that a lot of boys his age would have run away from the responsibility of fatherhood but it never occurred to him to do so. After his initial anxiety about Jean-Luc's fragility he became a wonderful, hands-on father, sharing the childcare with me when he was at home. In short, life could not have been better for us. Sometimes I pinched myself, hardly believing that everything could have worked out so perfectly. I was surrounded by love and fun and luxury.

Out of the corner of my mind's eye I glimpsed the political situation for Tutsis in Rwanda deteriorating, but the things going on outside my cosy little bubble didn't affect me and I continued to live my life in a state of happy and naïve ignorance.

My parents said very little about what was going on. Both were naturally cautious by nature and like everyone else they hoped that the unrest would simply evaporate so that our pleasant lives could continue. They were very protective of all of us and didn't want us to feel alarmed.

We heard whispers about young Tutsi men joining Paul Kagame's Revolutionary Patriotic Front, but they were in the Uganda–Rwanda border area, far from Kigali, so we never saw any sign of their activities. It wasn't the kind of thing that people discussed openly because the RPF was quite an underground movement at the time. My parents would not have allowed my brothers to join this organisation as they wanted them to focus on their studies.

Although I felt vaguely uneasy there was nothing tangible to worry about and my free, privileged life continued as normal. At the end of 1993 and the beginning of 1994 I noticed that there were more soldiers in the street, but because I was still very young none of them paid too much attention to me. They weren't sure if I was Rwandise or Zairian because I spoke very good French and Swahili (Zairian languages), and I made a lot of trips between the two countries. I felt that for as long as I had some sort of dual identity nobody could pin me down, label me a Rwandan Tutsi and cause me problems.

On the occasions when they did stop me and demand my identity card I did my best to shrug off their questions. 'I don't have it,' was my stock response, and because I was young the soldiers generally let me go without making a fuss.

Although tensions were increasing we also had grounds to be optimistic. In August 1993 Rwanda's Hutu president, Habyarimana, had accepted an internationally mediated treaty agreeing to share power with the Tutsi Rwandan Patriotic Front. The peace deal was bolstered by the arrival of 5,000 UN peace-keepers in the country.

'Now that the UN are here nothing bad can happen to us,' we all said, trying to reassure each other that everything was going to work out fine. Our Tutsi friends and neighbours said it was natural that some would oppose the peace deal, but that once everybody got used to it tensions would die down and things would return to normal. If Tutsis had had any inkling of what was about to happen they would have crossed the various borders out of Rwaanda in droves.

Optimistic by nature, I threw myself into being a mother and into my modelling, spending time with Christian, Jean-Luc and our families and socialising with a wide circle of young, fash-ionable and wealthy friends, Hutu, Tutsi and French. In our group nobody cared what background anyone else was from or how wide or narrow your nose was. We just wanted our nice, peaceful lives to carry on as normal.

We always ate, drank and danced in the most happening venues. Mostly these were calm, harmonious places to be, but I became increasingly aware of the presence of the Interahamwe in town, a motley group who organised anti-Tutsi songs and marches. The word 'interahamwe' means 'those who attack together' in Kinyarwanda.

The Interahamwe enjoyed strutting around the streets and using their group name at every opportunity. We were hearing the name more and more on national radio, and some of my friends who followed politics more closely than I did warned that no good was going to come of them.

My impression of the Interahamwe was that it was a rather amateur organisation, full of people with no jobs who had come from the farms in the countryside looking for work in town. Their outfit looked peculiar – red, green and yellow clothes, the colours of the Rwandan flag at the time. The leaders of the Interahamwe publicly appealed to their members' sense of patriotism, but behind the scenes were urging them to kill every last Tutsi 'invader'. I had no idea that their sole aim was to exterminate people like me, the Tutsis they referred to as 'cockroaches'.

Christian had been beaten up in Gisenyi in 1993 by Interahamwe. He was a target because he was so tall and had a distinctive, long nose, marking him out as a Tutsi. At that time Hutus and Tutsis were still cooperating but he was suspected of being a spy because he was travelling such a lot for his job. I was horrified to see a group of men attack him because of the way he looked. Fortunately he wasn't badly hurt, and I had tried my best to put the incident to the back of my mind.

One evening in January 1994 a group of us decided to pay a visit to Congrès National de Développement, site of the National

Assembly and a hotel. While most of the Rwandan Patriotic Front were stationed far from Kigali, the organisation's leadership and security battalion stayed in the hotel side of the complex while the UN occupied the National Assembly part. We knew some of the RPF soldiers and wanted to show our support for them. We were let in without any problems and felt reassured that they were in Kigali.

'Nothing bad can happen to us with you RPF boys and the UN here,' I said to one of the soldiers.

He shook his head sadly. 'Oh no, Leah, this is not over yet.'

'But we've signed the agreement,' I replied.

He looked uncertain. 'Let's hope you're right,' was all he said.

When we came out of CND we saw lots police in beige uniforms and red hats. I felt uneasy because people were watching us in the street. We couldn't have advertised our Tutsi identity and sympathies more clearly if we had walked out carrying banners supporting the RPF.

I shivered as some of the young men hanging around outside cast hostile glances in our direction. There was an expression on their faces that I didn't recognise and couldn't quite explain. After the genocide began I realised that it had been a lust for Tutsi blood.

Keen to get away, we decided to go and have a drink at a place we loved called Ramera, opposite the Amahoro Stadium. I hoped the people who had been watching us would just melt away. Christian was away again doing some pilot training in Nairobi. I wished he was by my side and felt vulnerable without him.

We ordered drinks and tried to relax but although no one said anything I could see that everyone was rattled. My instincts are usually good and I sensed that something horrible was going to happen before the evening was over. Suddenly a known Interahamwe leader, Jean Bizima, came in. He was wealthy and owned a garage. He must have been watching us leave the CND and followed us. He came and stood close to me. His hard eyes blazed with anger and I could smell alcohol on his breath.

He looked at me and sneered, '*Inyenzi.*'

Nobody had ever called me that to my face before. I was in a state of shock. My legs started to shake uncontrollably and I tried desperately to keep them still. I was breathing very fast and opened my mouth to speak but no words came out.

My initial shock was soon overtaken by anger. What made this man think he could insult me and get away with it? I had as much right to live and breathe freely as he did. I decided that the only way to deal with this horrible man was to fight back.

'How dare you call me that?' I replied in French, trying to keep my trembling voice steady.

'You lied to me and said you were Zairian when really you're just a cockroach,' he said, hissing as he rolled the word '*inyenzi*' around his tongue.

'I never said anything to you,' I retorted.

'You are a cockroach,' he repeated, enjoying baiting me and not able to think of anything more original to say.

My friends sat watching, open-mouthed.

'I'm not going to stay and listen to this rubbish, I'm going home,' I said angrily. Bizima stepped away from our table but he did not leave.

'If you go home now you'll be in trouble. Bizima might follow you. All of us who went to CND are in serious trouble; things are not good today,' one of my friends whispered to me.

There had been an anti-Tutsi demonstration that day and feelings were running high. Lots of Interahamwe and their supporters had got drunk after the demonstration. The marches happened regularly in certain parts of town; I tried to keep away from those areas and to block out the sound of the Interahamwe songs and chants calling for the destruction of Tutsis.

I felt that evil was building up all around me and was overwhelmed by the urge to run away to somewhere safe and peaceful.

'Tomorrow I'm going to Zaire,' I declared impulsively.

'Oh, Leah, don't you know what's happening in the streets of Ruhengeri and Gisenyi? Terrible attacks on Tutsis. These Interahamwe can be controlled here in Kigali, where the UN are, but not in other parts of Rwanda,' said another friend.

Maybe she was right that nothing too awful could happen in Kigali. I couldn't decide whether it would be better to run or to stay put.

Bizima returned to our table and touched me on the back of my neck. The hairs on my back stood on end. I felt as if he had electrocuted me. I couldn't stop myself from yelping even though I didn't want to give this vile man the opportunity of seeing me react to his taunts.

'Let's go to my sister's compound,' my friend Triffine said. 'We should be safe there.'

Her sister lived very close by. But once we stepped into the compound, before we managed to reach Triffine's sister's apartment, Bizima arrived with a menacing group of men.

'Oh no,' said Triffine. 'We're not going to sleep tonight. I thought they might come after us. You might be better off keeping your mouth shut, Leah. The more angry you make them, the more they'll try to get back at you.'

Bizima was so stuffed with rage he reminded me of a big, fat mosquito heavy with human blood. He spat on the floor.

I had regained some of my strength and composure and ignored Triffine's words of advice.

'Listen, Bizima. You need to stop calling me a cockroach right now. What kind of ideas have you put into your head? For a start I want to tell you I'm not Rwandise so please don't call me these terrible names.' I took out my Zairian travel document and waved it in front of his face. 'And if you don't shut up I'll show you how Zairian people can fight.'

'He's drunk too much, Leah, he won't listen to you,' said Triffine, trying to hush me.

As she had predicted, my remarks enraged Bizima further. Suddenly he grabbed my hair so hard that he pulled a clump out of my scalp, making it bleed – I still have a bald patch there today. I was in agony and the pain made me scream but I was just as angry as he was. I took one of my shoes off and started hitting him with that. Then I kicked and punched him as hard as I could. I had never laid a finger on another human being before and was amazed at my behaviour, but something inside me drove me to keep on hitting, harder and harder.

'Look at this cockroach, I could snatch her in one minute,' he snarled, slapping me hard across my face. I slapped him back and because he was drunk he fell. He was soon back on his feet and started beating me with his fists and kicking me with his heavy boots.

Triffine knew Bizima and implored him to stop. But he ignored her and two of his Interahamwe friends joined in with beating me.

'*Inyenzi* are not just from Rwanda, they are outsiders like her too,' said Bizima. 'Your Zairian travel documents don't impress me, Leah Inyenzi.'

A Tutsi man called Giturki, who had heard the commotion, arrived in the compound with some of his friends and to my enormous relief rescued me. His friends picked up Bizima and threw him into the street, where he jumped into his red Toyota sports car and roared off. I was covered in bruises and shook with fear.

For the first time I had felt the burning hatred of the Interahamwe for Tutsis like me. I was used to being loved, not loathed. On the surface I was full of bold talk but inside I felt sick and more threatened than I'd ever felt in my life. Before Bizima, Kigali was solid ground for me. Now I felt that the earth I loved was cracking beneath my feet.

'Maybe he'll think twice before he attacks an innocent girl next time,' I said to Triffine, angry tears springing into my eyes.

'Hush, Leah. You need to be careful. You should stay away from this area for a while. It is a big Hutu area.'

'But Triffine, we must stand up for ourselves. They are calling us *inyenzi* to get a reaction. But it doesn't mean that we've all turned into cockroaches.'

My friend Robert's father was an important soldier in the army. 'Oh, that's not good,' he said, shaking his head, when I told him what had happened. 'I'm going to tell my friends about this. We must make a complaint.'

The complaint was filed and a few days later Bizima came to Triffine's house to apologise. He looked sheepish and without making eye contact he said, 'I'm sorry, I drink too much.'

I accepted his apology. I can see his face still, wide and harsh and unsmiling.

I never went to Ramera again. I knew that it was no longer a safe place for Tutsis. I heard that there were lots of other attacks the same day Bizima came for me. I was lucky because the area I was attacked in was quite civilised. In some of the townships people who were attacked were killed outright.

From that day on I became acutely aware of the rising tensions and looked at everything differently. Before, I had been sleepwalking through Kigali wrapped in my little cotton-wool world. Now I was awake and alert to every nuance. Hutus and Tutsis were still mixing, as they always had done, but I could feel a palpable difference in the air.

Maman's cousin was married to a Hutu soldier who started giving us advice about where particular trouble spots were at particular times. 'Don't go this side today, don't go that side today, make sure you're indoors by six p.m.,' he constantly warned us, his brow deeply furrowed.

If we visited Ethiopian or Somalian friends we could see that they had become nervous in case they were targeted as a result of entertaining us. The number of roadblocks between Gisenyi and

Kigali increased and I began to shake every time we had to pass one of them.

I was the last person in my family to visit Goma, a couple of months before the war started. I went to visit Nyadera, the man I adored and who had taught me so much. I wasn't touched on the journey out of Rwanda but there were so many roadblocks that instead of taking the usual two hours it took five or six. The country I knew so well was becoming unrecognisable. When were things going to return to normal?

My great-grandparents greeted me in the traditional way with milk. I brought sugar for them as a gift.

'Leah, my beautiful one, how are you? How do you feel to be a little mother?' my great-grandfather asked me.

'It's easy for me, Grandpapa, because Maman is there. I don't have to do it all by myself. I'm sorry I couldn't bring Jean-Luc to see you but travelling is very difficult at the moment. I'm sure everything will calm down again soon and get back to normal though.'

'You need to be careful right now, Leah. Tell that *papa* of yours to come back to Zaire until everything is finished in Rwanda.'

'Well, Kigali is different from other parts of Rwanda, we don't really see too much trouble in the capital,' I said. I thought it best not to tell him about the recent beating I had received from Bizima. Their house was very peaceful and I enjoyed a few days of quiet pampering. It would be a long time before I experienced such tranquillity again.

All of us were now in Kigali, apart from my brother Timotei who was studying in Kinshasa. A Hutu friend of mine warned me to keep away from Gisenyi and said there was going to be big trouble there. Everybody thought that if there was going to be a problem it would be in an area like Ruhengeri or Gisenyi, but that Kigali would not be touched. I talked to my parents about going back to Zaire, but the whole family was well settled in

Kigali now and they both believed that because of the presence of the UN Kigali was probably the safest place to be. I knew that my parents were generally right about everything and I desperately wanted to believe them.

CHAPTER FIVE

There was nothing remarkable about 6 April 1994. The day began just like any other. It was *kakunguzi* – a kind of farewell to Rwanda – although of course we didn't know that as the sun rose in the sky. The weather was beautiful, and people moved around freely, laughing and chatting to each other. There weren't even as many roadblocks as usual. I was a happy, carefree seventeen-year-old with a head full of frivolous thoughts.

I dropped Jean-Luc off with Maman and then went to the market to buy meat, milk, sugar, soap, chicken, green peas and some salad. Then I returned to pick him up as I had decided to take him with me to the photoshoot.

'Are you not going to eat here with us tonight?' Maman asked.

'No, but thank you, Maman. I'll wait for Christian; he's due to fly in to Kigali Airport later on and we'll eat together.'

Christian had recently gained a licence to fly small 'taxi' planes locally. He was flying from Changugu to Kigali and was due to arrive at the airport at 6.30. I had told him I'd be with friends in a café near the airport belonging to my friend Josephine. He was going to meet us there and all three of us would go from there to our house, which was about fifteen minutes away from the airport.

Maman was wearing a colourful traditional African wrapper. Her hair was tied back neatly and as always she looked fresh and elegant. She was forty-five years old but looked much younger. As I left she was gathering up her things to go to the bank. We hugged and kissed goodbye as we always did.

'Bye, Bébé, see you tomorrow,' she said. 'I think Jean-Luc needs to eat some porridge. I didn't have any in the cupboard for him.'

'Bye, Maman. Don't worry, I'll feed Jean-Luc,' I said.

Both of us were rushing and our exchange was mundane. Neither of us had any sense that this was the end of our lives as we knew them. In the weeks and months that followed, that image of my busy, beautiful Maman was freeze-framed in my mind. As I climbed into the car I spotted my twelve-year-old brother Sans Souci crouching on the floor in the back of the car. He hadn't been feeling well and so had not gone to school that day.

'Sans Souci, what are you doing? Get out now and go back into the house. I'm in a hurry and I'm going to be late for work,' I said sharply.

'Oh please, Bébé, take me with you. I know you're going to work at the airport. You know how much I love to watch the planes; please take me.' He looked at me beseechingly with his beautiful, dark eyes.

'No, Sans Souci, I can't take you today, go back inside right now.'

Looking cowed, he scurried back into the house. For as long as I live I will regret that moment.

The photo shoot started at 2 p.m. It was very straightforward work, adopting different poses with the beer in my hand. The venue was the restaurant on the roof of the airport. It was a nice place to do a shoot because it was light and airy and offered good views across Kigali. I enjoyed the work because I liked being photographed and it was a very easy way to earn money.

Everything seemed normal at the airport. The streets were still quiet and peaceful but I shivered a little. After the tensions of the last few months things felt a bit *too* peaceful, and I wondered when the Interahamwe were planning their next demonstration.

Josephine was a beautiful, light-skinned Hutu with a dazzling smile. Her café was right across the road from the airport and was attached to her house. She was famous for the lovely soft meat she cooked.

It was 5 p.m. We all chatted lazily, everyone smiling and joking. But there seemed to be a lot of soldiers on the streets. I knew the President wasn't in the country and presumed the soldiers were guarding the airport area in his absence.

A friend called Pierre called and said he had got as far as Chez Lando, just a few minutes away from Josephine's place, but that he had been held up by lots of roadblocks.

'Don't worry, we'll wait for you,' I said breezily. 'See you soon.'

There was a lovely ambience in the café. Jean-Luc was in my arms and we talked idly about future social arrangements and hopes that the current tensions in the country would subside.

The airport was so close that I got a good view of the President's plane coming in to land. It was a beautiful private plane with the national flag on it. Not too many planes took off and landed at Kigali Airport and everyone knew that the President was due to arrive back in Kigali that evening accompanied by the President of Burundi, Cyprien Ntaryamira. One of my friends mentioned that he could see the President's plane flying towards the airport. We all looked and saw the distinctive flag on his jet.

Suddenly there was the loudest explosion I had ever heard and the plane burst into flames as we watched, gasping and screaming. The flames turned the whole of the sky an angry orange. Nobody could speak. What we were seeing had paralysed us all. I felt as if invisible hands had wrapped themselves around my throat and were trying to strangle me. I was choking and spluttering.

I had watched many Hollywood movies but I had never seen anything as horrific as this. It was almost impossible to believe it was happening.

Before any of us could absorb what we had just witnessed, grenades started to explode. People were running and screaming in the streets: 'Don't kill me, don't kill me!'

I could see members of the Interahamwe chasing after them. Those who were running away were covered in blood. After years of studying the Bible as a child the only word on my lips was 'Apocalypse'. I was convinced the world was about to end.

We all sat glued to our chairs in a trance-like state. Josephine had the radio playing and within minutes an announcement was broadcast that the President's plane had been shot down by Tutsis.

'We're finished!' I managed to stutter. 'None of us can survive now.'

It has never been discovered exactly who was responsible for the explosion. It is thought that Hutu extremists, suspecting the President was finally about to implement the Arusha Peace Accords ushering in a power-sharing government between Hutus and Tutsis, were behind the attack, although of course we had no idea about any of this at the time.

Within a few seconds of the plane being shot down we heard lots of shooting from behind the café. My throat tightened with panic. Now the eerie calm earlier in the day was starting to make sense. I pulled Jean-Luc closer to me. There had been incidents in Kigali before but nothing like this. Idle banter and the tinkling of glasses stopped. Everything good and happy in Josephine's place was now stone dead. All of us were frozen into horrified paralysis. The delicious smell of grilled meat mingled with the bitter smell of gunsmoke and charred plane.

Josephine grabbed hold of my arm. 'Leah, come, come into my house. Be quick now, you must hide.'

'Hide, what do you mean?' I mumbled. I looked at her in a daze, wondering how she had managed to stay so calm and composed with so much chaos all around. She ushered Donata, Jean-Luc and me into her house, along with a few other Tutsi diners from her restaurant.

I could see UN vehicles driving around madly in the street outside. They seemed to be as surprised and disorientated as we were. I knew that Christian was due to arrive at the airport at any moment but I blocked all thoughts of what might happen to him from my mind. I started kissing Jean-Luc all over his face. I was so relieved that I had him with me instead of leaving him with Maman. I knew that I had to call her to make sure she was OK.

'Josephine, please can I use your phone?' I begged her. She nodded. Shakily I dialled Maman's number.

She answered, sounding as dazed as the rest of us. 'There's a lot of killing in our street. Stay where you are, Bébé. The whole of our road is full of blood.'

'I'm at Josephine's place, Maman, near the airport,' I said, my voice shaking.

'Oh my God,' she said. Then the phone went dead.

I could hear grenades exploding in the background. I ran my hands through my hair. I wanted to push time back to the relative peace we were enjoying just a few minutes before. What was happening was too immense for my brain to cope with. There was no space for thoughts. The horror all around us blotted out everything.

This sudden outbreak of killing had turned the little capital of Kigali into a gigantic place. The walk to Maman's from Josephine's place usually took me ten to fifteen minutes, but I felt that if I attempted it at the moment it would take me more than a year to reach her home.

'Come, Jean-Luc, we need to hide,' I managed to say calmly. I knew that if he heard the terror in my voice he would start screaming. I clutched him very tightly to my chest, hoping that I could transfuse love into him by having his skin and breath so close to mine.

Josephine pushed us urgently into her house. She saw me looking over at the injured people screaming in the street, wondering whether or not I should run out to help them. She clamped her hand firmly to my forearm and reminded me about the shape of my nose.

'No, Bébé, don't even think about it. Your baby needs you. You know exactly what they'll do to you if you go outside. The Interahamwe are everywhere. They will slice you to pieces. Don't look behind you, just get in the house now.'

I peeped in terror through Josephine's bamboo fence and screamed silently when I saw that a beautiful young woman had had her stomach slashed open. She lay on the ground groaning.

'Let's see how a Tutsi baby looks,' laughed one of the Interahamwe, who had her blood on his hands and clothes. Nothing about him seemed human. This horrific scene was being played out just a few yards away from me and I could see and hear everything horribly clearly.

He and one of his accomplices cut the poor woman as easily as if they were unzipping a jacket, and then nonchalantly walked off. It was clearly a deliberate act not to put her out of her misery immediately but instead to leave her to a slow and painful death.

'That woman who is dying on the ground is a Hutu. They don't even know or care who they're killing now they have the taste for blood in their mouths,' said Josephine, shaking her head despairingly.

When my own stomach was cut later, it was that woman's contorted face and mashed body that flashed through my mind. I couldn't understand how anyone could do that to a pregnant woman. In Rwanda everyone respected pregnant women. They were carrying the future.

I could hear her groans getting weaker as the life drained out of her.

'I'm afraid that poor young woman won't be the only one,' said Josephine grimly.

'Oh my God, Josephine. Don't talk that way. What about Maman, Papa, my sisters and brothers, and Christian? His plane was supposed to land now. He couldn't have survived . . .'

My voice sounded unrecognisable, a hysterical, high-pitched babble.

'Don't think about all that now, Leah. There are still good people and I am sure they will be helping the people you love to stay safe, just as I am helping you.'

Suddenly I lost control of my bladder. Then I vomited and felt my period suddenly start. My body was having its own personal earthquake in response to what was going on.

'Please, Josephine, let me go out there,' I begged once again.

'Leah, don't be silly. If you stay here and hide you can live, if you go out there you will die. Your baby needs you to stay alive: it's as simple as that.'

I had never heard such steeliness in Josephine's voice. She was very businesslike, and was impatient with my naïvety. 'I beg you not to move from here, Leah. Do you understand me?'

I nodded. My brain had frozen over. All I could think of was how and when they would kill me. Tiredness, hunger and all other normal human functions were suspended. Everybody responded to this terrible fear in different ways. I started asking myself how I could have brought a baby into a crazed world like this, a world that seemed to be coming to an end.

Surely no God could give me a child only to take him away again so quickly, I said to myself. We all believed that God left Rwanda that day. According to many Rwandise it was a long time before He returned.

Inside Josephine's house she was the only one who remained calm.

'Let's eat,' she said.

'What?' I cried. 'How can you think of food at a time like this?'

'Leah, I think you're going to be here for a while. I don't want you starving to death.

'I'm going to go outside and see what's happening,' she said. 'I'm a Hutu and I can show my ID card, I should be OK.'

Out in the street she found some UN soldiers. I had become friendly with some of the UN peacekeepers, a young man called Luc amongst them. He was short with lovely green eyes and was very easy to talk to. He spoke slowly, thinking carefully before he let the words come out of his mouth.

We often met up and went out together in a group of friends. He had a good heart and it made me feel very safe spending time with him. Not all Rwandise people spoke good French, and Belgian UN peacekeepers like Luc, enjoyed spending time with good French speakers. He used to come round to Maman's house and played ping-pong with various members of the family.

Now Josephine told Luc, 'I'm hiding Leah and a few others but I don't know how long they'll be safe in my house. Can you get them out as soon as possible?'

'We'll see if we can come back for them tomorrow,' said Luc. Both he and his partner looked pale and sick with shock. 'We can't do anything now. It's mayhem out here.'

She came back into the house. 'I've spoken to Luc, he's going to try to come back and rescue you tomorrow. Stay hidden until then and try to stay calm. There is plenty to eat and drink in the house. And at least now Luc knows you're here. I have to go, it isn't safe for me to stay around here any longer. There's too much killing outside.'

'Thank you, Josephine,' I said weakly. I could see by the terrified expression on her face that she feared the worst for us but was trying her best not to show it. Josephine was a moderate Hutu who opposed the Interahamwe. This stance put her at almost as much risk of being killed as Tutsis like me.

'Please don't leave us,' I whimpered as she turned to leave. She had been a rock since the plane exploded and I couldn't see how any of us would manage to live without her guiding us.

'Leah, you'll be OK, you'll find a way out.'

All I could see outside were people running and screaming and killing and being killed. That evening launched a terrifying orgy of death. Hutu fathers murdered their Tutsi wives and children. The killers stopped being human, they had become animals. It was as if a spell had been cast on Rwandise people: both victims and killers had entered a zombie-like state. I stared helplessly at Jean-Luc, not knowing what to say or do.

Those who did not acquiesce to the bidding of the Interahamwe usually perished. It was almost impossible to make a stand. We watched with horror through the fence as some friends of ours – a Hutu husband and Tutsi wife – were caught. The Interahamwe demanded that the man kill his wife. He refused, saying, 'Kill me, I will never kill the woman that I love so much.'

The Interahamwe murdered the couple's children in front of them before ripping the unborn baby out of the wife's womb and leaving her to bleed to death. Then, when they felt he had witnessed the maximum possible horror, they killed the husband too.

Donata started screaming hysterically when she witnessed this.

My initial shock and panic had subsided. I had moved into survival mode. I slapped Donata hard across her face to quieten her down.

'You need to be quiet right now. Stop screaming and I will save you,' I said. I was surprised by my authoritative tone. I looked her hard in the eye. I didn't realise how literally she was going to obey me.

When a disaster like this strikes I believe that people divide into two groups, those who give up and become passive because they are overwhelmed with hopelessness, and those who actively fight against what is going on. Already I was aligning myself with the second group. Two others like me were trying to work out what to do next. The rest had become hysterical lumps of jelly and just wanted to kill themselves.

The road in front of Josephine's café was already filling up with dead people, so passing Interahamwe assumed that the area had

already been 'cleansed' of Tutsi 'cockroaches' and didn't bother
searching inside Josephine's compound.

Rwanda's Hutu prime minister, Agathe Uwiliyingimana, was
a moderate and sincere woman loved by Hutus and Tutsis alike.
She didn't survive for long. Although the plane carrying the
President was believed to have been shot down by Hutu extremists, it was convenient for the Interahamwe to lay the blame for
it at the door of the Tutsis as an excuse to launch the killing.

'We're going to finish you, you killed our president,' sang the
Interahamwe as they marched through the streets. I shuddered.
I had been brought up to be a good, God-fearing Catholic and
I kept saying, 'Where is God? Where is God?'

As one Rwandise singer put it much later, 'God goes and gets
busy everywhere else, but when it comes to Rwanda He loves to
sleep.'

I wasn't aware of it at the time, but as I crouched sweating and
shaking with the other terrified Tutsis in Josephine's place a trans-
formation was taking place in me. I had been forced to grow up
quickly when I became pregnant with Jean-Luc, but now that
process was being completed. I had already witnessed too many
terrible things that a girl of my age should never see and I was
going to witness much more. As the screams filled the air outside,
Bébé Leah was melting away like an ice cube in the sun. A tough,
scarred adult was taking her place.

We all hid in different rooms; muffled sounds of wailing could
be heard throughout the house. Everybody in Rwanda listened
to the radio, and a notorious presenter called Cantono on the
national radio station had done his very best to stir up hatred for
Tutsis amongst Hutu listeners. 'Open up your eyes and go and
kill all the cockroaches,' he exhorted over the airwaves. What
chance did we have, with messages like that being broadcast over
and over again?

We hardly dared breathe. We trembled violently because we
could hear so many guns being fired and so many screams. All of

us thought that we were going to be next. There seemed to be some sort of terrifying order in the chaos outside. This outbreak of killing could not be happening by chance. This was no spontaneous, random outpouring of hatred against Tutsis.

After a few hours the commotion in the street subsided. Some people in Josephine's place said, 'There's too much blood, we need to take our own lives. We have no chance. Better to be killed by our own hands than hacked to pieces by the Interahamwe.'

'What kind of talk is that?' I snapped. 'Luc knows that we're hiding here. He will come and rescue us as soon as he can.'

Night fell. The electricity had been cut; in any case we would have been too scared to let any lights show that there were human presences still in Josephine's house. The place was well stocked with beer and fizzy drinks and tentatively people started to sip some drinks. Josephine had lots of meat in her kitchen but none of us could bear to touch it. Nobody said anything but we all felt the same, that there was too much human meat in the street. Eating the flesh of a cow at a time like this would be like eating a human.

As the hours of the night passed exhaustion blunted the terror we were all feeling. I had no idea what had become of my beloved family and Christian but I was in too deep a state of shock to think properly about them. The only way I could keep going was by pushing all thoughts about what had become of them to the back of my mind, to be dealt with later. Humans can only take so much pain, and my mind was helping me to survive by blocking out thoughts of the people I loved most.

I had always been good at staying calm in a crisis and to my relief this quality was not deserting me now. I remembered climbing a tree as a child to get a tennis ball caught in the branches. I got the ball but fell hard out of the tree on to my stomach. All the children around me panicked, thinking that I had been terribly injured, but I lay there calmly and reassured everyone:

'I'm just going to lie here quietly for a minute or two and then I'll be fine,' I said, steadying my voice. I'd managed to make myself, as well as the others, feel better and wanted to use the same soothing logic now. As the people hiding in Josephine's place continued to debate the merits of suicide, Donata momentarily broke her silence.

'I'm too young to die!' she wailed.

All of us were in our teens and twenties. Josephine's was one of those happening places beloved of young, fashionable people.

I stood up and started speaking like some kind of leader.

'We're all too young to die, and we're going to get out of here,' I said firmly. 'Let's forget this nonsense talk of taking our own lives. Luc will make sure we don't perish here. We just have to be a little bit patient. Look, we're still alive when all these people are dead. That's got to be a good sign. Please don't lose faith, we'll find a way. '

I paused for a moment and could see that people were actually listening to what I was saying. 'The truth is, I am not meant to die now. If there is a God He did not give me a son for six months just so he could take him away.'

I cut up some of Josephine's bedsheets to use as nappies for Jean-Luc as I only had one spare one with me, then I tried to settle him down for the night.

Eventually we all drifted into an uneasy sleep, punctuated by the sounds of people screaming and groaning outside.

I woke the next morning to the sounds of the Interahamwe singing and chanting, 'Come and clean the cockroaches out of your house. Wake up, your house is dirty and needs to be cleaned out.'

Rwanda was a highly organised and well-run country. I had never actually seen a cockroach because the houses I lived in or visited never had such creatures scuttling around inside them. Occasionally I had seen pest-control vans parked outside a building where they were eradicating an infestation of these black, shiny insects. To be called a cockroach in Rwanda meant you could not be tolerated.

Thankfully Jean-Luc had slept soundly. He looked up at me with his big, beautiful eyes and gurgled. He was my little bit of sanity in the middle of all this madness.

There was nothing to do but wait for Luc to arrive. Nobody spoke because there were no words to describe how we were feeling, and nothing we could do to make things any better.

The sounds coming from the street were getting worse and worse. We had no real idea what was going on beyond the part of the road we could see from Josephine's compound. The terrible screams continued and the piles of bodies grew bigger.

What if Luc doesn't come back? I kept saying to myself over and over again. If we stay here much longer we'll either be chopped to pieces or when the food and drink run out we'll die of hunger and thirst.

We sipped drinks and nibbled food without any appetite. Each minute felt like an hour. I was starting to work out a plan of escape if Luc didn't return, and thought that maybe we could creep out of the back of the compound under the cover of night and then try to find a way to get out of Kigali using back roads and tracks. I had been wearing expensive, high-heeled shoes when I arrived at Josephine's. I kicked them off, deciding that if we were going to escape on foot I'd be better off barefoot than in this kind of impractical shoes.

At eight that evening we heard the door opening. We gripped each other's hands in terror, wondering if the Interahamwe had found our hiding place. But to our delight and relief it was Luc with some other officers. I rushed up to him and flung my arms around his neck.

'Thank God you came, Luc, thank God, everything will be all right now.'

Luc had a haunted expression on his face that I had never seen before. He said, 'Please, Leah, there is no time for that. You have to hurry and get in the truck. I'm not taking Hutus, only Tutsis. The road is hell, travelling is not easy.'

'You're taking everyone who's here, we're all Tutsis.'

He nodded briefly. 'It's very bad outside. I want to say one thing before we leave this place. Please don't look in the street.'

CHAPTER SIX

As Luc hurried us out I couldn't resist the human impulse to look, though I had a pretty clear idea of the scene in the streets from peeping through the gaps in the fence of Josephine's compound. Bodies were piled up by the side of the road. I looked away, managed to control the urge to vomit and held Jean-Luc more tightly, burying his head in my chest so that he wouldn't see any of this. The spirit of death was everywhere; we still lived but we were inhabiting a place of death. I was sure I could hear the souls of the dead crying out.

This bore no resemblance to the Kigali I had known for so many years, a place of civilisation with graceful streets and calm order. I couldn't understand what kind of collective insanity had overwhelmed the people of Rwanda to make them butcher their neighbours in this way. I thought of all my kind, intelligent Hutu friends and couldn't imagine any of them ever getting involved in a brutal massacre. I know many books have been written about the genocide and why it happened but to this day I cannot comprehend what took people over, how easily a human switch can be flicked, turning people from kind friends into cold-blooded killers.

'Hurry,' said Luc nervously. 'Get into the truck.' We clambered in obediently, feeling terribly exposed, after the relative safety of Josephine's place, to be out in the street in full view of people who would have liked nothing better than to hack us to pieces. The truck was covered with a UN tarpaulin which prevented our enemies from seeing in and us from seeing out. All seven of us from Josephine's crouched into the truck. We collected other people from the neighourhood too and all of us crouched down. I could hear the Interahamwe singing. They sounded animated and untroubled.

I prayed that Luc would take us to the airport so that we could just get out of the country before anything worse happened. But it was not to be.

'We're going to Chez Lando,' he said quietly. There was so much tension in his voice it sounded as if his vocal cords were about to snap. Chez Lando was a fancy hotel and nightclub where I had spent so many happy evenings laughing and dancing and singing. They grilled the best chicken in Kigali.

My wish was for the sky to open up so that I could disappear. I felt totally hopeless and out of control. I could hear that the Interahamwe were arguing with the UN as the truck set off on its short journey. My heart pounded each time the truck stopped, presumably at roadblocks, and I pulled Jean-Luc closer to me. The whole town smelled of death, putrefying flesh and fear.

We supported each other inside that truck. When one person looked as if they had reached their limit, another with a little more strength stroked their hand gently and whispered softly, 'Hang in there.'

It was strange that Jean-Luc never cried. All the babies knew instinctively that they had to be quiet. Every so often I peeped out through gaps in the tarpaulin where it had ripped. Every time I looked out I saw the same sickening sights. When we approached my family's neighbourhood I couldn't help but look in case I saw someone in the street who I knew, or even a family member. I saw no one living, only more bodies. As we passed my parents' house I saw Papa's car right outside the house. The house looked exactly the same as it had a few days before, but Papa's car was completely burnt out. I gasped. Images of my lovely *papa* being blown to pieces as a grenade hit his car jumped before my eyes.

'No, no, no,' I cried under my breath. I didn't want anyone to hear me weeping and wailing. Maybe they all escaped, I kept saying to myself. I've got no proof that Papa and the rest of them have been killed. Papa is smart, he and Maman have many Hutu friends, I'm sure that like me they have had help to escape. I squeezed my eyes shut and tried to push all the terrible thoughts away. Please let them be OK, please, please, I prayed.

It took us about two hours to reach Chez Lando, a journey that was usually no more than twenty minutes. We had interminable stops at roadblocks while Luc negotiated with the Interahamwe and handed over money to them. Why were the UN playing by the rules of the Interahamwe? Like many Tutsis I had felt very confident that they would protect us from harm. Instead they seemed completely powerless in the face of the atrocities being committed.

Until the plane exploded I always saw the house Jean-Luc, Christian and I shared as a place of safety, our cosy little refuge from the world. But now that house had become poisoned for me. It was the last place I wanted to be. I knew that nowhere in Kigali was safe for Tutsis. Once again I pushed all thoughts of my family and Christian out of my head. I didn't feel strong enough to think about what could have happened to them. I squeezed every last ounce of mental energy into thinking about the best way I could protect my precious baby.

I knew it would be impossible to arrive at the wreckage-strewn airport and simply get on to a flight unless the UN helped us, but having seen how powerless they were I didn't hold out much hope that they would save us. As the truck crawled along the roads I tried to calculate which would be the safest way out of the capital. I had no idea whether or not the killing had spread beyond Kigali, but instinctively I thought we would probably be safer in the countryside. Just get out and get as far away as you can from all of this evil madness, I said to myself.

Finally we arrived at Chez Lando. Jean-Luc looked up at me with his big, trusting eyes and smiled. I tried to take strength from him before looking at the terrible scene inside this once-beautiful nightclub.

The first thing I saw was more dead bodies piled up outside. When is it going to be my turn? I thought to myself. But wait, I've survived so long, maybe I can survive a little bit longer, I argued silently. I was discovering an energy I didn't know I possessed. One moment I was overwhelmed by feelings of hopelessness and the next I felt stirrings of hope that we could get out of this mess alive.

Chez Lando had been transformed into what I can only describe as a mad camp. The luxurious fixtures and fittings were still intact but with the scenes of chaos superimposed on the place it was almost unrecognisable.

Luc led us to a bedroom. 'Wait here, Leah. I want to see if it's safe to take you to Hôtel des Mille Collines which is more secure than this place. But the road is full of Interahamwe. I don't know if it's safe enough for us to pass that way.'

'Luc, why is the UN not doing something to defeat the Interahamwe? We all thought we would be safe with you here, but we're not. Not at all.'

Luc hung his head. 'We have orders not to attack them unless they attack us first, and they are not attacking us – they are attacking you – so we must not intervene. *Je m'excuse, Leah.*'

I shook my head incredulously. How could they describe themselves as peacemakers when they were only bystanders? In the weeks and months that followed I was often haunted by Luc's voice in my head saying, *'Je m'excuse Leah, je m'excuse.'*

It was pouring with rain that night and Luc hoped the bad

weather would drive some of the Interahamwe off the streets. The rain turned the blood pink and it mixed with the orange earth. The bodies had started to bloat so that they became unrecognisable. Everybody was panicking.

'What's going to happen? I'd rather they caught us now than prolonged the agony,' said one woman, sobbing.

Luc had very honest eyes and couldn't hide his fear. 'Leah, I can't promise, but if I can get you to Mille Collines we might be able to airlift you out of this mess.'

'You have to get us out, Luc,' I begged. 'Can't you say I'm your girlfriend? You know we won't survive if you leave us here.'

'I'll try, Leah, but it's not easy. I'll be back soon.' He turned and walked away.

I heard a general at the Chez Lando reception say to another soldier, 'The only people who are moving out of here are white people. Rwandise are going nowhere.'

I felt sick when I heard this. Somehow Luc would have to find a way to get us out.

Around midnight he returned. I was overjoyed to see him. 'Thank you for keeping your promise,' I whispered.

He had brought me a pair of his trainers to wear. Because he was small for a man they fitted me perfectly.

'We need to move quickly, right away,' he said. 'While the road is clear.'

We climbed back into the truck, travelling slowly because the rain had made driving conditions difficult. To my enormous relief there were fewer roadblocks than there had been on the way from Josephine's. Jean-Luc slept in my arms and Donata trembled silently.

Whenever the truck was stopped the UN handed out money or drinks in the hope of preventing the Interahamwe from asking difficult questions about what or who was in the truck. The strategy seemed to work.

I had spent time at Mille Collines before. It was a place where diplomats and politicians went to and was famous for its pool. I wondered whether it too would now have bodies piled up in the driveway. Thankfully I saw nothing like that. There were lots of people there but it looked remarkably similar to the way it had the last time I'd visited. Luc hurried us past Reception and into a room where we were told we could hide.

One of the people who had hidden with us at Josephine's was also a model who worked for the beer company. I later heard that she survived and escaped to Belgium, but I don't know what became of the others after we left Chez Lando.

'Leah, this place is safe for now. The Interahamwe have not penetrated. Let's see what happens in the next day or two,' Luc said.

It was wonderful to be in a clean, calm, ordered place with no blood and no bodies and no Interahamwe. But there was an atmosphere of menace. I knew we wouldn't be able to stay for too long here. Death was not as close as it had been at Josephine's and Chez Lando, but it hovered just beyond the walls of the hotel compound.

'You see, Donata, I said I would get you somewhere safe,' I said to her, trying to sound positive. Donata gave me a silent, twisted smile.

We were sharing a big room with other families and were given milk and biscuits, tea, Fanta and bread. Nobody wanted to eat though. The same thought was in everybody's mind: that eating food felt like eating the bodies of the dead. Nobody said much. We were all shocked into silence.

The water and electricity were miraculously still working but because the water was contaminated by dead bodies it was no longer of drinking quality. The first time I tasted the beer I had been advertising was at Mille Collines. Because my stomach was empty it made me very sick.

'Let's sleep now,' I said to Donata, laying Jean-Luc carefully on the bed. I had a shower, using the good hotel soap. I tried to

scrub the odour of death off my skin. Then I lay down on one
of the beds, but my sleep was punctuated by screams and groans:
everyone in the room was having nightmares.

Paul, the manager of Mille Collines, was well known in Kigali.
He was a very kind man and was doing his best to help us all.
While we were in our room we had no idea how many others
were sheltering there as we were advised not to wander around
the hotel.

The next morning I left our room to look for some milk for
Jean-Luc and the other children in the room. While I was there
I heard talking between the UN, Paul and some of the
Interahamwe leaders, who had been allowed inside the hotel
while the marauding mob of foot-soldiers were being held outside the hotel compound. One of the leaders, a man I knew as
Jean-Baptiste, was the most horrible man I had seen in my entire
life. He had red, bulging eyes and looked like a monster. He spat
in front of the UN soldiers, not caring what they thought of his
behaviour.

He was speaking in his very bad French and I thought to
myself, That must be how Satan looks. People said he had a
family. How could someone with a family behave like that? I
used to think that people with families were good, sensible,
decent people, but that was not what I had seen in the last couple
of days. I was terrified that people like him were inside the hotel,
apparently negotiating with the UN.

'We have been told that you have *inyenzi* in here.' The word
'*inyenzi*' was no longer hurtful to me. It had become a word that
meant 'my people'. If I see a cockroach scuttling across the
ground now I cannot kill it because I feel like I'm killing a
member of my own family. I shuddered and crept back to our
bedroom.

At that moment I was certain I was going to die, but I did not
know how or when. Would I die with a bullet and be lucky, or
would they cut off my head or limbs? Before, machetes were

normal farming implements. I never dreamed they could be used to cut people into pieces.

A family friend who lived near my parents was also hiding in the hotel. When he saw me he hugged me, his eyes full of tears.

'Bébé, I'm so sorry. Your papa's car was found completely burnt out. It was hit by mortar fire.'

'I saw the car. I know it looked bad, but how do you know Papa died in there? Maybe he managed to jump clear just in time.'

He shook his head sadly. 'I don't know, Bébé.'

I started screaming, 'No, no, how can you be sure?' I put my head in my hands and said over and over again, 'Papa, how will I manage without you? You gave me so much and taught me so much.'

I cried until I had no tears left. 'What about Maman and the rest of the family? Are they dead too?' I whispered.

'I have no news of them. Maybe they made it,' he said.

Hearing the news about Papa made me more determined than ever to get out of Kigali. There was no time to grieve. With chaos and killing all around there was no space inside my head for any more pain. I decided not to tell Donata as she was in such a fragile state. I prayed that somehow the rest of the family had survived and tried to focus on how we could escape from the hotel if Luc failed to help us. Day after day I scanned the lobby area, looking for him, but there was no sign of him. I wondered if he had already gone back to Belgium.

Eventually, after a week of waiting, crying and panicking, he appeared.

'Luc, thank God you're here. I prayed that you wouldn't leave us. Have you managed to arrange a flight out for us?'

He shook his head miserably. 'I'm so sorry, Bébé. The Interahamwe are outside. We can't take anybody.'

'What's going to happen to us?' I said.

He shrugged and stammered, 'The situation is looking very bad, Leah. We have to leave.'

'You can't leave!'

'We have to. We're leaving tonight.'

'Please, please take us with you. You know we won't survive here.'

'I can't,' he said and started crying. 'I have to go.'

I told Donata that we were going to have to leave by ourselves because the UN weren't going to save us. Donata refused to budge. She folded her arms across her chest and kept shaking her head.

'Donata, this place is not safe. It's up to you whether or not you come with me, but if I'm going to be killed I would rather die resisting.'

A lady in Mille Collines gave us a traditional Senegalese dress called a *boubou*. Rwandise women don't wear this kind of outfit so we hoped we would look foreign. Donata and I were both wearing jeans and T-shirts that showed off our tall slim bodies. Tutsi women have very different bodies from Hutus – generally we are long and slender, while Hutus are shorter and broader. We gratefully put on the Senegalese robes to conceal our shapes and our true identity. Donata continued to be mute so I didn't have to worry about her giving us away with her local accent, but it was important for me to sound foreign.

'Just speak French with an Arab accent, say you're Senegalese and are working for the UN,' urged the lady who gave us the dresses. 'These Interahamwe are illiterate and they won't know any different.'

I went back to our room and told everybody there was no point waiting for the UN to save us. 'If we want to survive we have to leave now,' I said grimly.

Old people were saying, 'How can we move? We can hardly walk.'

'I can only take those who can walk,' I said quietly. I was amazed by how calm and businesslike I sounded. At this moment the only thoughts in my head were of how to ensure that Jean-Luc, Donata and I survived.

I knew a back way out of the hotel. We crept down to the pool and jumped over the back gate. I strapped Jean-Luc to my back.

'Come, Donata,' I said as she hesitated.

For almost a minute she stood and looked at me and then with a deep sigh she clambered to the top of the wall and jumped down on to the soft earth on the other side. To my relief there were no Interahamwe in view. I assumed they were all still crowded around the front entrance of the hotel.

Sixteen of us escaped that way. We crawled towards the main road and then went to hide in a Pentecostal church that was full of dead bodies. It was too terrible to be in such a place, but common sense told me that we would be safest in places where there were fresh killings because the Interahamwe were unlikely to return there. In that way the dead protected the living.

And this was how we spent our first few days on the run: hiding with rotting corpses, their faces still contorted in agony. As we tried to sleep I was sure that I could hear their troubled souls crying out.

CHAPTER SEVEN

Our plan was to hide by day and travel by night. But we had to wait in the church for three days, surviving on some old biscuits and Fantas we found in the kitchen. Every night we tried to leave but the Interahamwe were too close by. I wanted to reach a farming area with small houses where I thought we could be safe. Instinctively I thought that if we could pass through some back roads we would get to the market that they call Nyagasambo and we'd be safe. Although I was terrified of how the Interahamwe might torture us if they caught us, I no longer feared death itself. Being so close to so many dead bodies had taken the terrible mystery away.

Eventually we crept out and took the back roads towards the bush. But even in the bush there were mutilated, decomposing bodies strewn everywhere. The Interahamwe were terrifyingly efficient. It seemed that they had left no area untouched.

The people we escaped from the hotel with went in all different directions. Sometimes we walked with others who were fleeing, at other times Donata, Jean-Luc and I walked alone. People rarely spoke to each other. Like washing, eating and changing our clothes, conversation had become an unnecessary extra, not needed for survival.

Papa's kind face kept floating before my eyes. I blinked to try to flick it out of sight. As soon as I shook his image out of my mind, Maman's face filled the space. I saw her laughing and chattering as she prepared to go to the bank in the hours before all hell broke loose. When I tried to blink her away Christian floated in front of my eyes, smiling kindly.

You need to go on, for Jean-Luc's sake, and the only way to do that is to think about nothing except how to cheat death, I told myself firmly.

After two exhausting days of trudging through the bush and back roads, somehow managing to avoid the Interahamwe, we arrived at a Catholic church, the Church of Nyamata, on top of a hill, where many people had sought shelter.

I prayed that here we would be safe. As we walked up the path I could see a couple of nuns in the doorway. Surely nothing could happen to us while they remained in the church, I thought to myself. They would not permit the Interahamwe to cross their threshold.

The nuns gestured to us to enter, although they didn't seem very friendly. The atmosphere was hushed. Everyone was very quiet because the church was in such an exposed spot on top of the hill. The body of the church was crowded with people seeking refuge, and we found our way to a small side room where confession was heard. I was relieved not to be crowded together with all the other desperate souls. I couldn't bear to see their pain.

Most of the nuns in Kigali were Hutus. One of them approached me and asked suspiciously, 'Where are you from?'

'I'm from Senegal,' I replied quickly. But I could see she didn't believe me. I saw none of them show any kindness to anyone, not even the small children. They passed tea around wordlessly and we drank it gratefully. Jean-Luc and Donata dropped off to sleep. I closed my eyes but immediately reopened them when I heard the nuns whispering to each other in Kinyarwanda.

'We must tell them.'

'No, we can't do that.'

'We can't let them be killed.'

'Why not? We know these people are only cockroaches.'

My blood froze. The Interahamwe must be near. I knew we had to get out fast. There was no point hoping that the nuns who were suffering a crisis of conscience would be able to persuade the others to do the right thing. I stood up and shook Donata awake.

'Things are getting very bad, we have to leave,' I whispered.

Donata kept on shaking her head. She did not have the physical or emotional strength to move. Once again she wanted to stay and give up. I made a gesture of a throat being slit.

'Donata, if we stay here we'll be killed,' I hissed.

A few others who had come into the same room saw and said, 'What are you talking about? We're in a church, we must be much safer in here than outside.'

I shook my head. 'Believe me, this place isn't safe, I'm going.'

Two other women followed Donata and me. One of the nuns saw us leaving but didn't try to stop us. I think she was the one telling the others not to give us up to the Interahamwe. I had never seen anyone with such a sad expression on their face as that nun had. She knew exactly what was about to happen.

Leah, you have to at least die trying, you can't just sit there and surrender, I kept saying to myself, to try and give myself some courage. You have to fight until the end.

Just a few minutes after we crept out by a back door I heard the most terrible screams coming from the church. The sounds people were making were more like animals than humans. Donata looked at me in amazement as if to say, *How did you do that?* After that she rarely questioned my instructions.

'Let's just get out of here,' I said to her wearily.

I still don't understand how servants of God could usher people into the house of God so they could be killed. But there was so much about all of this that I didn't understand. I decided that the less I thought about what was going on and the more I focused my energy on getting out, the better things would be for us. Unlike many Rwandise people I had travelled abroad, growing up in Zaire, visiting Burundi, Kenya and Belgium with my parents. I knew there were other worlds beyond this hell and that kept me going. I think some of the others gave up because they couldn't see beyond the blood that was filling the streets and rivers of Rwanda.

We tried various routes out of Kigali but it looked as if the entire city was ringed by roadblocks. Kigali had become one big coffin, with the lid slowly but surely shutting on all of us. We were tired, hungry and terrified but a small, stubborn voice inside me made me determined to carry on. I decided that if we couldn't find a way round the roadblocks we would simply have to go through them. I planned out a few stories in my head to tell the Interahamwe policing them. Maybe I could charm our way through these terrifying barriers.

My heart pounded and I felt sweat stick my *boubou* to my back and run down my chest, a river of drops pooling in my belly button. I tried desperately hard to calm my shaking legs and walked confidently up to a checkpoint.

'Oh, where are *inyenzi* reaching now? They are giving us too much trouble. I wish I didn't come here. I wish I could reach home,' I said irritably.

'Where is home?' asked one of the Interahamwe suspiciously. He was dressed in the brightly coloured uniform and was clutching a club studded with nails. His face looked cruel.

'Goma,' I replied without flinching.

'What are you doing in Kigali?' he asked me.

I knew a Burundian Hutu professor who was married to a French-Malian woman who was light-skinned like me. I decided it was time for some name-dropping. 'I'm visiting my brother-in-law Lionel; he's a well-known Hutu professor. Do you know of him?'

The man had obviously not heard of him but didn't want to appear a fool. Wearing the *boubou* and speaking French with a French accent helped me a lot.

'Where is your passport?'

'They took it over there at the other checkpoint.'

My story worked well. The man looked at me carefully, considered what to do for a minute that felt like an hour and then signalled for us to pass. I was flooded with relief. Maybe we're going to make it, I said to myself.

We weren't allowed to pass all the checkpoints so easily. The rebels held all the cards. But if they believed you were not Rwandise, you weren't treated too badly.

At some checkpoints they shouted to me to remove my shoes so that they could check if my feet had a Hutu or Tutsi bone structure. I pretended not to understand a word of Kinyarwanda. Once they hit me with the back of a gun.

I cried out in French, 'Why did you hit me?' Then I gave the story about my brother-in-law the Burundian professor. 'All we are trying to do is get home. We're looking for the way to go.'

Very few people in Rwanda had managed to get hold of traditional Senegalese clothes like the ones Donata and I were wearing after the genocide started. These clothes really helped to protect us and over and over again I gave silent thanks to the woman in the Hôtel des Mille Collines who had given us the *boubous*. Sometimes I changed my story at the checkpoints and said I was a UN staffer or a charity worker from France. I tried to squash my nose as much as I could so that I looked more like a Hutu. Alas I did not have access to the cotton wool I had used in Zaire to stuff inside my nostrils.

We all looked like the walking dead, and more so with each passing day. Our bodies were unwashed, our teeth unbrushed. We had been infected by all the death and madness in the air. I felt as if I was clinging on to my sanity by my fingertips.

Those who killed looked crazy, possessed. And so did the

victims. Everybody in Rwanda had gone mad. We hid whenever we saw killings. After the Interahamwe killed people they ground them into the earth by putting their foot on the dead person's stomach, in exactly the way you would crush a cockroach underfoot. They genuinely believed that we Tutsis had no human qualities at all and were vermin that needed to be destroyed.

We survived by eating underripe bananas and raw potatoes, anything that was not poisonous that could fill our stomachs, however horrible it tasted. I chewed some of this disgusting food to soften it before placing little bits in Jean-Luc's mouth. I had hardly any breast milk left and I had to find a way to give him enough nourishment to survive.

It must have been a combination of my ability to speak different languages, to think on my feet, the Senegalese clothes and my sheer determination to survive that finally got us to the outskirts of Kigali alive.

CHAPTER EIGHT

Donata had become very weak and we couldn't find any more tough bananas to chew on. We spotted a farmer's hut in a field of mud where they grew rice and tea, and went inside to rest there for a while. My milk had all but dried up but I let Jean-Luc suck from my breast whenever he wanted to and he managed to stimulate a few drops of milk to flow.

After a few hours I woke Donata.

'We need to make it to the road. We have to keep moving. It's dangerous for us to stop for too long.'

Donata dragged herself off the ground reluctantly. I felt very sorry for her because she was so sick and weak and because she had spent so long dragging around behind me when all she really wanted to do was to lie down and die.

At first the road was deserted, and I relaxed a little. Then suddenly a ferocious group of Interahamwe appeared armed with machetes. I felt so sick that I thought I was going to vomit my heart up.

I turned to Donata and said, 'Donata. I don't think we're going to make it. You can see they are ready to kill. I think today is our day to die.'

Donata shrugged. Even if she had been able to talk, what was there to say? I was running out of lies and I was so tired. My feet were swollen and I was weak and dizzy with hunger.

'How are you?' I said to one of them.

'You're weak, aren't you? Too weak to go any further,' he said, looking me up and down. I avoided looking him in the eye.

I had given up on false accents and just spoke Kinyarwanda. My voice sounded weak and reedy. I knew it was all over and I felt almost relieved. Every hour since this madness started felt like a week. The constant not knowing when death would come was over at last. My head filled with images of my family and Christian: maybe after my death I could be reunited with the people I loved. I noticed that the thug was carrying a gun and hoped he would be kind enough to let all three of us die by the bullet rather than hacking us to pieces.

Then he exclaimed, 'Bébé Leah? Can it really be you? You look very different from the last time I saw you.'

In my daze of terror and weakness the man's face hadn't registered as one I knew. But suddenly I realised that the man I assumed was going to end my life was an immigration officer called Manu I had met when I used to go to parties in Gisenyi.

'Now I am going to kill you,' he said in a loud, staged voice. He came up very close and whispered in my ear, 'How on earth did you end up here? I'm not going to kill you. I'll try to save you, but you need to play along.'

All I could do was look hopelessly into his eyes and nod feebly. I had no idea whether or not Manu had the power to save us. I was so weak that I felt detached from everything that was happening and felt certain that even if Manu didn't kill us somebody else would. I had lost all hope.

Manu gestured to one of the others to give us some sweetcorn they were grilling. 'Here, you can have your last meal,' he said scornfully. 'You look half starved, Bébé,' he whispered.

The sweetcorn tasted juicy and delicious. I had never eaten anything so good in my entire life. The Interahamwe had also been grilling potatoes which Manu tossed in our direction. I chewed bits of potato to soften them and then placed them carefully in Jean-Luc's mouth. He was such a good boy. Even though he was starving he did nothing more than whimper occasionally.

Manu started boasting to the others about how he was going to kill us by cutting our stomachs open. 'These people haven't eaten for a long time. Eating a big meal now will make them feel very ill,' he said cheerfully to the other Interahamwe gathered around. He told one of them to open the boot of a blue Volkswagen Golf parked near by. 'I'm going to put them into the boot, then I'm going to rape this one,' he said, gesturing towards me.

At that moment another group of weak people trudged up the road and the other Interahamwe went off to see whether they were friends or foes.

'There are so many roadblocks, but I'll try to get you through,' Manu whispered.

Having ascertained that the group were Hutus, the Interahamwe let them continue on their journey and returned to the sport of Tutsi-baiting.

I didn't care about anything any more. I was so tired of running that I just wanted to die.

Manu gave an Oscar-winning performance, describing in graphic detail what he was going to do to us. He appeared to be the boss and the others seemed to believe him. We were exhausted and as soon as the boot was shut on us all three of us fell asleep. I hoped I would never wake up again. I had no idea where we were going or what would happen next time we saw daylight.

I woke up sweating an hour later when the boot opened. We had arrived at some sort of army camp and a group of Interahamwe appeared, curious to see who was about to be tipped out of the car. Manu threw Donata and me on to the ground and then put Jean-Luc roughly in my arms. He started to cry but I held him tightly and said with all the strength I could muster, 'It's going to be all right.'

I told Donata weakly, 'We're lucky to be here at the camp where they have lots of weapons. We will be killed with the bullet rather than the machete.'

A group of Interahamwe walked up to us to see who Manu had captured. They kicked and prodded us roughly and then one of them commanded me to crouch on all fours. 'You will make a nice table,' he snarled, pushing his booted foot down hard into my spine. Just right to rest my bottle of beer on.' The other Interahamwe laughed.

'Don't worry, I'll deal with them,' Manu said to the others. They nodded and wandered off back to their hut. They'd lost interest in Manu's cargo – just another group of cockroaches.

Manu looked at me and winked as if to warn me that what he was about to do was part of his performance for the benefit of the other Interahamwe. Then he took up his machete. I looked him in the eye. I had no idea what he was going to do to me with it. Even though I knew death was close I felt terrified of pain.

'Please don't hurt me, Manu; can't you shoot me?' I said trembling.

'Just play along,' he whispered. I had seen too many of the Interahamwe with a mad, faraway look in their eyes when they killed. Manu's expression was not like that. He looked concerned and in control.

Slowly and deliberately Manu brought the machete down on both of my legs. Donata clapped her hand over her mouth and passed out. I felt no pain but watched with a strange, detached interest as my blood spurted on to the dusty brown earth. I didn't realise it at the time, but Manu had cut me in such a way as not to cause too much damage. It was only after I got out of Rwanda that I started to feel pain from my wounds. In the same way that

I was managing to block out terrible thoughts of what had happened to Christian and my family, most of the time I felt nothing of the physical pain and emotional trauma of being cut. I began to realise that the human body and mind can be kind. When there is too much pain for any human being to bear it is blocked out, filed away to be dealt with at a later date.

Manu left the three of us lying on the ground. The day was hot but we were all so still it looked as if we had been frozen into the earth.

'Let's leave the cockroaches there for a while and go and have a drink,' he said to the other Interahamwe.

The others were already drunk but Manu was completely sober. As he walked into the guards' hut he spotted a calendar from the beer company with my photo grinning out of it.

'Hey, I've just realised who our prisoner is. It's Bébé Leah, the girl on the calendar. She's not a cockroach, she's Zairian,' I heard him exclaim.

'Oh yes, Bébé Leah, the beauty of Zaire,' chimed in one of the others.

'We should bring her in.'

When I heard this I felt a surge of happiness. As I lay bleeding on the ground in a twisted pile with Donata and Jean-Luc, I felt a renewed urge to live.

Some of the Interahamwe carried us into the office. They peered at me and rubbed some of the grime from my face to try to get a better look at me.

'Oh, Bébé Leah, that is you!'

'Yes, that's me. I was working on another beautiful calendar for you and got trapped while I was trying to go home.' I tried to turn the whole thing into some kind of black joke but felt too weak. 'Look, you can see the gap between my front teeth. It really is me,' I insisted when they looked doubtful.

They kept looking at the calendar and back at me.

'Bébé, it certainly is you. We'll do our best to get you home.

Manu will take you in his car and see how far you can get.' I
could hardly believe what I was hearing. With the Interahamwe
as our escorts, surely we would make it to the border.

There was a piece of cloth in the hut and he handed this to me
to tie around my wounds.

It was dangerous for Manu to travel too far out of his own area
though. Different Interahamwe controlled different areas and they
could behave in an unpredictable way when others encroached
on to their patch. He drove for another twenty minutes and said
it would be too dangerous for him to take us any further. He
dropped us on the main road.

'Manu, I don't know how I will ever be able to thank you.
You know you have saved three lives and that is the greatest thing
that any human being can do, especially when we are drowning
in killing.'

'Bébé, take care. I will pray for you and hope that you can get
back across the border into Goma. Gisenyi is very bad. When
you reach there take care.'

Donata and I looked at each other and beamed with relief. We
knew we had been mauled inside the mouth of a lion and then
miraculously spat out.

'I think we're going to make it, Donata. We've been lucky, and
we're not too far from the border now. I know we're sick and
weak, but after all this we must find a way to reach safety.'

She nodded and gave me a sad half-smile.

The road was littered with bodies. People had been cut when
they were trying to run. Trying to find a space on the ground to
walk without treading on a dead body had become normal. All
I could think about was to keep moving forwards. I knew that
whichever route we took we would encounter the bodies. They
were like autumn leaves; you clear them one day but more fall the
next. We had seen bodies throughout our journey but in this part
of Rwanda it seemed that the killing had been much more
intense.

'Donata, we're going to go through the bush, it will be safer there.'

She had fallen and cut her leg badly while we were walking.

'Let me pee on it, it's supposed to be a way to make wounds better.'

She looked horrified. I peed on her and she screamed as the urine stung her. I hoped it would disinfect her wound, but she looked unconvinced. In our previous lives such an act would have been unthinkable but now it seemed almost normal behaviour.

There were children and babies sitting next to their dead parents as we walked. Flies were greedily crawling over their faces. Some hungry, wretched children started following people who were walking down the road. Some mothers had abandoned their babies because they couldn't carry them. As a mother devoting every fibre of my being to protecting my own precious child, I had a heightened sensitivity towards other babies.

'Donata, let's try to at least take one or two of these poor little things,' I said.

She looked at me as if I was completely mad.

I picked up one boy of about two who was clinging to his dying mother. Blood was pouring from the woman's abdomen and from the way her legs were splayed open it looked as if she had been raped.

'I'm going to look after your baby for you. I promise you he will be in good hands, I will do everything I can to save him,' I whispered. I picked up the boy and cuddled him so that she could see and then gently closed her eyes so that she could die. I hoped I had given her some peace to leave the world with.

A few minutes later we found two babies who looked like twins who were trying to suckle from their dead mother. To my amazement Donata picked them up. They were four or five months old and smelled very badly of urine.

I took Jean-Luc and the older boy and Donata carried the twins. None of the children made a sound. Donata was like a robot, her face a blank mask concealing whatever was going on in her soul. We moved off the road into the dense undergrowth alongside it, hoping we might be safer there. There were plenty of cacti, and long grass where we could hide if we heard anyone coming. And lots of shallow, dirty ponds alive with leaping, croaking frogs. I hoped the noise of the frogs would conceal the sounds of our footsteps. I loathed frogs because of the harsh, tuneless noise they made, which set my teeth on edge. The creatures I really loved were butterflies, but it seemed that they had fled too. Since our journey had started I hadn't caught sight of a single one. As children we used to put two pieces of white paper on a little wire and wave them around. Plenty of butterflies would come, thinking there were other butterflies around. Where did they go? I wondered now. The birds had fled too; I couldn't hear them singing. Perhaps what they saw broke their little hearts and they decided to migrate to a kinder country.

The horrible thing we did see all the time was dogs eating people's bodies.

Sometimes the Interahamwe removed organs after they had already killed people. On our journey I had seen one of them pull out a heart and stamp on it saying, 'I'm stamping on a cockroach heart.'

I had never heard of rape in Rwanda before but now it was everywhere. Sometimes they raped women while they were alive, at other times after they were dead.

Wherever people were caught they were told to sit in the road, and then Interahamwe would sit on their heads and break their necks. Sometimes they urinated in people's mouths, other times they severed their heads from their necks. They were often drenched with sweat from the sheer exertion of chopping off so many limbs.

We stumbled along for a while but didn't seem to be getting

very far. I sensed that we were wandering around in circles and would have to get back to the road if we were going to move forwards. What on earth had I been thinking when we picked up the three children? It was madness to think I could save them. We were all going to perish together.

It was around six in the evening when we returned to the road. We saw people there who were sick from drinking bad water. They were vomiting and doubled up with diarrhoea cramps. Many sank down with exhaustion and died where they fell.

As we walked along I saw a roadblock, a wall of Interahamwe barring the way with guns, machetes and grenades. Whenever we snatched some sleep my nightmares always featured these roadblocks. We joined another group of people, hoping that we might be able to slip through. I couldn't work out if it was better to be at the front, in the middle or at the back. Would they get fed up by the time they got to the back of the line and just move everyone on? I decided our chances would be better if we hung back. Donata and I lowered our heads in the hope that we wouldn't be noticed.

My heart sank when one of the Interahamwe cried out, 'Hey!'

I couldn't believe my eyes when I saw it was Bahati, a Hutu taxi driver I knew from Gisenyi. Often when I had been partying there and had been too tired to walk across the border back to Goma he had driven me home. I had always liked him although I didn't know him well. I wondered how he would behave towards me.

'These cockroaches are mine. I know exactly what I'm going to do with them,' he said. Manu had used the same tactics, and I prayed that Bahati too would try to save us. I felt a heavy sense of responsibility towards all the children and I wanted to keep my promise to the dying mother of the oldest child we had taken.

Bahati smacked my bottom and groped my breasts to show the

other Interahamwe that he meant business. I winced. It was impossible to know whether or not I could trust him. He bundled us into his yellow Renault taxi. I remembered the last time I had been in the taxi, before I had Jean-Luc. I had been out with friends in Gisenyi and had spent the evening laughing and joking. Bahati had taken me back over the border to Goma. It felt like a lifetime away.

'Bébé Leah, don't worry. I cannot have your blood on my hands. I will not harm you. The situation is very bad here. If you don't join in with the killing you get killed. It was not my choice to be part of this mess. You look terrible, like a dead girl walking. I didn't know you have a baby. I would like to get to Zaire myself.' He was talking so fast I could barely catch what he was saying.

We made very slow progress along the road because there were so many people walking – a big, sad exodus. Then we reached another roadblock, where Bahati made the same speech to the Interahamwe about how he was going to kill us.

'No, *we'll* kill them, leave them here. Why didn't you put them in the boot?' asked one of the Interahamwe suspiciously.

'No, these are mine,' insisted Bahati. 'I'm going to rape this girl so much and I know exactly how I'm gonna do it.'

I was panicking that they would make him rape me in front of them.

Bahati came and shouted in my face and spat at me. 'I wanted you very, very badly for quite a long time. Now I've got you. I'm not going to kill you in front of these people, I know exactly how I'm going to do it. These *inyenzi* I will kill them myself,' he snarled, and rubbed his hands together in anticipation.

I saw him looking thoughtfully at the babies and children I had with me. I hadn't considered their ethnic origins but even at a young age the fatter, flatter Hutu noses and the long thin Tutsi noses could be distinguished from each other. How strange to be hacked to pieces because of the shape of your nose. It was like one of the French satires I'd studied at school, only it was real. I hoped that the fact that I was looking after Hutu children might help to save me.

'First of all I'm going to rape these two,' Bahati boasted to his friends, gesturing towards Donata and me. I saw the glint in his eye. He looked as if he meant it. There was a truck parked close to the roadblock. 'I'll put them in the truck and take them somewhere a bit more private.'

His friends looked doubtful but then shrugged and turned away. He pushed us into the truck. I was shaking from head to toe but tried not to let him see how terrified I was. Jean-Luc was whimpering in my arms. Donata looked paralysed with terror.

'I'm not going to kill you,' he hissed under his breath without taking his eyes off the road. I'll try to get you out of Rwanda but I don't know what is happening round the next corner. At each roadblock the Interahamwe make up their own rules.'

I relaxed a bit but in these circumstances it was impossible to trust.

'Just kill me, Bahati,' I said wearily. 'I know you will kill me better than the others, without cutting my head off. I don't want to die by the machete.'

'Bébé, you're going to live,' he said confidently.

Before we reached a place called Biyumba there was a big roadblock. I could see that Bahati wouldn't be able to control the situation here. The Interahamwe signalled impatiently for us to get down from the truck.

'These cockroaches are mine, I know what I'm going to do with them,' Bahati repeated hopefully.

He hit me very hard on the face to show the others that he meant business. I was holding Jean-Luc. Donata stood there mutely; I don't think what was going on even registered with her any more. As horror piled on top of horror, each day Donata regressed. She had entered a childlike state and needed almost as much looking after as Jean-Luc.

Bahati took out a long, terrifying knife and cut me on my leg. Blood spurted but once again I felt no pain. Donata collapsed at the sight of so much blood and I slumped to the ground feeling overwhelmingly dizzy.

Jean-Luc slept through the whole thing. He was amazingly still.

At that moment a group of Interahamwe walked up to us. 'Should we kill them?' asked one.

'No, these cockroaches are already dead,' Bahati said dismissively.

'Well, just leave them here, we don't have time to take dead bodies.' The Interahamwe turned round and walked away.

'You need to be strong,' Bahati whispered, and walked away.

When the coast was clear we tore up parts of our by now ragged, filthy Senegalese *boubous* to use as bandages for my slashed legs, and started walking. Blood, dust and tears mingled into an unsightly paste that clung to our filthy bodies. We hardly had the energy but somehow we moved forwards. We had to reach a place called Ruhengeri before we could cross the border.

'We're going to go through the forest,' I said to Donata. 'I hope it will be safer than the road.'

We reached an abandoned village that had many bananas on the trees and decided to stay for the night. We found some banana juice in one of the mud-and-straw huts, and drank it greedily. It looked as if the people had left in a hurry. A traditional pot made out of mud and used to cook beans was kicked over on the floor. There were some raw beans but we had no water to cook them with.

'Nobody must cry,' I said sternly, hoping the babies would understand from the tone of my voice, even though they didn't know the meaning of my words. I needn't have worried because nobody had the energy to cry. We lay down on the mud floor and tried to sleep. I was trying to feed all the babies although I had hardly any milk and my breasts felt very painful. It was a quiet place and for once I couldn't hear the Interahamwe singing their evil songs. Nothing breathed in the bush. At that moment I felt as if all Rwanda was dead.

CHAPTER NINE

When I woke up the next morning I decided to have a look outside. I walked for a few minutes to see if it would be safe to return to the road, and froze when I heard footsteps crunching through the undergrowth. I watched in terror from behind a tree, waiting for the figure to pass. But as I watched I thought there was something familiar about the man I was hiding from. I realised it was Habi, a Hutu farmer who had a depot in the market in Gisenyi and grew his crops in this area.

Habi was a lovely man, kind, chatty and always cheerful. But now everyone had become dangerous to me, even gentle souls like Habi. He was wearing a black leather jacket, with distinctive fabric patterns on it. I recognised it from the market and stepped out from behind the tree. Despite the fact that I looked very different from the way I had looked just a few weeks before he recognised me straight away.

'Bébé Leah! What on earth are you doing here?' He looked me up and down. 'I'm so sorry,' he said. 'I can see that you have really suffered. These are terrible times. This place is far too dangerous for you.'

I relaxed because I could see that he was concerned about me.

'I'm trying to cross the border into Goma, Habi. How is the road ahead?' I asked.

'Not good, not good at all.' Habi looked very sad.

'What is it, Habi?' I asked. 'You look as if you have suffered too.'

'I've lost everyone, Bébé. You know my wife was a Tutsi. She and all the children have been slaughtered.'

'I'm so sorry, Habi,' I said.

'That is the case for so many people. I am not alone with this grief. People are behaving very badly in the street.'

'I know,' I said. 'I've come all the way from Kigali.'

'Really? I didn't think it was possible to make that journey and survive. How are things there?'

'Everything is very bad there, people have gone crazy. It is as if everyone has been given a pill that infects them with a disease of madness and makes them happy to go out and kill their neighbours.'

'Where are you staying?' he asked.

I pointed to the hut we had been sleeping in.

'Come to the place where I store my potatoes; you will be much safer there.'

He came back to the hut with me and saw Donata and all the babies.

'Bébé, what are you doing with all these little ones?' Then he gasped and fell to his knees, weeping.

'Habi, what's the matter?' I asked.

'Oh, my God, it can't be? Are you a witch, Bébé, bringing people back from the dead?'

'What are you talking about, Habi?'

He started shaking.

'That one, Mutoni' – he pointed to the biggest boy we had picked up – 'he's my son. I thought he was dead. Where did you find him? How long have you had him?'

'Three or four days. He is a very good child. He was sitting by a dying woman. I'm sorry, Habi, I think it must have been your wife.'

'Yes, my neighbour told me she and the children had been caught. But I had no idea any of my children had survived. God bless you, Leah, how can I ever thank you? They are trying to force Hutus like me to kill Tutsis but I will not. I will do everything I can to protect you.'

He sobbed as he hugged and kissed his son. I cried too but Donata's expression didn't change. I realised that this was the first time I had witnessed any happiness since the killing started.

'How did you manage to travel with these babies?' Habi asked when he had recovered himself. 'It's hard enough to move around by yourself. Surely taking on all these extra children has held you back and put you in more danger. That is why their mothers left them by the roadside: they knew they couldn't run with them.'

'They're human, that's why,' I replied quietly. 'Now that I am a mother myself I understand how precious children are. If Jean-Luc was left by the roadside because I had been killed, I hope some other mother would pick him up and care for him.'

'Wait here. I'll be back. I'm going to help you.'

Donata was really terrified of all Hutus. Although she still wasn't talking, the expression on her face said that she feared Habi would betray us.

At first I felt confident that he would help, but as the hours passed and there was no sign of him I began to panic. Perhaps he would abandon us to starve to death or be found by the Interahamwe, or maybe he would tip off the Interahamwe and tell them to come and kill us. He himself might even return with a machete and kill us one by one. In these unreal times it was impossible to have any certainty about anything. Some Hutus I had known to be decent human beings before were now so infected by the constant exhortations to kill that their morality had completely disintegrated. It was hard to know just by looking into their eyes who still knew the difference between right and wrong and who had completely lost their way.

After three hours that felt like three days Habi returned, with a truck piled high with potatoes. He was dressed in the brightly coloured uniform of the Interahamwe. With him were two other men I did not recognise, also dressed in the Interahamwe colours.

'You have to hide under the potatoes. Be quick and be quiet,' he said. I was flooded with relief and gratitude that he'd returned, but was still unsure about whether or not he would ultimately betray us. Even if he didn't, maybe the other two men would.

'Bébé Leah, I will try to help you cross Ruhengeri into Gisenyi, but it won't be easy,' he said. 'It's one of the worst places for killing.'

I cursed myself for thinking I could beat the Interahamwe and get out of this hell alive. Why hadn't I just given up on 6 April and stayed in Kigali to die? People we had met on the road on our journey out of Kigali had said it was impossible for Tutsis to survive Ruhengeri.

The two men in Interahamwe uniforms sitting in the front with Habi didn't even turn round to look at us as we clambered into the truck and lay down, holding on to the babies. The smell of the fresh earth that had fallen from the newly dug potatoes filled my nostrils. It was a joy to inhale something honest and full of life after the weeks of rotting human flesh.

Habi turned the key in the ignition and we set off down the bumpy track. I closed my eyes, clenching my fists to try to stop myself from shaking. Every time the truck was stopped at a road-block my heart lurched. Habi gave the same story each time – the potatoes were destined for Interahamwe troops in Gisenyi. The men at the roadblocks demanded that he hand some of the pota-toes over to them. Each time he gathered up potatoes to give to the Interahamwe I held my breath. Each time he was waved on.

Then the truck stopped again, but I couldn't hear the usual agitated sounds of the Interahamwe. It was very dark and there was no electricity so I had no idea where we were. Surely we hadn't crossed Ruhengeri so easily? Habi jumped out of the truck.

'Bébé, we made it. We're on the outskirts of Gisenyi. You must stop here for a while and I'll see if it is safe to continue.'

'Thank you, Habi, thank you. I can't believe we've made it so far.'

It had taken us just a little over an hour to cross the shark-infested waters of Ruhengeri.

Habi lived in this area and knew it well. He left us in an abandoned house that I suspected belonged to the Interahamwe.

'I'm going to see how the road is and I'll come and tell you,' he said. 'I may be a while.'

He left us in the house for about six hours. He handed us Fantas and bananas and we almost relaxed. I felt reassured that he had left his son with us. I breastfed the babies whenever they cried. My milk was still depleted and I'm sure the quality was terrible, but thankfully it hadn't dried up completely. I wondered if the Fanta would make it fizzy for the babies.

We all dozed off and were woken by Habi's return.

'The road is clear at the moment. Let's try and get to Gisenyi.'

He said he'd been going backwards and forwards with his truck of potatoes in the hope that the men on the checkpoints would be used to seeing him and would just wave him through when he had us in the back.

His strategy worked and he wasn't stopped once. Within an hour we had reached Gisenyi. But my joy at getting so close to the border with Zaire was short-lived. All around us was madness. The place was bursting at the seams with bodies and people running. I had spent a lot of time in Gisenyi over the last few years, crossing backwards and forwards between Zaire and Rwanda. It had been my favourite place to go to swim at the beach with Christian. But now there was so much tension in the air; nobody knew what was going to happen next. In my mind

I had imagined that somehow Gisenyi would be untouched and we could be safe.

I burst into tears, and Habi hugged me and tried to comfort me. 'This madness will be over soon, Leah, and the Gisenyi you love will return,' he whispered.

He dropped us outside my uncle's house. I'd often stayed there when I had danced in Gisenyi with the Commandores. I looked around anxiously but could see no Interahamwe.

'I think you'll be safe. The Interahamwe have killed everyone they found there so they won't be coming back for a while. Now I must leave. I will take my son. I will never be able to thank you enough for saving him.'

'It's nothing, Habi. I will never be able to thank you enough for everything you've done for us.'

He shrugged and smiled shyly. Then he picked up Mutoni and was gone.

My uncle's house was large, cool and tranquil and I had always loved spending time there. But as soon as I stepped into his compound I could see that terrible things had been happening. In the last few weeks I had seen too many dead bodies to count. Of course it was devastating to see such evidence of brutality and the only comfort I had was that none had been members of my own family. I knew that what I was about to find would change all that. Once again I clenched my fists tightly to try to steel myself for what was ahead.

My uncle had a large water tank in his garden. To my horror I could see an arm and a leg hanging out of it. I turned away quickly and felt nausea rise in my throat.

Since we had escaped from Hôtel des Mille Collines I hadn't had access to a proper toilet. I went into my uncle's bathroom and caught sight of myself in the mirror. I almost screamed because I was totally unrecognisable. A wild-eyed skeleton zombie stared back at me. My hair was matted, my face smeared with dirt and my cheeks sunken with hunger and fear.

I recognised the bodies strewn around the house – members of my uncle's family and some of his servants. It looked as if they had struggled for their lives and I wondered if despite everything I too would struggle to defend my last breath when my turn came.

The house had been looted and the contents of drawers and cupboards were pulled out and scattered everywhere. I thought of how much pride my uncle and his family had taken in maintaining order and beauty in their lovely home, and how quickly all the love they'd put into the house had been destroyed. I wondered if similar things had happened at Maman and Papa's house in Kigali.

Donata sat herself down in a chair in the living room and sobbed quietly. I felt too numb to cry. The children, as usual, remained silent, staring at me with their glassy, innocent eyes. I laid them down on one of the sofas.

I tried desperately to block out images of my family, but I couldn't help wondering if Maman and my sisters and brothers lay slaughtered in our family home in Kigali. I shook my head hard to try to physically shake the image out of my brain.

Towards dawn we all dozed off. I think it was almost noon when we woke up. I was amazed when Habi returned just after 7 p.m., as soon as darkness fell. He had brought more bananas and water for us. I could hear the now familiar, chilling sounds of the Interahamwe marching and singing.

'You mustn't stay here. The Interahamwe are all around. They may come back and check this house. You must leave as soon as the marchers have passed,' said Habi. 'Then you've got a chance to get across the border.'

I could see nervous sweat dripping from his forehead. If he was caught talking to us, bringing us food, trying to keep us alive, he too would be hacked to death.

'Good luck,' he said and hurried out, melting into the darkness.

The one room I hadn't been into was my uncle's bedroom. I thought I would lie down on the bed for a few minutes and gather some emotional and physical energy before we tried to run for the border. But any kind of resting was impossible. The room was full of dead bodies. Suddenly I heard a faint coughing sound coming from right underneath me.

Oh my God, what is that? I thought. Can the dead cough? Is it a member of the Interahamwe hiding and waiting to kill us?

The cough sounded weak rather than menacing and I called to Donata to help me lift up the heavy, old-fashioned bed to see what lay underneath. As soon as Donata saw that there were bodies in the room she refused to enter, but somehow I managed to persuade her.

'Come, Donata,' I said sternly. 'I can't lift this bed alone.'

I yelped with surprise when I saw that the cough belonged to one of my uncles, a big, broad man called Jean who was a prominent member of the Tutsi-dominated Rwandan Popular Front.

'Oh Leah, is it really you?' he croaked. Donata ran to get him some of the Fanta Habi had brought for us. I hugged him and he gulped the drink gratefully.

'I'm so happy to see you, Jean. You're going to be OK. We're all going to make it.' I lifted him up and cradled his head in my arms.

Momentarily he pulled himself up and then slumped back on to the floor and groaned.

'I saw everything happen but I couldn't do anything.'

'Don't talk, don't think,' I said, amazed by my authoritative tone. 'We need to escape very soon. A Hutu brought us but we don't know if any of the Interahamwe watched us come in. This place isn't safe, we have to leave.'

I didn't ask my uncle for details of the massacre that had taken place here but I knew from the freshness of the blood that the bodies hadn't been dead for long. I think he'd been under the bed for just that day. 'Just leave me here, Bébé,' he said. 'Maybe they won't come back and I will be able to die peacefully.'

'You know I can't leave you, Jean, we still have a chance to make it to Zaire.'

Finally I convinced him to go with us. I gathered up the babies, shouting at Donata to rouse her from the stupor of terror she had fallen into and we crept out.

Just before we reached the border, we were caught by the Interahamwe.

At first I thought I was dead and that was the reason why I couldn't move. I could still hear sounds though, and couldn't understand how this could be if I had passed over to the next world. The smell of rotting corpses was more overpowering than I had ever known it.

I heard a rough voice say, 'Cockroaches don't die that easily. Look, there's still one moving. No point killing it – it's going to die itself.'

I don't know how long I had been lying in the pit of corpses in Gisenyi before I regained consciousness, but when I did I knew with certainty that I had many dead bodies above me and even more below me. I was some sort of macabre sandwich fill-ing, a crumpled up bit of breathing tangled into the dead. We had been attacked in the evening and now the sun was high in the sky so I guessed I'd been lying there for about eighteen hours.

I was too scared to surface in case I got killed. The bodies felt so heavy on top of me and I thought that here was probably as good a place as any to drift towards death. At last I could be reunited with my family and Christian.

At that moment I heard a pitiful little voice calling, '*Maman!*'

Jean-Luc could only say a couple of words and 'Maman' was one of them. Very few babies in the area would have been taught French words and I knew immediately that he was my beloved son.

I couldn't see properly from underneath the tangle of bodies but managed to glimpse him cradled in Donata's arms. The other two babies were by her side, sitting mutely. She looked as if she was waiting for death.

I struggled to get out from under the pile of bodies. They were heavy and I felt weak and breathless as I tried to stand up.

As I tottered to my feet I came face to face with a man dressed in a scruffy T-shirt and jeans. His eyes flared and his gaze was icy. Despite the heat of the day I shivered. I could see that other men like him were dragging piles of bodies out of the way, killing those people who still breathed before throwing them on to trucks.

'You who can be found alive after all this: if you can't die with all these bodies I don't want your blood on me,' he hissed.

He started to step backwards away from me as if I possessed some strange power that could curse him on the spot. And then he turned tail and ran away. I scooped Jean-Luc up from Donata's arms and covered him with kisses.

'My precious, precious baby,' I said over and over again. He looked as if he'd just woken up from a long and peaceful sleep. I hoped he had.

'We're not supposed to die yet,' I whispered to him. 'And I promise you we won't be parted ever again.'

Donata looked as if she'd just seen a ghost. Then a slow smile spread across her face and she started tearing strips of cloth from her *boubou* to wrap around the wound on my abdomen where I had been slashed just before I passed out. She had torn so many strips off this garment in the last few weeks that it had changed from a long dress into a short one.

The bleeding had stopped and my stomach was covered with dried blood. But the wound looked as if it could reopen at any time.

The Interahamwe who had been piling bodies on to trucks had driven off. The road ahead was clear and I could see the border. I recognised the familiar outline of Goma in the distance – the promised land.

Wearily we started climbing the hill behind the university. I was in a dream-like state. I didn't want to look behind me, where the piles of bodies lay and the Interahamwe prowled. I looked ahead at the sweet green grass of the hill we were climbing which stretched towards Goma and freedom. I inhaled the smell of living, growing nature, uncontaminated by the stench of dead bodies. If I kept my eyes firmly fixed ahead of me I could pretend that all this killing had never happened. The grass and trees and plants looked exactly as they had always looked. As we climbed we bumped into some students, some of whom looked as if they were of mixed Hutu and Tutsi origin, who were also trying to cross. Alex, a Tutsi student, said he was going to join the RPF.

After being dragged through hell for weeks to get to the border that represented the difference between life or death for us, I was suddenly overwhelmingly exhausted. All emotion had been wrung out of me and I was no longer even sure what the difference between life and death was. Life, recently, had felt a lot how I imagined death to be.

It took us almost an hour to reach the border. We were crouching and creeping behind shrubs and bushes as we climbed the hill, in the hope that the Interahamwe wouldn't see us. I couldn't understand why there were none of them around. Everything was eerily quiet. This part of Gisenyi felt empty.

We headed for the place known as the market border, thinking that there might be fewer Interahamwe there than at the main border crossing. In fact there was just one bored-looking guard lounging on a plastic chair at Immigration on the Zairian side.

'Where have you come from?' he said, not batting an eyelid at our horrible appearance. I assumed he had seen many others in the same state as us in recent days.

'*De Kigali*,' I answered. I began speaking in French. I had stopped speaking Kinyarwanda, partly to try to conceal my Tutsi roots and partly because I had grown to hate the language in the

last three weeks. Each word of it that I spoke felt as if I was spit-
ting out poison.

'Where are you going?'

'Home.'

'Where is home?'

'Goma.' The word had never sounded so beautiful to me.

He nodded our bedraggled group across the border. With just
a few steps we had left hell behind us.

CHAPTER TEN

I don't know what I had expected to find when I reached Zaire. But after the first few moments of elation the familiar feelings of horror returned.

The town was almost unrecognisable. It was heaving with refugees who, like us, had found a way to cross the border. There were desperate people everywhere, Hutus and Tutsis. They had turned my beloved Goma into a gigantic human anthill.

In my horrific flight out of Rwanda, for some reason it had never occurred to me that Zaire would be flooded with the people I had tried to flee from as well as many others like me. Goma was full of security people, army and police, and somebody said that any Interahamwe who crossed the border had to hand over their machetes and other weapons to the *gardes civiles*.

But there was life and music too. Zairians laughed and chatted and bought food from the street stalls. I shuddered when I saw Interahamwe trying to sell cars they had looted from wealthy Tutsis they had killed.

Bloated, bleached-white dead bodies floated all over Lake Kivu. The Red Cross had brought in water tanks because nobody could drink from the lake. I'd hoped I would feel safe here and have a chance to rest and recuperate in the tranquil environment of my parents' house. I'd thought that in the sane surroundings of Zaire I would somehow be able to pull myself together and try to rebuild my shattered life for the sake of Jean-Luc. But instead I was overwhelmed with that all-too-familiar sensation of wanting to run. I decided not to visit my grandparents because I didn't want them to see me in this terrible state. Also I didn't want them to hear bad news about my family.

The wound in my abdomen kept reopening and although she still wasn't speaking, Donata led me to the hospital. She seemed to have regained some of her composure, while I could feel mine ebbing away. I had made superhuman efforts to hold on to my sanity and to avoid an explosion of grief that would have left me in a crumpled heap on the floor. What had kept me going was the thought of reaching Goma and being safe once more. Now that I had achieved what I had set out to do, I had no fight left in me. My spirit felt crushed.

The general hospital was surprisingly empty. I'd expected it to be swarming with refugees in a similar or worse state than mine but one of the nurses explained that most of the refugees were in camps and were receiving medical treatment there.

A doctor I had known since I was a child treated my wounds. He shook his head sadly when he saw my injuries. 'Everything is madness,' he said. 'But don't worry, Bébé. Not too much damage done. The wound will heal by itself. I'm going to prescribe some antibiotics to make sure you don't get an infection. You'll be OK.'

'Thank you, Dr Mutembo,' I said.

Back on the streets of Goma all was chaos again. Some of the Rwandise women had started to prostitute themselves in order to survive. I decided that I couldn't stay here. As we walked out of the hospital my weary brain was whirring. How could I get out of Goma? I had to keep on running until I could see no more Rwandise. Only then would I be safe, I told myself. The three students we had crossed the border with had left us to join the

RPF. For them that was a way to take back some control over their lives.

We had all been taken by surprise when the outbreak of killing began in Kigali but I was determined that this time I was going to be ready. I didn't want to be a victim again and somehow I would find a way out of Goma as soon as possible. As I looked around and saw Interahamwe members in the streets I shivered. I was sure it would only be a matter of time before this killing disease that was wiping out Rwanda would infect Goma.

When I was growing up I had rarely thought about my Tutsi background, apart from when I was the subject of the occasional playground jibe. But now I felt uneasy as a Tutsi in my home town. I wasn't a Bantu, a proper African, so I wasn't welcome. I felt that Zairians were looking at me differently. Or maybe I was looking at them differently, stripped of my childhood confidence and innocence about the way human beings could get along with each other.

I spoke to a few people in the streets, asking them innocently what was happening, to try to find out their views of the situation. Mobutu supported the Hutus and the general belief in Goma seemed to be that it was the Tutsis who had caused all the problems that were now affecting the nice life people had in eastern Zaire.

The last thing I wanted was to be questioned about what I had been through in the last few weeks, what was really going on in Rwanda, and worst of all what had become of my family. These were all things I couldn't bear to think about and I was far too traumatised to put my experiences into words. The only way I could keep on moving, breathing, eating, was to block everything out.

With a heavy heart I decided to take the twin babies to a place called the *foyer social*, a kind of reception centre, in an area called Tungane. Donata and I walked slowly along the streets. We were so weak we could hardly put one foot in front of the other.

I wept as we parted from them and they cried too. In just a matter of days they had become part of our sad, depleted little family. The place was set up to care for refugees and I knew they would be safe and looked after there. It broke my heart to leave them, though I didn't even know their names. I didn't feel like they had become my own babies, but at the same time I was very attached to them. I had breastfed them with the few drops of milk I had left and tried to show them some love and warmth in the middle of so much cruelty. The staff promised to look after them. I could see that they were looking after a lot of parentless children and babies.

'Thank you, *chérie*,' said the woman I gave the babies to. 'You have done a wonderful thing to rescue these babies.'

'Any mother would do the same,' I said.

'Let's go to my house,' I said wearily to Donata as we walked away from the *foyer social*. 'Maybe we can wash there, find some food, rest for a while and plan what we should do next.' I felt as if I would be able to sleep for a hundred years.

Donata seemed happy that we might at last have a permanent and comfortable place to rest.

The house looked exactly the same as when I had last been there, a couple of months before. I was relieved that at least one thing had remained the same. Of course I had no keys with me so we had to break in. Thankfully the house hadn't been damaged in any way in our absence. Nobody seemed to have looted people's homes, but had gone obediently to the camps. At first people in Goma responded generously because they had no idea that the refugees were going to become a permanent fixture.

I walked around the house, touching familiar, well-loved objects: Maman's favourite vase, the pictures on the wall. Then I sank to the floor and for the first time since 6 April I sobbed and sobbed. This home had been so lovingly created and protected by Maman and Papa. I could hear the laughter of my sisters and brothers echoing around the walls. We had had so many happy times here. Now everyone I loved was destroyed. Donata tried her best to wordlessly comfort me. She took me in her arms and wiped away my tears.

'We have to get out of here quickly,' I said as soon as my sobs had subsided. 'Tutsis are being blamed for everything and the people of Zaire might turn on us soon the way the Interahamwe did. But first we must eat and rest.'

To my relief there were beans and rice stored in the house so we could cook. Maman had always made sure that her cupboards were well stocked, prepared for any eventuality, although she had never dreamed of this particular one. There was water, but it was impossible to drink because it came from the lake clogged with bodies. But the water from the rainwater tank looked clean and we used that instead, heating it with an immersion heater in a bucket. I was so happy to be able to wash my baby and myself at long last. I scrubbed and rinsed myself over and over again. There was so much dirt on my body that one wash couldn't shift it. I found some of my old clothes in my bedroom cupboard, clean and ironed.

I threw the remains of my tattered *boubou* in the bin. I never wanted to see it again.

I decided to keep everything just as I had found it in the house, in case any members of my family came back. In fact I should have sold everything while people still knew that my parents owned it. Later someone else took it over and didn't pay us a penny because I had no documents to prove that it belonged to my parents. This is a common problem in many parts of Africa, where property ownership is often not backed up with formal documentation. Because of this lax approach it can be hard to contest ownership if somebody else lays claim to your land and property.

Donata and I cooked a feast of rice and beans and ate greedily. I ran my fingers along the kitchen cupboards and the big sink. The familiarity of these things comforted me. I fed Jean-Luc the rice and he kept opening his mouth to have more and more of it.

'Poor baby, I'm sorry you've been hungry,' I said to him. 'When I start eating again my milk will come back properly and it will fill your tummy, I promise.'

He gurgled as if he knew exactly what I was saying to him.

It was so nice to feel full, and a novelty to eat off plates. Donata looked very contented as she cleared our plates away. She had begun to speak again haltingly.

'Let's stay here, Leah,' she said. These were the first words she had uttered since I had told her to remain silent three weeks ago.

'Donata, you can stay here if you want but Jean-Luc and I are leaving as soon as I can work out the best way to get out of the country. Anyone can see that the Rwandan conflict is spilling over into Zaire. Who knows whether or not the Interahamwe will start their killing here? Last time I trusted what everyone said about the UN protecting us, but look what happened. I'm not going to get caught out again. Look after Jean-Luc. I'm going out to see if I can find a way out of here for us.'

Donata looked miserable but didn't try to dissuade me.

I walked down one of Goma's main streets, trying to work out how we could leave the town, when suddenly someone screamed, 'Bébé Leah, Bébé Leah!' I cringed that someone was calling my name. I wanted to keep my head down while I was in Goma and not let anyone I knew from the past know that I had returned. I remembered the bad songs about Tutsis that had been sung at my primary school and felt very uncomfortable.

I looked to see who was shouting. To my amazement it was Josephine.

She rushed towards me and embraced me warmly. 'Oh Bébé, am I pleased to see you! Where is Jean-Luc?'

'He's at home with Donata.'

'Thank God you all survived. You're smart, Leah, I knew you'd make it. Come and sit and have a drink with us. I've thought of nothing else but you and the others hiding in my café. Did they make it?'

I shrugged. 'I don't know. We became separated from them. Do I look as if I could sit and have a drink with you, Josephine? I'm not feeling very good. I have a lot of pain from where they cut me. I must go.'

She looked hurt by my sharp tone.

'*Ma chérie*, I'm so sorry about what has happened to you. But I know you, Bébé, you're a strong girl, you'll be OK.' She kept on stroking my cheeks and saying over and over again, 'Poor baby.'

Josephine had tears in her eyes. She told me that she had driven straight to Goma after she left us and had no news of what had happened to anyone stranded in Kigali.

As I walked away from her I realised that I had turned her offer down because I wasn't ready to sit down with a Hutu, even though Josephine was my friend. I never would have thought in that way about a friend before but now I trusted no one. I could see that she was surprised by my reaction. At the same time as feeling angry with Josephine because she was a Hutu and Hutus had killed the people I loved and nearly killed me too, I no longer felt worthy of her company. I was starting to believe the Interahamwe propaganda: I was a Tutsi cockroach who did not deserve to sit with someone like Josephine. My self-esteem was in shreds.

'I'm so grateful that you told Luc to come and fetch us, you helped me so much. Thank you, Josephine,' I said, trying to sound less hostile. 'You know Luc had to leave Rwanda.'

'Oh, I wondered what happened to him, I'm glad he got out safely. How did you get out, Bébé? I know so many people didn't make it.'

I couldn't bear to hear my pet name any more. It brought back too many painful memories. I could never go back to being Bébé Leah again; she was dead.

'It's a long story, Josephine. I'll have to tell you about it some other time.'

Josephine started to cry. I think she felt ashamed about what had been done to the Tutsis.

'Leah, remember not everybody is bad like those Interahamwe. You need some time to heal.'

Seeing Josephine brought back all the memories of how everything had started: the plane, the machetes, the people screaming, hiding under her bed. It was all too painful for me to think about.

'I'll come by later and if you're still here I'll join you for a drink,' I said. I had no intention of returning and hurried away quickly.

I walked down Goma's main street, still trying to think of a way to get out of Zaire. I thought that if we could just reach Nairobi we would be safe. I had so many happy childhood memories of holidays to Kenya and felt sure that Kenya would be far enough away from Rwanda and Rwandise people for me to feel safe once more. All I wanted to do was to get out as quickly as possible.

Suddenly I remembered that there were big trucks that carried petrol to Tanzania. They parked up not far from where I was. I assumed that the trucks would drive through Kenya on their journey. I had no passport or papers to say I was Rwandise or Zairian. Everything that proved who I was back in Kigali. Even if we could hitch a lift with one of the truck drivers, how could we cross borders without travel documents?

I wandered around the streets in a daze. As I stumbled past exiled Rwandise, my hand protectively covering my wounded abdomen, a plan began to form in my dazed mind. I knew where the office in Goma that issued travel documents was. Maybe I could get documents for Donata and me today so that we would not lose any time.

I searched the faces of the lorry drivers parked off the main street. I was trying to find somebody who looked kind. Many of the drivers looked stressed and anxious to get out of Goma as fast as they could.

I noticed a driver with twinkling eyes, who grinned at me in a friendly way. I decided to try my luck with him. The trucks had enough space underneath them to sit and many of the men made small fires in portable stoves and cooked food for themselves. I was used to seeing women prepare food and I marvelled at how skilfully and efficiently this man was preparing rice and vegetables. He didn't look Zairian or Rwandise, and the fact that he appeared to be a foreigner and unconnected with the recent events was very appealing.

He stood up and came towards me. He looked as if he was in his early thirties and was tall and friendly.

'Hello,' I said, trying to look normal and carefree as I approached him even though I felt neither. I had managed to make myself look presentable, putting on one of my favourite hats that I had found in a cupboard in our house, a cute French beret, fresh jeans and a newish pair of shoes.

'Hello, sister,' he smiled back. He was obviously not Zairian or Rwandise because he didn't seem to understand what I was saying to him. He spoke Swahili to me although it sounded very different from the Swahili I had grown up speaking. Somehow, though, we managed to communicate in two different variants of the language.

He told me that he was Tanzanian and was heading across the border into Kenya. I saw *TZ* written on his truck and hope surged.

He extended his hand. 'I'm Mustapha, nice to meet you,' he said.

I hadn't discussed all the terrible things that had happened in Rwanda with anyone but I decided that Mustapha was a man I could tell my story to. I also thought that if he understood what had happened to me he might be more willing to give us a lift out of Zaire.

'I've been having a lot of problems because of the war in Rwanda,' I said.

'I'm sorry to hear that you've had such a rough time, sister,' he said. 'Here, take this Fanta. Would you like to come out for a meal with me? You look half starved.'

'Thank you for the kind offer but I've just eaten,' I replied. My voice sounded weak and croaky, and I suddenly realised how little I'd spoken in the last three weeks. So much energy had been used on keeping myself and everyone else silent to avoid detection by the Interahamwe as we tried to creep out of Rwanda. I had hardly had any conversations at all except at the checkpoints.

'Where are you heading for, Mustapha?'

'Today or tomorrow I'm going back to Tanzania,' he replied.

'Are you going to pass through Rwanda?' I asked nervously, thinking that if that was his planned route I would have to find someone else to hitch with.

'No. No, Rwanda is impossible at the moment. I cannot pass that way. I'm going to go through Bunagana in Uganda.'

'Oh good, that's good. Please, please take us with you.'

Mustapha looked slightly taken aback by the vehemence of my request.

'Who's "us"?' he asked cautiously.

I took a deep breath. 'It's my baby son and the woman who helps me to look after him. Mustapha, I am a Tutsi and somehow, I don't know how, I managed to get out of Rwanda alive. I have seen things in the last three weeks that no human being should ever have to see.'

He winced, as if he could physically feel my pain.

Then before I knew what I was doing I told him everything, about hiding in Josephine's place, Hôtel des Mille Collines, the husbands who had slaughtered wives, the Interahamwe who tried to help and those who longed to feel our blood on their hands.

Mustapha had come through Rwanda so he knew exactly

what was going on there. He listened carefully and touched my arm gently.

'I'm so sorry,' he said. 'Of course I'll take you, Donata and Jean-Luc. But you cannot travel without papers. I will wait in Goma until you've got some new travel documents.'

I embraced Mustapha. 'Thank you, thank you so much. Your kindness is better for me than any medicine.'

I walked back to our house, feeling some small seeds of hope in my heart.

All I wanted to do now was to go to sleep in Maman's bedroom so that I could try and feel close to her. I knew how much Maman had loved that house. As I walked into our compound I noticed how overgrown the garden had become and thought how sad Papa would be to see that the plants, trees and grasses he had tended so lovingly had grown wild and unkempt.

'Donata,' I said excitedly as I walked through the door. 'I've found a truck driver who has agreed to take us out of Zaire. He is travelling to Tanzania and passing through Uganda and Kenya. We will be safe travelling that way.'

Donata was still unconvinced about the need to leave Goma, especially now that she had a clean, comfortable bed to sleep in, access to water and a good food supply in Maman's cupboards.

But there was no way she could dissuade me. My mind was fixed on going to Kenya. I knew that that was the place where the UN had airlifted people to, because Luc had told me that the UN were trying to fly as many people out of Rwanda as possible. If we can just get to Kenya we will be safe and everything will be OK, I kept telling myself. In my mind memories of my blissful, childhood holidays in Mombasa merged with my knowledge of Kenya as the nearest stable country that people were running to. I was unable to think more than one step ahead of what was happening now. It took a long time to persuade Donata but eventually she agreed to come with Jean-Luc and me.

I went down to the immigration office and told them I'd lost my travel document. They gave me a new one with Jean-Luc written in mine, and I also got one for Donata. We got express papers that were processed the same day. The documents were equivalent to a visa allowing us to enter Uganda, but they didn't permit us to travel into any other countries.

I rushed to tell Mustapha.

'Great,' he said. 'We'll leave at five tomorrow morning.'

'Thank you so much,' I said. Then I went home, fell into bed and dropped off to sleep almost immediately.

The next morning we arrived at the lorry very punctually: I didn't want to risk Mustapha leaving without us. I had packed a few clothes I had found in the house and some gold and silver jewellery that I planned to sell to keep us going. Mustapha was still cleaning his teeth and was surprised to see us so on time. He was very smiley and cheerful and I decided that anyone who could behave like that at such an early hour must be a very good person.

I used the name Leah Mukaisa, one of the names my family gave me, a good Zairian name. I wanted to try to erase as much of my Tutsi identity as I could.

I no longer looked like the Bébé Leah who smiled out of billboard posters clutching a glass of fake beer. But I didn't mourn that Leah. I felt that the only way I could survive was to block out my past and make a new start in a completely different place. No Rwanda, no Tutsi, no Bébé Leah. I wanted to run as far away as possible from everybody who knew me. I deliberately didn't knock on the doors of our neighbours. I knew they would deluge me with questions that I wouldn't be able to cope with. I didn't want to see them or anybody else.

Donata, Jean-Luc and I squeezed into the passenger seat by Mustapha's side. We passed through Rutshuru. This normally calm, ordered place was transformed by the blur of refugees walking aimlessly, hopelessly. I knew that each and every one of them had their story to tell, but the thought of hearing about any more suffering made me feel physically sick. When we reached the Kiwanja area Mustapha stopped the truck and bought us Fanta from a little stall.

'Thank you, Mustapha, you're very kind. I will drink it but I can't give this to Jean-Luc. He is too young for Fanta. Now that I have started to eat and drink again my milk is coming back.'

He was a very soft-hearted man. As I sat next to him in the truck I decided that he was an angel who had been sent to heal me. I don't know why I had initially talked to him and trusted him but my instincts told me that he was a safe person.

In Rwanda I had been terrified of everyone. Being able to trust is a very important part of being human, and in his kind, quiet way Mustapha was teaching me how to trust again. He was a genuine Good Samaritan. If you are bitten by a poisonous snake you need to find an antidote to the venom fast, and Mustapha was that antidote. Just being in his company soothed my pain. He was a kindly father figure to Donata and me. He wanted to make us feel better and it was clear that he wanted nothing in return.

For much of the time we drove in silence but it was a calm silence without any stress in it.

'We will cross to Bunagana in the morning,' said Mustapha.

'That's great,' I smiled. I knew I would feel much better once I was over the border. Although I was taking the antibiotics pre-scribed for me at the hospital in Goma, my wounds had become unbearably painful. My brain had blocked out my physical pain while I struggled to stay alive and get out of Rwanda but now that the immediate danger had passed the pain had become over-whelming. I had some paracetamol and took that, longing for Maman to be by my side. She knew how to fix any pain I had. I took a deep breath and tried to push my image of her, prepar-ing to go to the bank the last day I saw her, right out of my mind. Donata had also developed bad sores on her legs in the course of our journey through Rwanda and she too was in a lot of pain. I tried to sleep as much as possible on the journey, cradling Jean-Luc securely in my arms.

Mustapha could see that both of us were suffering. When we reached a heavily forested area near the Ugandan border he pulled the truck over and jumped out.

'Here I think I'll be able to find something good that grows that can help to heal your wounds.' He smiled.

He returned ten minutes later, carrying an armful of leaves that he instructed us to rub on our wounds. We obediently did what we were told and miraculously the pain began to subside.

Mustapha started to have diarrhoea soon after we started our journey. At first he said nothing but kept on stopping the truck and disappearing off into the bush without any explanation. I became paranoid that he was secretly meeting up with bad people who were planning to kill us.

After one of these mystery disappearances I plucked up the courage to ask him what was going on. 'Why are you going all the time into the bush, Mustapha?'

He hung his head and said shame-facedly, 'I'm having bad diarrhoea. It must be something I ate in Goma or Rutshuru.'

'Oh,' I said, grinning. 'That's a big relief. Of course I'm sorry about your diarrhoea but I thought you were disappearing to plot something against me.'

He smiled weakly. 'Don't be silly. I want to help you, not cause you harm.'

Mustapha continued to make unscheduled visits to the bush. He looked increasingly unwell.

'I'm too weak to drive, Leah. You will have to take over from me.'

'Mustapha, you're crazy. How can I drive a big lorry, a petrol tanker?'

'Listen, Leah, do you want to live or not? You want to get as far away from Rwanda as possible. And my boss says I have to get this lorry back to Tanzania in two days' time or I'll lose my job. We have to keep moving somehow.'

'But I don't know how to drive,' I lied. I was terrified at the prospect of being in charge of such a huge vehicle, and worried that I might end up killing us all in a terrible accident.

'Leah, you're a survivor, you'll find a way to do this. We need to continue on our journey or we'll all be in big trouble.'

'OK,' I shrugged. 'Show me what I have to do.'

Falteringly Mustapha explained to me how the controls worked. I climbed into the driver's seat and set off juddering. After a while I did get the hang of it. The controls were actually straightforward and of necessity I learned fast.

I had to drive the lorry for the whole night. I felt so young and small behind the oversized steering wheel but Mustapha shrugged the whole thing off as if it was all perfectly normal, in the hope of making me feel more relaxed.

'Just imagine that you have to run for your life and the only way you could do it is if you drive.'

And so, with Mustapha clutching his stomach and moaning gently, Jean-Luc dozing fitfully in Donata's arms and me, a skinny seventeen-year-old, at the wheel of the juggernaut petrol tanker, we entered Uganda.

CHAPTER ELEVEN

Mustapha drank plenty of water and by the end of the day he was feeling better.

'I think these bad bugs have passed through my system now. I'm starving. My stomach is completely empty. Let's find something to eat.'

He came back with *matoke*, a plaintain that is boiled for a long time and eaten with a sauce, some bananas and some meat.

I looked at the meat and felt as if I was going to vomit. I edged away from it as though it was going to jump out of Mustapha's hands, pick up a machete and assault me.

'I can't eat meat,' I cried. 'It reminds me too much of the human flesh I saw.'

'OK, if you can't eat meat, Leah, none of us will eat it,' he said apologetically. 'Let's find chicken instead.'

'I can't eat chicken either, it's still too close.'

'OK, we'll all eat fish then.'

'Thank you, Mustapha, you're so kind.'

Mustapha bought some fish and prepared that and the *matoke*. All the truck drivers had become good cooks. After living on a diet of little more than bananas in the last few weeks, everything tasted heavenly. I had forgotten how good well-cooked food could taste.

I was trying to feed Jean Luc with some *matoke* and soup and was praying that he wouldn't catch Mustapha's diarrhoea. He made little noises with his lips that sounded almost like 'Yum, yum, yum' when he had finished eating. He too appreciated tasty food.

'You can sleep in the local hotel across the road, I'll sleep in the truck,' said Mustapha when we'd finished eating. 'I've booked a room there for the three of you. In the morning we'll leave early so that we can get to the Kenyan border before it gets too late. We'll have to try and work out a plan to get you all across the border because you don't have papers.'

Mustapha had chosen a simple guesthouse for us but it had comfortable beds and warm water in buckets to wash ourselves with. Everything he said and did made me feel safe. I felt terrified at the prospect of being separated from him.

The next morning we set off early to get to the border.

There were many refugees walking along the road, carrying their belongings. I couldn't tell which backgrounds they were from but I assumed that many were from Rwanda.

'Leah, I might not be able to help you cross. There are people you can pay who smuggle people without papers across the border. You might have to try that way if I can't persuade anyone to let you cross with me.'

He dropped us off ten minutes away from the border in a busy, bustling area with lots of people selling food. The brightly coloured clothes and scarves of the women, the mouth-watering array of fresh fruit and the dazzling sunshine made me feel dizzy. My head was still pounding and somehow the sounds of happy, normal people going about their business disorientated me.

I watched people laughing and talking and striding forwards purposefully and thought, Whatever terrible things happen, the human spirit rises and seeks out happiness.

I smiled at Mustapha; something had made me seek him out rather than any other driver. Despite everything I too was leaning towards happiness, like a flower craning its slender neck towards the sun.

'I'll see if I can give money to somebody to help us cross. Don't worry, we'll make it,' I said to Mustapha, trying to make my voice sound as bright as possible. I embraced him. 'I hope we'll see you on the other side,' I said, gesturing towards Kenya. 'Thank you so much for your kindness and everything you've done for us. You have helped me more than you can ever know.'

Mustapha smiled and shrugged. 'It was nothing,' he said shyly. He gave me some money to help me to bribe our way across the border through one back route or another. 'Good luck, Leah,' he said. Then he climbed back into his truck and drove towards the border. My heart sank as the lorry moved further and further away from us. He and his vehicle were our salvation.

I watched what was going on around me carefully to see if I could work out what the people without papers were doing to get across the border.

Some people were discreetly giving money to young men with pedal bikes and then climbing on the back of the bikes and heading off in the direction of a forested area. I assumed the bikes were some kind of smuggling taxi.

I approached a man standing next to his bike. His hand was shading his eyes and his head was swivelling from side to side like a bird's, trying to spot potential customers.

I walked up to him as casually as I could and said, 'How much?'

He looked me up and down and then turned to Donata, who was holding Jean-Luc, before replying. He named his price. I nodded my head and he said, 'But you'll never cross in those clothes. The two of you will have to dress like Ugandan village women. We have to pretend that we are returning to our village in the forest.'

I looked down at my fashionable jeans and T-shirt and at Donata's Western-style dress, which we had changed into at my

home in Goma. He pulled a couple of dusty, sweat-stained traditional Ugandan dresses out of a bag and told us to go behind
some trees and get changed.

Then we clambered on to the back of the bike and headed
towards the forest.

After we had passed through the village our smuggler pointed
us in the direction of the Kenyan side of the border. 'Take that
path and you'll find yourselves just beyond the border. Good
luck,' he said. Then he jumped back on to his bike and disappeared, probably to collect more desperate, paperless people.

It had taken an hour to cross. We walked towards the area our
smuggler had pointed out, where I could see a throng of chattering people. I looked around and saw Mustapha standing by his
truck, waving and smiling.

'Leah, welcome to Kenya,' he said softly when he saw us, and
laughed. 'How did you do? How did you manage to cross?'

'I paid a man with a bike and he took us the back way,' I said
simply.

'You are something else. You are a crook and a bad girl.' He
laughed affectionately. He was relieved because he hadn't wanted
to leave us stranded, but he had a deadline to deliver his petrol.
Even Donata laughed. She too was very slowly beginning to trust
and to regain a little bit of her sense of humour. She had even
started to say a few words, although still seemed happier when
she was not speaking.

'So you see we are Ugandans now,' I laughed, pointing to our
new outfits. At that moment I felt elated.

Mustapha was a person who found a lot of joy in the simple
things of life. It was he who elicited the first laughs from Jean-
Luc. He had smiled from when he was a couple of months old
but during our flight out of Rwanda entertaining him had been
the last thing on my mind. Mustapha threw Jean-Luc up in the
air and he laughed and laughed. I will always think of Mustapha
as my guardian angel. Had I not met him so soon after leaving

Rwanda I think I would have sunk into a deep despair that I may not have been able to climb out of. Mustapha's quiet, kind actions showed me humanity at its best.

He promised to take us as far as the capital Nairobi, so we all clambered back into the truck that had by now become like home. The battered old seats and the driving controls were like trusted old friends.

'We're heading for Nakuru by nightfall, and then tomorrow we reach Nairobi,' said Mustapha. My plan was to stay in Nairobi. I was hoping against hope that I might find some members of my family there.

We started driving as night fell. The roads in Zaire were poor, but the main roads in Kenya were perfect. There were cacti and big, shady trees everywhere, along with plentiful tea crops.

We passed through a place called Kisumu, where the temperature suddenly dropped.

'Not much further now and then we'll stop for the night,' said Mustapha. 'You see the lights shining in the distance? We will rest there.'

As he drove he described the hotel we were going to stay at. 'You will sleep on the softest bed with crisp, white sheets and have your own bathroom.' From what he was saying the place sounded even grander than the Sheraton!

The hotel wasn't quite like the Sheraton but it was very comfortable. Mustapha paid for everything for us. He did this without fuss or fanfare. Usually when men do that they want something in exchange, but he didn't. He spoke to us fondly about his wife and his three children and how much he was looking forward to seeing them again. He was very easy about everything and didn't make me feel like he was doing anything much for us. I couldn't stop thanking him.

'If something like this happened to one of my sisters, I would hope that someone would do the same for them.'

'I'll never be able to repay you.'

The hotel had a proper, warm shower. It was blissful. I sat down in the shower and let the water run over me. I cried and cried as I tried to scrub myself clean, feeling that I would never be able to wash away the imprint of the dead bodies on top of me and underneath me.

But however many times I washed my body it would not be enough. I wanted to take my brain out and scrub it with a tooth-brush to remove all the horrible memories. I prayed that Jean-Luc was too young to remember any of what we'd been through.

Donata came and knocked on the door, worried about how long I was taking. When she got no response from me she sum-moned Mustapha.

'Leah, come out. You have been in there for a long time, we're worried about you.'

Eventually I emerged and got dressed. Mustapha offered me some water to drink from the pipe.

'Mustapha, it's dirty water. I can't drink it.'

Because I had seen so many dead bodies in the water in Goma I felt I would never again be able to trust tap water again.

'No, no, Leah, it's pure water from the mountains.'

We dined on delicious beans and *matoke* and then fell into bed. As Mustapha had promised the bed was indeed soft and com-fortable, and Donata, Jean-Luc and I all enjoyed a deep, dreamless sleep.

The next morning we set off at five. The road zigzagged through dazzling forests and mountains. Eight hours later we reached a town.

'I'm tired, Leah. Will you take the wheel for a while?'

'I'm scared of driving along these narrow, winding roads, Mustapha. We'll plunge down the mountain if I drive.'

'If I close my eyes we'll end up down the mountain anyway. Just drive for a little while, Leah. We have stopped more than I usually stop and I need to reach Tanzania or I'll be in trouble with my boss.'

I could see how tired he was and I agreed to take over. How could I refuse Mustapha? He was a man with a pure heart who just wanted to help other human beings. Although he was a Muslim he didn't believe in having more than one wife.

'Two wives, do you want to drive me to an early grave? I can't afford to feed my family as it is. Muslims only agree to having more than one wife if they can support the wives equally and all the children. Can you imagine if you follow the Koran you have to sleep with one and then go next door and do the same with the other one? It's impossible.' We both laughed at the idea of Mustapha bed-hopping.

I marvelled at how well he knew the areas we travelled through, understanding how the land worked as well as the rules and regulations. He knew where to find the cleanest water, the best food, and the most effective traditional medicine in the bush. He showed me how a piece of bark was much better for cleaning teeth than a toothbrush.

We slept in the truck and the following morning we rose early so that we could get on the road to Nairobi. But when I woke up Mustapha had his head buried in the engine. I could see that he was frowning.

'Oh dear, is there a problem with the truck?' I asked.

'Yes. I think I can fix it but it will delay us by some hours. My boss in Dar es Salaam expected me back yesterday. Oh well, never mind, these things can't be helped. Even if I get the sack I know I have done something good in my life, helping all of you.'

We sat around in the shade. Finally at 5 p.m. Mustapha declared the truck fixed. 'I think we'll be out of here by six,' he said. He bought some food for the journey and we set off.

We reached Nairobi around 10 p.m. From outside it looked so beautiful with all the lights. Kigali had always had lights but they went out on 6 April. I was excited to see the ordered, illuminated outline of Nairobi. Surely nothing bad could happen to us here.

In the Mille Collines everyone was talking about Nairobi as some kind of paradise. It had always been an important place in my childhood, the place where all the top students went to, where all the good businesses were and where all the best clothes were sold.

I felt momentarily elated but then another emotion washed over me, sweeping away my joy. Mustapha was such a powerful force for good and after all the evil I had witnessed I didn't want to let him go. He was my saviour and I wanted to cling on to him for ever.

'Leah, I'm going to take you to an area called Kirenyaga. Here, you will find a cheap hotel and you can sort things out. There are many refugees in this area and they will be able to advise you about what you should do.'

I woke Donata and told her, 'We've made it. We're in Nairobi.'

She rubbed her eyes sleepily and then grinned as she looked out of the window.

'Thank God,' she said.

Mustapha booked us into a lodge and said he would come and say goodbye in the morning.

Nairobi was full of tall buildings, noise and traffic jams. Everyone seemed to be hurrying. I was too tired to notice much of what was happening around us and once again all three of us tumbled into bed.

The following morning Mustapha arrived early bearing gifts – two cups, two plates, a Thermos, milk, bread and sugar.

'Thank you, thank you, Mustapha, you always know exactly what we need,' I said.

He looked me in the eye and said, 'Mama Leah, I have to go but I know you'll make it. The police here in Kenya are very tough and you need to be on your guard against them. They will stop you for no reason and give you problems.'

I shuddered. The thought of having to deal with any more men in uniforms terrified me.

'Come on, let's go to the market and I'll buy you fish so you can cook.'

We followed him obediently. He bought me a little petrol stove from one of the stalls and showed me how to use it. Then he dug into his pocket and gave me $50.

'That's all I have. If the police stop you, you must tell them the truth, that you are Rwandise. Whatever you do don't say that you're Zairian or they'll try to send you back to Zaire. They know they cannot return people to Rwanda at the moment.'

'Please don't go,' I whimpered.

'I have to go, but next week I'll be passing through here again and I'll look for you, I promise.'

And off he went.

CHAPTER TWELVE

I felt all the strength drain out of my body. But I knew that, if we were going to survive, it was down to me to act. Donata was still saying little and seemed incapable of making any decisions. I wiped away my tears.

'Stay here, Donata, I need to find out what we have to do next. I'll take Jean-Luc with me,' I said, trying to sound as confident and in control as possible.

The lodge was pleasant enough. We had a clean room to sleep in and shared cooking and bathroom facilities. There were Rwandise business people there and white people too. I was reluctant to get involved in too many conversations about the horror we had fled from but I did start chatting to one Rwandise man who looked kind. His name was Paul and he showed us where the refugee camp was.

'They will support you there; they'll give you some money, some food and blankets and help you try to trace your family,' he said.

Many of the Rwandise in the lodge had been out of the country when the troubles started and they were eager to hear eye-witness accounts.

'I'm sorry, I really can't talk about it,' I said.

They saw the pain in my eyes and asked no more questions. I felt as if my eyes had become small TV screens showing anyone who looked at me exactly what had happened.

As I approached the refugee camp, which was not too far from the place where we were staying, a Rwandise man started chatting to me and told me what I needed to do.

'You must register yourself with United Nations High Commission for Refugees. You can't walk around without papers or the police will make trouble for you. UNHCR will give you displaced-person documents.'

We went into a long, long queue and eventually we reached a desk with a tired-looking white man sitting behind it.

'Do you want to come into the camp?' he asked.

'No, no,' I said hurriedly. The thought of being surrounded by Rwandise terrified me.

We were given some money, a packet of beans, a pot, some plates and some cups, and given $50 per week to survive on. We were told that in the next few weeks the UN wanted to move many of the refugees receiving support in Nairobi to a camp in Sudan. The thought of being stuck in the desert did not appeal at all. I hadn't grown up in a desert area, but surrounded by earth at its most fertile. I couldn't imagine that I would be able to adapt.

Everybody said to me, 'Sister, you don't want to go to the Sudan border. It's the desert and people die there.'

Although I believed that everyone I loved was dead, I did what many other Rwandise people were doing and posted up the names of my family and husband on the Red Cross missing-persons list in the hope that at least some of the refugees who had fled to Nairobi might have some news about what had happened to them all. I told myself over and over again that nobody had survived, but I couldn't help harbouring a glimmer of hope that maybe some of them had. I tried my best not to think about my family and what had happened to them but I couldn't banish all thoughts of them from my head and longed to be with them again, especially my beloved Maman. I was not surprised but was still engulfed with disappointment when I got no response to my Red Cross posting.

I tried to make the best of the situation I was in and was thankful that we had a roof over our heads and didn't go hungry. I felt we were now a safe distance from the crazed men with machetes and started to relax. There were quite a few small children staying with their parents in the same lodge as us, and sometimes we sang songs like 'Frère Jacques' together. Jean-Luc was too young to join in with the singing but clapped his hands together and laughed whenever the other children started to sing. He was able to sit up by himself now and was taking an active interest in the world around him, gazing intently at new people and sights and laughing at almost anything.

After my initial relief at being out of Rwanda, unease and despair set in. It was very hard to work out how to survive daily life. I was seventeen years old and until a few weeks ago had led a sheltered, cosseted life, frequently turning to my parents for advice about how to deal with one situation or another. If only I could turn to one of them now and ask, 'What should I do, how should I respond to this problem?'

I did not have the wisdom or the experience to always make the right choices and just had to do the best I could.

When Donata first came to stay with us in Kigali she was my servant, but that was no longer our relationship. We had become as close as sisters; we shared clothes, did each other's hair and slept in the same bed. We never discussed what had happened to us in Rwanda though. It was too painful a subject to broach and I was sure that Donata was trying as hard as I was to block the whole thing out.

I had spent the day undoing Donata's braided hair. When we'd finished I said to her, 'Go and wash your hair and I'll get some fish in the market.'

Donata nodded happily. I had agreed to do her hair in a different style when I returned from shopping.

The market was only a few minutes away and shortly after I arrived there someone from the lodge rushed up to me and said breathlessly, 'Come quickly, Leah, Donata is bleeding badly.'

My mouth dropped open. Just when I thought we had reached safety, disaster had struck.

'What are you talking about? Has she been shot, or stabbed? Where is she bleeding?'

'From her eyes, nose, mouth, ears.'

I didn't know it was possible to bleed from such places, and raced back to the lodge, leaving my package of fish at the stall. The only condition I knew of where that might happen was ebola.

Oh, please God, no, I said to myself. If it's ebola Donata will almost certainly die and Jean-Luc and I will probably be infected too.

I was appalled when I reached our room to see that Donata was indeed bleeding profusely. It was as if there was a fountain spurting inside her head with such force that it had to gush out from every available exit. She was unconscious.

Someone at the lodge knew someone with a car, and we rushed Donata to Kenyatta Hospital, a dirty, chaotic place overflowing with human misery.

'Please don't let her die, not now, after all we've been through,' I begged the doctors, who I could see looked puzzled by her condition.

Her head had turned red. Sticky blood coated her face and clung to her teeth.

'We'll do our best, but we don't know if we can make her better because we're not sure what's causing the bleeding,' said the doctors. The Swahili I spoke was very different from Kenyan Swahili and the doctors laughed at what to them was a very strange way of speaking their language. They confirmed however that it wasn't ebola, to my enormous relief.

'There is no point in you staying here. Go home and come back later. Maybe your friend will be better by the time you come back,' they advised me.

I squeezed Donata's unresponsive hand and whispered, 'You're going to be fine. Don't give up now.'

I walked despairingly out of the hospital with Jean-Luc in my arms. I couldn't understand how one minute Donata was well and the next moment she was almost dead. I don't think God wants me to have any luck, I said to myself.

I began to silently plead with Him to spare her life. Donata and Jean-Luc were the only people I had left in the world. Donata and I had been through a horrific ordeal but together we had survived. I was inconsolable at the thought of losing her now.

I walked towards the bus stop. If God exists, perhaps He heard me sobbing. Just at that moment a gleaming white Toyota Celica pulled alongside me and the driver started speaking to me in a language I recognised as Kikuyu, although I was unable to speak it.

I looked helplessly at the driver. 'Me not understand,' I replied falteringly in English, a language I only knew a few words of.

'Oh, where are you from?' he asked in English.

'No English,' I replied, hopelessly.

'Where you from?' he continued in English.

I couldn't answer. I tried Swahili. 'Please, I'm not in the mood to chat.'

'Where are you going?' he asked in Swahili.

'We're staying in Kirenyaga, we're heading back there now.'

'I'm going that way, let me drop you,' he offered cheerfully.

I had no idea whether or not this was a man I could trust but at that moment survival was not uppermost in my mind.

Wearily I climbed into the passenger seat and held Jean–Luc close. At least I can save myself the bus fare, I thought.

My mind was racing and I hardly thought about the driver. How would I bury Donata if she died? I didn't have much money and I certainly couldn't take her back to Rwanda or Zaire. I started crying. The driver looked alarmed.

'Whoa, hold on a minute, let me go and buy you something to eat. Beautiful girls like you don't cry easily.'

I turned and looked at the man through my tears. He was in his mid–thirties and obviously quite wealthy. His hair was close–cropped, his clothes were expensive and his face was handsome and not unkind. He told me his name was Kamal.

He parked outside a local café and we went inside, where he ordered some cold drinks. In the hope that he might help us I decided to tell him my story, everything from our time trapped in Josephine's place to all the near–misses with the Interahamwe and our various border crossings. Kamal looked horrified.

'I assumed you were Kenyan when I saw you walking along the street. I had no idea that you'd escaped from this terrible, terrible situation in Rwanda. You poor girl.'

We talked for over an hour. Kamal told me that although he was now a wealthy man he had very humble roots. He had lived on the streets, surviving on his wits, and had built up his fortune by doing odd–jobs for Western tourists in Mombasa. He was popular with them because he was always honest.

'I know what it is to suffer and I don't like to see other people suffer,' he said. He thought hard for a few moments and then said, 'I have to sort out some business matters but I'll be back at four and we can go together to see your friend Donata. Hagakan Hospital is one of the best hospitals in Nairobi. I want her transferred there by ambulance. I will make some calls now and make sure it's done immediately.'

'Thank you, Kamal, you are very kind indeed. If Donata is in a good hospital her life may be saved.'

He dropped Jean-Luc and me off at the lodge and told us he would be back just before 4 p.m. to collect us.

'Everything is going to be OK,' I told Jean-Luc, who looked up at me with his big, trusting eyes and gurgled. 'There are many bad people in the world but also guardian angels like Mustapha. I think Kamal is another one.'

Hagakan Hospital was lovely, like walking into a fancy hotel. Donata was sleeping peacefully in a nice clean bed in a private room with a doctor at her bedside.

'We've given her some scans and there doesn't seem to be any fundamental damage. What has happened to her could be the body's way of responding to extreme trauma,' explained the doctor.

Within a week she was better, sitting up in bed, talking, eating and cuddling Jean-Luc. To my relief she was talking normally again, the way she always had done. She remembered little about our ordeal in Rwanda and was reluctant to talk about whatever she did recall.

Kamal took us to the hospital every day to visit Donata. I sobbed with gratitude when she was discharged.

'How can I ever thank you, Kamal? I'm so sorry that I have no money to pay you for your kindness,' I said.

'Don't even think about that,' he said. 'I've been blessed with money and I'm just happy to be able to help. I'm going to Dar es Salaam to sell some cars – that is my job – but I'll be back soon,' he said.

He gradually gained my trust. He moved us from the first lodge we stayed in into a more luxurious one, and again he insisted on paying all our bills. He also took us to church every Sunday.

'I can't believe that Donata has made such a good recovery,' I said, smiling at Kamal. 'We owe you a lot. I think our luck is changing and now everything is going to be just fine. I'm going to make us all a nice cup of tea to celebrate.'

The last thing I remember is filling the kettle from the tap. Then I collapsed. The kettle fell with me, the spilt water gathering in a pool around me.

CHAPTER THIRTEEN

I have no idea what Kamal thought of me collapsing so soon after Donata. I'm sure he wondered what on earth he was getting into! Donata told me later that he took the whole thing in his stride and calmly returned to Hagakan Hospital with me laid out in the back of the car.

'You have to make her better, whatever it takes,' I remember hearing him say as I lay, barely conscious, on the cool white hospital sheets.

When I regained consciousness a few days later I had lost the power of speech, and when I tried to express myself by writing a couple of words in a notebook found that I could no longer write. I had been struck dumb and illiterate. Strangely, I didn't mind at all. I did not want to think any more, nor to shoulder any more responsibility; in fact I wanted to do absolutely nothing. Using gestures I made it clear that I could not be parted from Jean-Luc. He was the only person that mattered to me in the world. He remained in the bed beside me and I managed to wash him and feed him although I couldn't speak to him. It was almost pleasant to lie back in clean whiteness and stuff my brain with pure nothingness. I did not feel scared of my altered state. Instead I felt rather relieved, as if my nerves had been strung as tight as catgut for weeks and now everything in my mind and body could slump into a state of relaxation.

I felt as if I had built myself a brick room and climbed inside it with Jean-Luc, enjoying its peaceful emptiness. I was aware that Donata barely left my bedside, constantly mopping my forehead with a damp cloth, her tears splashing on to the sheets.

As in Donata's case, the doctors could find nothing physically wrong with me. 'Your condition is a response to the extreme trauma you have experienced. Your body is shutting down to try to heal. Lie back and let nature take its course,' said one of the doctors.

When people found out that I was in hospital, they came to see me. In the first lodge where Mustapha left us I had become friendly with some of these Rwandise people. Donata had told them that I had carried three babies along with my own through the genocide and I had quite a few Rwandise visitors who prayed for me and praised my courage with the babies.

Most of the time I was unconscious. My only memory is of being happy where I was and of never wanting to leave this comfortable, womb-like place.

The doctors treated my wounds, which had still not completely healed. They checked me for all sorts of diseases, including HIV, because blood from my wounds had mingled with the blood of others. Miraculously all the tests came back negative. Once again I had been incredibly lucky.

After three weeks I started to get better and was discharged from hospital. I could speak falteringly but I still couldn't read or write. Kamal had visited faithfully every day. Like Mustapha, he asked for nothing in return for helping me.

'Leah, I'm so happy to see you're getting better,' he said. 'I feel you're like a daughter to me. I want only the best for you.'

After I was discharged he began the painstaking process of teaching me to read and write from scratch. I had always been a very able student at school, but now the words swam before my eyes like hieroglyphics. Gradually my powers of literacy returned. It's strange what trauma can do to the mind.

The first time I saw how bad things were in Rwanda was on the television in the hospital. I watched in horror as injured people fled Rwanda and told their stories. It was hard to believe that we had made it out alive. I felt both relief and guilt that I had survived. Why had I got out when others hadn't? Every time I saw those terrible images of people suffering I felt enraged that one group of people could inflict such agony on another because of the shape of their noses. I decided that there was no hope left in Rwanda. It looked like Sodom and Gomorrah to me, like the biblical end of the world. I decided I never wanted to return there and switched off the news.

As my recovery progressed I became increasingly scared of Rwandise people. I was convinced that I would be attacked in the street, and my sleep was disturbed and sweat-soaked.

Kamal did everything he could to make me feel at ease. 'Now that you're better, Leah, I want to show you all the nice places to go to in Nairobi. You need to forget what you've been through.' He took us to live music shows and to all the best parks and cafés.

He was kind to Jean-Luc and clapped when he took his first faltering steps at the age of nine months. I wished Christian and Maman had been there to witness this. I had a photo of Christian that had been in my handbag when I was at Josephine's place and I'd kept it safe. I decided it was time to start showing it to Jean-Luc so that even though Christian was dead he would always know who his father was and how much he was loved by him. Every day I showed Jean-Luc the photo, pointed at it and said 'Papa' to him over and over again.

'Your *papa* loves you very much,' I said to Jean-Luc, trying not to cry.

I knew I should be counting my blessings that Jean-Luc and I had survived and were now leading a comfortable life in Kenya, but I felt wretched. Although I was extremely grateful to Kamal for his kindness and generosity I was feeling increasingly unsettled in Nairobi as more and more Rwandise refugees arrived. I was also beginning to worry about Kamal's intentions. Although he had made no approaches to me, he was always very affectionate in a fatherly kind of way, and I wondered if he was going to wait until I was eighteen and then try his luck.

'I'm not happy being in Kenya, Kamal. It's not far enough away from Rwanda and I just don't feel safe here.'

'What?' he said. I could see that he couldn't believe I wanted to walk away from the nice life he had provided for me even though I had nothing. 'Listen, Leah, I'm going to Germany next month on business. Wait until I come back and we'll talk. Don't make any hurried decisions.'

I agreed to wait until he returned from his trip, but the weeks rolled on and there was no sign of him. He had paid the rent for the lodge we were staying at several weeks in advance, but now another payment was due and I had no money to cover it. All I had with me was the jewellery that I planned to sell in an emergency but I didn't want to use it to pay rent on an expensive apartment in Nairobi.

I was keen to be independent rather than financially reliant on Kamal. Maman and Papa had always drummed it into me that I should work hard for everything I received and not be dependent on charity.

We had put our names down on a UNHCR waiting list to go to Canada to start a new life, but the list was extremely long and none of the officials could give us any real indication of when or if our turn might come.

I was beginning to see less and less of Donata, because she had started a relationship with a young Rwandise man of mixed Hutu and Tutsi origin called John. I was happy for her but found it hard to understand how she could trust anyone with Hutu blood in them so soon after witnessing the atrocities perpetrated by Hutus. To me it was a kind of betrayal. The three of us had become such a tightly bonded unit that I had assumed we would be together for ever.

I felt the familiar urge to run intensifying inside me. Every time I saw Rwandise people I wanted to put as much distance between us as possible.

I left Jean-Luc with a Somalian friend who lived near by and went into town to try to sell some of my jewellery. I had decided that Kenya wasn't far enough away from Rwanda, and my new plan was to go to South Africa – as far away as I could get from Rwanda without leaving the continent. I had spoken to a couple from Cameroon at the same lodge. They said they travelled regularly to South Africa and that the journey was not difficult.

'It's a wonderful place, Leah. It looks like Europe, with good roads, nice buildings, electricity and clean water, but now that Mandela is liberated it is a place of freedom for black Africans.'

'It sounds perfect, and it is very far from Rwanda. I think Jean-Luc and I will try to reach that place.'

I sold some of my jewellery and then decided to go and find Yusuf, a friend of Kamal's who I had met a few times, who worked in town.

He greeted me warmly and we chatted for a while.

'Yusuf, do you know what has happened to Kamal? I thought he would be back from Germany by now but there is no sign of him.'

'I'm afraid I know as much as you, Leah. I too thought he would have returned by now.'

'I'm leaving Nairobi, Yusuf. I can't wait until Kamal has returned. I feel that it is too dangerous for me here. There are too many Rwandise and I don't know who is my friend and who is my enemy. I feel as if I'm in a trap and don't want to leave it too late to run like I did in Rwanda. I want to try to get to South Africa. I believe Jean-Luc and I will be safe there. I want to find a place where we can put down roots and I can enrol him in a nursery.'

'I'm sorry you're leaving, Leah, and Kamal will be sad to find you gone when he returns, but I do understand why you feel you need to move on,' said Yusuf. He reached into his trouser pocket and pulled out a hundred US dollars. 'Here. This is all I have at the moment, but take it for your journey. I'm sure it will come in useful.'

'Thank you, Yusuf,' I said, hugging him. 'You've been very kind to us.'

When I returned home and collected Jean-Luc from my friend's house I could see that he wasn't well. He kept pointing to his nose and seemed to be having trouble breathing. The thought of anything bad happening to my precious baby filled me with terror. I looked up his nose and saw, to my horror, that one nostril was stuffed with raw meat and the other with peas.

I tried to remove them but they were wedged tightly inside his tiny, delicate nose. I was terrified of causing him damage by pulling too hard.

'What happened to you, Jean-Luc?'

'Abdi,' he whimpered. Abdi was my friend's son. He was just a year older than Jean-Luc.

'Blow, Jean-Luc, blow,' I cried. But he was too little to know how to do it. In the end I rushed him to hospital and one of the doctors extracted the food. Although it was a relatively minor incident it really threw me and made me feel it would be bad luck to stay in Kenya any longer.

'That's it, we're leaving,' I said, starting to pack our belongings. The Cameroonian couple had explained that they took a bus to Dar es Salaam in Tanzania and from there travelled to Zambia and then South Africa. Jean-Luc was almost one year old. He could say words like 'Maman' and 'hello'. He was hearing a mixture of French, English and Swahili and I'm sure he was very confused. He was running around all over the place and I needed to watch him like a hawk. He was entranced by the world around him and was constantly looking and pointing at things. His innocence and enthusiasm for life kept me going.

I knew that crossing the border would be difficult as I didn't have papers. But gradually I was adjusting to the fact that I was now living a back-road life. I had become like a criminal, hiding in the shadows. I was learning the secret way past every border. Somehow I would find a way to get to where I needed to be.

The prospect of leaving Kenya cheered me up. I was relieved that I would soon be leaving behind a country that was gradually filling up with Rwandise people. I hadn't travelled much in Africa, visiting only Burundi and Kenya, and was excited at the prospect of going somewhere new. I knew very little about other African countries, and that was part of their appeal.

South Africa held an idealistic glamour for me and I was convinced I'd be safe there. We had learned about apartheid at school and I had gone to hear Mandela make a speech when he visited Zaire. He spoke English so I couldn't understand what he was saying, but I was very impressed all the same. He was wearing one of those brightly coloured shirts he favours and Mobutu was by his side. The speech was replayed endlessly on television and there was a big party in Goma that day.

Mandela was Papa's biggest hero, along with Fidel Castro.

I told Donata excitedly that I wanted us to travel to South Africa. I thought she would agree to come with me, and the vehemence of her refusal surprised me.

'I don't want to go to Europe or Canada or South Africa. In fact I don't want to go anywhere. I'm going to stay here,' said Donata. 'I want to move on with my life. I want to get married and have children with John. I believe I have a chance of happiness and I don't want to lose it.'

I felt as if I'd been hit by a truck. I had become accustomed to her being more or less glued to my side. The fact that Donata and I would no longer be together was very painful for me. Perhaps being with me was too horrible a reminder for her of everything that had happened to us in Rwanda, I reasoned. But it didn't take away the feelings of hurt and rejection that I had.

'OK, Donata, you must do what is best for you, but Jean-Luc and I must move on. I don't feel safe here in Kenya any longer.'

Donata lowered her head. She didn't want to look me in the eye. She moved in with John soon afterwards and I saw her even less. Then one day she and John left suddenly without telling me. I think she was too scared to tell me what she was doing and it was too difficult for her to say goodbye.

Although I was devastated, it made me more determined than ever to hurry out of Kenya and get on the road again. I went to buy the bus ticket to take me to the Tanzanian border from Nairobi's dusty, crowded bus station. Now all I had to do was work out how to sneak out of one country and into another.

CHAPTER FOURTEEN

Another border, another dusty road crowded with travellers, traders and optimists convinced that a change of territory would transform their luck for the better.

With Jean-Luc in my arms and a small bag of clothes and other essentials on my back, I decided to use the same approach I had tried so successfully in Goma with Mustapha. I found a driver who looked friendly and approachable and walked up to him as confidently as I could.

'Excuse me. I'm trying to get across the border,' I said, smiling as sweetly as I could. 'I'll give you money if you can help me to cross.'

'Are you crazy?' he asked.

'No, I'm not. I don't have any papers. I have no choice but to find other ways to cross.'

I wasn't sure whether or not I could trust this man. I didn't have the same instinctive feeling and had decided to make up a story, to put as much distance as possible between me and my Rwandan identity.

'My name is Leyla,' I said, choosing a good Kenyan name. My Swahili had improved and I could now speak good Kenyan Swahili. 'Somebody has stolen my bag with my passport in it, so I have to find another way to cross the border.'

The driver seemed to accept that I was an ordinary Kenyan woman just trying to visit Tanzania.

'Oh, that's bad luck,' he said, smiling. 'The customs people on the border aren't too bad. If you can pay me fifty dollars for your passage you can climb in and we'll see how we get on.'

I nodded and grinned. I felt much better knowing that I was on the move again. Moving made me feel safer; staying for too long in one place was too risky. I handed Jean-Luc to the driver while I climbed into the truck. Mustapha's truck had always smelled fresh, but this one stank of stale tobacco, an odour that made me want to retch.

With this driver the deal was strictly business. Unlike Mustapha he didn't offer to share any of his food with us. I bought grilled bananas and sugarcane in the street before we set off.

The border-control officials sat on white plastic chairs. They looked as if they were wilting in the heat and didn't have the energy to challenge anyone.

The driver said a few words to the official in a language I did not recognise and we were waved through.

I smiled broadly. 'I'm free again, I'm free,' I whispered to myself. I felt I could breathe more easily now that there was some extra distance between me and all the Rwandise who had congregated in Nairobi.

I relaxed back into the seat and closed my eyes. I missed Donata so, so much. Although we had never talked much I had always trusted her and valued her loyalty. Crossing borders without her was much harder because I had to hold on to Jean-Luc the whole time.

We travelled all the way to Dar es Salaam with only a couple of brief food and toilet stops. It took the driver the whole day and night to reach the capital but he was very strong and didn't seem to tire. He certainly didn't waste his energy on conversation and only uttered a handful of words to me throughout our journey.

The first thing that hit me about Tanzania was the heat. Every step was like walking into a hot wall. Despite the stifling temperatures the Tanzanian women were wearing long black robes, and the men had similar white robes. The Muslim women kept all of their faces covered too, apart from their eyes. I nicknamed them 'African ninjas'.

I was so hot I wanted to remove all my clothes and walk naked. I stripped down to a vest and a wrapper. Everyone looked at me as if I was completely crazy.

'I don't know Tanzania very well,' I said to the driver.

'Tanzanians are very kind. Go to Peacocks Hotel, it's just at the end of this road they will look after you there,' said the driver.

I thanked him for getting us across the border and headed in the direction he had pointed to. It was a very nice hotel and as he said the Tanzanians I met seemed very kind and friendly. A man who was staying there could see that I was suffering from the heat.

'You need to drink hot tea, it will cool you down,' he said. It sounded like a very strange theory to me but I took his advice and to my amazement I did feel a bit cooler afterwards.

The food was very different from what I was used to, with many people eating big plates of chicken with spicy rice. I was used to eating much plainer food – boiled potatoes and vegetables. Everyone ate with their hands and because I had never done this I wasn't sure what to do.

The people in Tanzania were very polite and welcoming. They seemed to be very honest and were willing to help when you had a problem. In Kenya I was always scared to approach people in case they tried to con me but I didn't worry so much about that in Tanzania. A lot of the restaurants were outdoors and men sat in the shade of mango trees, heavy with plump fruit, while they played chess.

Dar es Salaam is a seaside place with lots of soft white sand, so hot it singes the skin on the soles of your feet. The heat of the sun was shooting into the centre of my head like a gun firing piercing bullets. I worried that the intense heat would trigger the nosebleeds I had suffered from as a child. I knew that, especially now Donata was gone, I had to remain healthy for Jean-Luc's sake.

I met a couple with two children who told me they were from Zambia although to me they looked Zairian. I started to talk to them but decided not to tell them that I was Rwandise. Instead I said I was Zairian.

'Could you help us get to Zambia?' I begged. 'Unfortunately I don't have a passport.'

'Yes, we're going back, you can come with us. We will buy a family ticket and if you pay your share we will include you in our ticket. But what are you going to do when you reach the border with Zambia? The immigration people do check when you're in the train.'

'I don't know, maybe we will hide in the toilet,' I replied, deciding that I'd cross that bridge when I came to it.

We spent a week in the hotel, trying to work out what to do. Immigration officials were poorly paid and they often visited hotels to check up on the guests' immigration status. If they found you didn't have the correct papers they could arrest you and take your belongings and then you had to find someone to pay bail money.

I didn't go out much as I wanted to stay close to wherever the air-conditioning was. But unfortunately I didn't manage to prevent the nosebleeds; it had been ten years since I'd suffered from them. Then Maman and my sisters fussed around, taking care of me. Now I was all alone. I missed my family all the time but at those particular moments I ached for them more than ever. If only Maman was here now, to pinch my nose and make it stop bleeding in that magic way she had.

I hated having time on my hands because then it was impossible to shut out thoughts about the people I loved. Nightmares about what had happened in Rwanda, and the faces of my family and Christian, continued to invade my sleep.

Jean-Luc sometimes cried out in his sleep. I wondered what kind of dreams he was having. He had become very attached to the photo of Christian and liked to have it beside him when he went to sleep. I was careful never to promise him that one day Christian would come back, but wanted to make sure that an image of his father remained in his mind.

'Look at Papa. Isn't he handsome?' I often said.

Each day that we were in Dar es Salaam the heat became more and more unbearable. I thought a cold shower would help me lower my body temperature but a cold shower in Dar es Salaam was a hot shower. My nosebleeds continued. We were on the fourth floor and I had to get the receptionist to give me cold water from the fridge. He gave me two jugs of iced water and put my wrapper in the freezer to cool it off. Then I wrapped it around my head and managed to stop the bleeding.

I knew I wouldn't be able to survive for long in this heat and that I needed to continue as soon as possible with my journey towards safety. After a week the family I had become friendly with had worked out all the details of our trip. I still said nothing about my previous life and they continued to believe that I was a Zairian girl on her way to Zambia.

'We'll book one of those little private carriages on the train, and when the ticket man comes to check we'll help you hide in the toilet so you don't need to show your travel documents,' said the wife. Kamal had bought me nice clothes in Nairobi so I didn't look like a refugee trying to dodge border controls. Jean-Luc was also well dressed. I bought him second-hand Dolce & Gabbana jumpers. I knew all the good names and exactly which brands from Europe to look for in the market in Nairobi.

I had seen trains in movies but had never stepped on to one.

I was excited and apprehensive as we boarded. Tazar was written on the side. It was a huge thing, full of business people. I had thought the journey would last a few hours and had no idea we would actually be travelling for a few days. We bought ice-cold Fantas in the restaurant and gulped them down.

There was air-conditioning on the train and we played cards to help the time pass. I could see lots of cows out of the windows, and people working peacefully on their farms and washing themselves and their clothes in the small rivers. This looked like a part of Africa that had not known war.

'You know, Leah, it's not safe to cross the border illegally into South Africa at the moment. When they catch people trying to do that they throw them into jail,' said the wife.

'I'm sure I'll find a way. I managed to cross from Kenya to Tanzania without too many problems. There must be people who cross illegally. I'll watch what they do.'

The family accepted that I was determined to get to South Africa, whether or not it was a sensible idea. I felt sure that if I could just get to the furthest tip of the continent, I would at last feel safe and calm and could start rebuilding my life.

Once we had crossed the border the train terminated and we had to take a bus to the capital, Lusaka. I got chatting to some Zairians on the bus.

'What do you do in Zambia? Is it an easy place to find work?' I asked.

'We're traders, we sell carvings and sculptures,' one of them explained.

'We have our pitch outside the Lusaka Hotel. It's the place where rich people go. Sometimes business is good for us. Go down there with us and you will find people who can help you,' said one.

I talked to the traders outside the Lusaka Hotel and asked if they knew of any places to stay. There were a few Burundians amongst them; many had fled their own internal conflict on Lake

Tanganyika in boats. They recommended a cheap place on the outskirts of the city.

'Your baby is very cute. Where is the daddy?' a young Burundian woman asked me.

I showed her the photo of Christian.

'Oh my goodness, I know this guy. He's also from Burundi.'

'No, I think you're mistaken. This man is not Burundian and he died in Rwanda.'

'Oh, OK, you know best. People can look alike.'

'Where is this man you know, anyway?'

'He left just a few days ago. He was sleeping in the street and finding it very hard. I think maybe he went to Malawi.'

I looked at her disbelievingly.

'I'm not joking,' she said. 'I do know this guy. He was hanging around with a woman called Christine.'

I became very aggressive. It was torture to hear someone pretending that Christian was alive when I knew for sure that he was dead.

'OK then, if he's alive, what's his name?'

'Yusuf,' she said, with great certainty.

'You see, I told you he was dead. Christian was never called Yusuf, you've made a big mistake there. He was flying into the airport when the President's plane blew up. Nobody survived that.'

She could see how worked up I'd become and hurriedly changed the subject. 'I'm sorry. I didn't mean any harm. Christian really does look exactly like the Yusuf I met, but I know many people have doubles. Let's just forget it.'

I could see though that she was still convinced that Christian and Yusuf were one and the same person. I did not believe for one minute that Christian was still alive but her certainty unsettled me. Even though I was convinced that Christian was dead the idea, however impossible, that he might still be alive made my heart surge with joy. But having told myself for all these months that he was dead, the thought of building up my hopes only to have them dashed again was too much to bear. Don't be silly, Leah, you know Christian is dead. Don't go building your hopes up for nothing, I told myself sternly.

Behind the hotel there was a big market with lots of stalls crowded together. People were buying freshly cooked takeaway food and women were styling hair. In Rwanda people went to a hairdresser to have their hair done, but here a lot of Zambians were plaiting hair. You could have clothes made for you while you waited. They certainly did things differently here from the way we did things back home. In my culture people sat down and ate a proper meal, but here everyone was happy to eat on the go.

'You should go into the market,' the woman said. 'You will find many people there.'

'I'm scared of the market. I don't know why I feel that way,' I said quietly. I used to love the hustle and bustle of markets, with women hawking their wares and excited children weaving in and out amongst the pyramids of fruit and vegetables on display. But now crowds felt dangerous. Anybody could be in a crowd: a lunatic, a member of the Interahamwe wielding a machete. It was impossible to be safe in such a place.

'Wait until my husband comes and he'll take you,' she said. Both of them were selling bowls and ornaments made of blue-green malachite.

He returned half an hour later and we all headed off to the market. On our way there I could see sick people being wheeled around in wheelbarrows. I had never seen such a thing. She explained that that was how sick people were transported to hospital. I looked sadly at the people crumpled up in their makeshift ambulances. I knew there were infinite ways to suffer. I had thought that it was only in Rwanda that terrible things were happening, but increasingly I was beginning to understand that people suffered everywhere and it was people, not places, that caused human suffering.

Zambia was full of street stalls, and not as clean as Nairobi. At times I thought I was back in Zaire because Zairian music filled the streets. At first I didn't want to approach anybody in the market but after a while I gained courage and started chatting. Briefly I felt like the old, carefree Leah; I could make people smile and they were making me smile. The banter helped me forget what I had been through and the big, black boulder crushing my brain stopped feeling so heavy.

A second woman I got talking to came from Burundi. She was beautiful, with chocolate-coloured skin, and was smartly dressed in Western clothes. Her hair was plaited, with beads threaded through it at the end. She looked as if she was in her mid-twenties.

She heard me speaking French and said, 'Are you from Burundi?'

'No, no, I'm not from Burundi,' I replied, not wanting to volunteer any information about my origins or what I had been through.

Then she switched to Kinyarwanda and without thinking I replied in the same language, suddenly pulling myself up when I realised what I was doing. But it was too late.

We introduced ourselves and she told me her name was Claire.

'Where are you staying?' she asked, delighted to have found someone from the same region of Africa as herself.

When I told her the name of the hotel I had been recommended she tutted: 'Oh no, that's much too expensive and not very nice. There's space in my room. You and your baby can stay with me rent-free, it's really no problem.'

I was fortunate to meet many kind people like Claire, but it was not only me who received help. Many people throughout Africa had heard about the horrific events in Rwanda and tried their best to help those who had fled the horror. Claire was particularly supportive towards me because she too was a Tutsi and had suffered a lot in Burundi.

(Not everyone that Jean-Luc and I met on our journey was kind to us. Sometimes we knocked on doors asking for water when we were thirsty and people chased us away. But more often than not people were willing to help.)

Claire started asking me many questions about what had happened in Rwanda.

'I don't want to talk about it,' I replied, wincing.

'I understand.' She nodded. 'For a long time I didn't want to talk about what happened to me in Burundi.'

Thankfully she didn't push things any further. She could see that I was reluctant to talk about anything to do with Rwanda and turned the conversation to practical matters. She told me she rented a room in a guesthouse. She had a huge bed and at the front there was a verandah where she cooked.

She explained that she was Rwandise but had grown up in Burundi. Here in Zambia she worked in an Arab boutique. She loved to go dancing and went to clubs every weekend. She was really full of life. I marvelled at how joyful and carefree she was even though she hinted that she had been through terrible things. I wished that I could put our trauma behind me as effortlessly as she apparently had. Now I realise that her behaviour was her way of blotting out pain.

I showed her Christian's photo. 'This is Jean-Luc's father. We were teenage sweethearts but sadly he was killed at the beginning of the war,' I said.

In the beginning I had been too much in shock to think of showing people Christian's photo. At first Jean-Luc had been with Donata but now that he was always with me, people asked where his father was. I found it easier to explain that Christian was dead by showing people the photo. She looked briefly at the photo out of politeness, then she looked again more intently.

'Oh, I saw this guy,' said Claire. She was speaking with great conviction and I was completely taken aback.

'But that's impossible. I just told you he's dead. Believe me, I've been through a lot. Please don't upset me more by playing these tricks on me.'

Claire shrugged. 'OK, sorry,' she said.

Once again hope surged. Maybe I was wrong, maybe some-how, miraculously, Christian had survived.

'Where did you see him?' I asked more gently.

'He was here until just a few days ago but he said he was moving on. I think he planned to go to Malawi.'

'I would be interested in meeting this man who looks like Christian, just so that I can be sure it isn't him,' I said to Claire.

'OK, I'll ask a few people he was hanging around with and see if they know where he is now.'

As Claire and I chatted more I explained my plan to get to South Africa.

'But Zambia is a great place. You should stay here for a while and give it a chance,' she said.

'I'm sure it's great, but the truth is I would love to get out of here. Can you help me, Claire? I don't have any documents. I'm a refugee. I'm on the run and I can't rest until Jean-Luc and I reach South Africa. There I believe I'll be safe at last.'

Claire looked me in the eye. She could see that I was deadly serious. 'I know somebody who can do you a passport, but it will cost you,' she said.

'I have some jewellery that I will happily sell to buy a passport,' I said eagerly.

She took me to a shop next to the market that bought gold and I sold one of my favourite necklaces for $300. I had no regrets about parting from the necklace, as long as the proceeds got me to South Africa.

Then Claire told me about a Zairian man who produced forged passports. 'I think he's here in the market; I'll go and get him.'

She returned a few minutes later with a man she introduced as John. He was a shy, studious man, not the kind of person you would expect to be involved in this line of work. We spoke in Lingala.

'I can do the passport for you.'

'And how much will it cost us?'

'A hundred dollars,' he said quickly.

I nodded and prayed that the passport would work. He explained that he would have to take my photos to other people who make up the passport. He was obviously just a messenger boy. Claire said they bought genuine passports from Zambians and altered the photos inside them.

'Let's go back to my place now,' she said. 'I assume you're not planning on leaving this minute?'

I laughed. 'No, no of course not.'

Claire asked a few people if they knew where the man who looked like Christian had gone to, but nobody seemed sure. I was overwhelmed with disappointment but told myself that this man couldn't be Christian and so there was little point in trying to meet him.

Claire's room was clean and spacious. She, Jean-Luc and I all slept in her big double bed and cooked outside together on her verandah.

Staying with Claire was a breathing space for me. It was nice to do normal things like cooking and cleaning, and I couldn't stop thanking her for her kindness. But all I could think about was moving on.

We spent three weeks in Zambia while I sorted out my passport. I gave John a picture of myself and he did everything else. I was tired of sneaking through the bush from one country to the next. This time I wanted to go through the front door with my head held high, even if it was with a forged passport.

I celebrated my eighteenth birthday in Zambia. Claire cooked some special rice and beans and bought Fantas for all of us. I appreciated her thoughtfulness but I could not help contrasting it with my seventeenth-birthday celebrations in Kigali. My parents organised a huge party, a lavish barbecue for all our family and friends. Everyone was alive and carefree and none of us had any idea of what was to come. Papa had bought me a

Toyota, saying that now I was a mother I would need a nice family car.

Jean-Luc was changing every day. He scampered all over the place and it was hard to keep pace with him. He was full of fun and loved playing hide-and-seek with me. Claire bought him a red toy car and he refused to be separated from it. Claire's place was close to the airport and Jean-Luc loved watching the planes taking off and landing. Every time he saw one he pointed excitedly and cried, 'Plane, Maman, plane.'

When the forged passport finally lay in the palm of my hand, I felt apprehensive. I'd never been involved with any sort of fraud before and I felt sick to my stomach. But it was the only way I could think of to reach safety. I took a deep breath and put it carefully in my bag.

We got tickets for the Zambaz, the coach to Zimbabwe. From there it was apparently very easy to enter South Africa. In fact it all sounded a bit *too* easy.

I hugged Claire goodbye and we climbed on to the coach. It was spotlessly clean, with air-conditioning and all mod cons.

It only took us an hour or so to reach the border. Jean-Luc was sleeping peacefully when we arrived. We all climbed down from the coach to show our passports to the border guards. I took my passport out of my bag but at that moment Jean-Luc stirred, then woke up and cried out very loudly in French, '*Maman, je vais faire pipi.*'

'*Jean-Luc, arrête,*' I said without thinking. Zambians don't speak French and I was pretending to be Zambian. Reverting to French was a disastrous move on my part.

'Why are you speaking French?' asked one of the border guards suspiciously.

'I'm teaching my son French because his daddy is Zairian.'

I looked longingly at the big bridge between Zambia and Zimbabwe. They had been about to put a stamp in my passport on the Zimbabwe side of the border and now it looked as if my plans were ruined.

He didn't believe my explanation about the French and I knew I wasn't telling a very convincing story. He barked out more questions like bursts of machine-gun fire.

'Who is the President?'

I shrugged and hung my head. I didn't know.

More questions followed about Zambia's history and geography. Again I had no idea of how to answer.

They fined me and told me to go back into Zambia.

CHAPTER FIFTEEN

I had thought the whole thing had sounded too good to be true and it was. I wept as we were dispatched to the other side of the border.

'Oh Jean-Luc, if only you'd stayed asleep for just two more minutes, we'd be on our way to South Africa now,' I said exasperatedly. I called Claire in tears and told her what had happened.

'Never mind, Leah, get a bus back to Lusaka and we'll think of a different plan for you. It's not the end of the world.'

'Oh, but it's such a waste of money. I don't have anything more to sell,' I wailed. 'I've only got a couple of hundred dollars left to my name.'

Once in Lusaka we went back to John, the passport forger's assistant, to tell him what had happened and ask his advice about what to do next.

'Now they'll be checking you out if you try to get over to Zimbabwe again. This time you should go the back way, through Malawi and then from Malawi to South Africa,' he said.

'OK, I'll try that,' I said, brightening. He made it all sound very simple.

'I can show you the back way into Malawi.'

'Thank you, John, thank you,' I said, smiling for the first time that day. 'Can we leave tomorrow?'

'OK,' he said. 'It will cost fifty dollars.'

Jean-Luc and I always travelled light, with just a couple of changes of clothes that could be washed easily. Jean-Luc clasped his little red car tightly and a pair of plastic butterfly-shaped sunglasses. I classed these as our essential extras.

As we boarded the bus heading for Malawi, John explained that we needed to avoid the 'front door' of the border. Torrential rain lashed against the windows of the bus, some of it dribbling through gaps in the windows on to our hair and noses. It was hot and damp inside but no one wanted to open the windows too far in case we got completely soaked.

There was a girl on the bus who was travelling to her mother's village. We got chatting and I managed to speak to her in my basic Nyanja, one of the main Zambian languages, which I had picked up from the time I spent in the market with Claire. Thankfully the aptitude for languages that I had been praised for at school had not deserted me. Nyanja contained a lot of Swahili, which made it much easier for me to learn.

She asked where we were heading, and I briefly explained our story.

'Oh, so you don't have a place to rest on your journey. You and your baby will be very welcome to stay overnight with us,' she said.

'Thank you, you're very kind,' I replied.

We reached her home at around eight in the evening. She lived in a beautiful modern white house with red doors. Her family made us feel very welcome and offered John a bed too.

Her mother joked that every time her daughter came home on the bus she brought at least one of the travellers back with her. 'We don't mind having guests, we have plenty of room,' she laughed.

They cooked maize and fish and vegetables for us, and made porridge for Jean-Luc, and I had the luxury of a lovely hot indoor shower. We slept very well in soft, clean beds.

The house wasn't too far from the border and with a gift of bread and rice in our bags we set off early the next morning.

Even though Jean-Luc was heavy it comforted me to have him close to me. I carried him on my back and tied him to me. I used to sing 'Frère Jacques' to him and other French nursery rhymes I had learned from Maman. When he cried I used to sing, 'Bébé, sois gentil,' and he used to answer in English, 'And be good!'

Jean-Luc believed I was a magician. Sometimes I took big, long beans, pretended to bite them between my teeth while hiding whole beans in my mouth, then moved the cut beans and showed him how they had magically been restored to whole beans again. He never tired of that trick. I also found an Asterix book on our travels and read that to him as often as I could.

We had to walk twenty kilometres through the bush and it rained the whole night. I was exhausted but John kept up a steady pace. His lean, broad back and strong arms and legs looked as if they would never tire. I felt the $50 I had paid him to accompany us on our journey was money well spent.

'Let's rest under the trees for a while,' he said. We sat down, ate our bread and rice and dozed for a while. 'We can cross to Lilongwe in the evening when it's quiet,' he said calmly.

I was scared of the dark since fleeing Rwanda but said nothing.

At 6 p.m. we started walking slowly. It was too hot to walk by day so we rested then and walked at night when it was cooler, and there was less chance of being seen.

'How many hours will this take?' I groaned, envisaging another twenty-kilometre hike.

In the end it took us just a couple of hours to reach a village close to the border. John was very kind to me; sometimes he carried Jean-Luc and my bag to help me.

There was a group of people waiting to cross when we arrived in the village. 'Good luck,' the villagers chorused. They were obviously used to people congregating on their land before making a dash for the border. It was nice that people cared, but looking at their faces I could see they were thinking, Are they going to make it?

I looked down at myself. Even without a mirror I could see that I looked awful. I was a proper refugee. I was wearing some of Claire's clothes and a pair of her shoes that didn't fit me very well, and was begging for food. What would my poor Maman and Papa, who gave me the best of everything, think if they could see me now? Tears slid down my cheeks but I quickly brushed them away. This is no time to feel sorry for yourself, Leah, I told myself sternly. In the last few months I had done things I never thought I could have done in my life, and accepted help I would once have rejected.

'Time to go,' grinned John. I took a deep breath and we started walking through the bush with the rest of the group of illicit border crossers. To pass through the bush you have to use a stick to part the thick undergrowth. The rain had stopped but every time we moved some of the rich green vegetation aside we were splattered with the raindrops that had settled on it. The earth beneath our feet was soft and rich, birds sang and insects buzzed. I prayed that there were no snakes waiting to slither around our ankles. The bush is rich with plants that can both poison and heal, and with animals that accept the presence of humans and some that attack when disturbed. John could speak the silent language of the bush and, sure-footed as ever, led us safely through.

It took us about three hours to reach the first village on the Malawi side of the border. I was too exhausted to celebrate making it into another country. All the countries I had been through had merged into one exhausting blur and through the mental mist of each one images of the Interahamwe loomed, grinning and brandishing their machetes and nail-studded clubs.

The Malawian villagers were friendly. We gave them a small amount of money and they allowed us to stay in their guest hut.

John knew the area very well and understood how to negotiate with the villagers in a respectful way. In the middle of the hut they made a big fire to warm us up and dry us off. We grilled some sweet potatoes and filled our stomachs.

'Tomorrow we'll go to the market and take a bus to Lilongwe,' said John.

We huddled in a corner and closed our eyes. The rain was pounding against the flimsy mud walls of the hut almost the whole night. I couldn't stop shivering and clung on to Jean-Luc, desperately trying to transfer whatever body warmth I had into him.

At 6 a.m. John woke us up. 'Come on. Everyone who wants to go to Lilongwe, we need to buy a ticket now and get on the bus before the day gets too late.'

A few of us trooped obediently after John, bought tickets from a place not too far from the village and boarded the bus.

I had an image in my mind of Lilongwe as a gleaming, modern capital and was disappointed when we arrived in a dusty, run-down place with a very small airport.

'Is this really Lilongwe?' I asked John in disbelief.

'Lilongwe is not a proper capital any more. Blantyre is a nicer place, a sort of unofficial capital. But stay here for tonight and then afterwards you can go on to Blantyre if you want to. I'm going to take you to a place where you can sleep, but you will have to pay.'

'That's OK,' I said, assuming he was going to take us to a hotel or a guesthouse. Instead he took us to a one-roomed mud hut.

'Just give them ten dollars and you can sleep here,' said John.

'Are you serious? They can't expect me to spend ten dollars on this dump.'

'Leah, the nicer places in Lilongwe are much more expensive. Stay here for tonight and then tomorrow we'll see.'

'I'm so very hungry, John, and I'd love to wash my son.'

'Leah, just forget about that now.'

'Where is the toilet? I can't forget about using that until tomorrow, I need it now.'

John gave me directions. It sounded as if it was quite a long way away from our less-than-luxurious sleeping quarters. It was about ten minutes' walk and it was simply a deep hole splattered with excrement. I took a deep breath and used it. I had no choice.

'I need to go to the market,' I announced when I returned. I found some water and repeatedly scrubbed my hands.

'Oh, there is no market in this area,' said John. 'Why don't you rest now?'

'I can't take my son to that kind of toilet. I need to buy a bedpan for both of us. If you think I'm going to walk to that disgusting toilet in the middle of the night you can forget it.'

John shrugged and said nothing.

'How long do we have to stay here?' I asked.

'I don't know. We have to see who can help you.' John had seemed so sure of what he was doing on our journey to cross the border, but now he seemed less certain.

In the afternoon a woman arrived at the hut. She was middle-aged and had a mean face. She wanted money for everything, even for a glass of water. She explained proudly that she and her husband owned the place and that I was lucky I had come early otherwise I wouldn't even have been able to book a little corner of the hut for Jean-Luc and myself. I didn't see her being pleasant to anyone the whole time I stayed there. I couldn't understand how she could take pride in such a grubby little place. I would have been ashamed to charge money to guests for a hut like hers.

I was exhausted, hungry and dirty. I had spent two days without washing and was desperate to scrub all the dust and sweat of our journey off Jean-Luc and myself. During our journey out of Rwanda getting clean was the last thing on my mind, but ever since I'd fled I had developed an obsession with getting clean and staying that way.

I was begging the owner to let us wash, but the only place to shower was next to that smelly toilet. I couldn't bear it. I washed Jean-Luc outside quickly with a bucket of water the woman grudgingly brought for me, washed my face and my armpits and wiped myself dry quickly.

I picked up Jean-Luc and said to John, 'Please, I want to go somewhere where I can buy proper food.'

He took me to a nearby stall that sold chicken and chips. I chewed the tough meat first to soften it and then I gave bits of it to Jean-Luc. The chicken and chips tasted so good because we hadn't eaten properly for a long time. I bought Fanta to drink and looked around for somewhere to buy a potty.

'Leah, I will be in Malawi for a while if you need my help. I know the woman who runs the guesthouse very well; she's really not too bad.'

'Thank you, John, for everything. I could not have made that journey without your help,' I said.

We spent a very uncomfortable night lying on mats in the corner of the hut. The woman gave us some smelly, nasty grey blankets to cover ourselves with. Big fat black cockroaches ran over us. But because we had been compared with cockroaches I felt as if I couldn't kill them, so I picked them up wherever I found them and threw them out of the hut. Rats ran in and out too. I was frightened of them but tried my best to ignore them.

Jean-Luc developed a fever during the night. I didn't know if it was from drinking dirty water or from being in the rain so much. Back home he'd had everything he needed and I felt so bad that here he had nothing. Throughout our difficult journey he had smiled and accepted everything that was thrown in our path. He was a very sweet-natured boy. But now he lay limply in my arms, his little body clammy.

'Jean-Luc, you can't get sick, you're all I have in the world, my precious boy, you must get better,' I whispered, panic rising in my chest. If only Maman was here she would have known what to do, she would have made Jean-Luc better. There had been so many times during this journey that I had longed to have her by my side. As I mopped Jean-Luc's brow I physically ached with her loss.

I hurriedly got dressed and went out into the street. I stopped a woman and asked her where I could find a chemist's shop. The chemist said he was sure Jean-Luc just had a cold and not something horrible like malaria. To my enormous relief his temperature came down quickly after I gave him the medicine and after a few hours he began to improve.

Until disaster struck in Rwanda I had never lived outside my family home, apart from the months I spent with Christian after Jean-Luc's birth. Now I was forced to live in many strange places and to adapt to different people and customs. I felt very lonely as I walked back to our basic sleeping quarters. Living conditions didn't matter when we were facing death, but now that our lives were no longer in danger it was horrible to have to put up with such dirty, impoverished conditions. I closed my eyes and dreamed of the lovely home Christian and I shared with Jean-Luc in Kigali, and of our beautiful family homes in Bukavu and Goma. At that moment I would have given anything to be in one of those homes, sitting in the garden and watching Papa tending to the fruit trees and delicate plants.

CHAPTER SIXTEEN

I felt very negative about being in Lilongwe. I still had some money in my pocket and I wanted to try to buy something nice to tempt Jean-Luc to eat now that his fever was subsiding. I found a café that looked nice and clean and we sat down. I ordered a Fanta for me and a hot chocolate for Jean-Luc. A tall man who looked as if he was in his thirties walked up to our table and started speaking to me in his language. I had no idea who he was or what he was saying. I tried to communicate with him in the bits of English I knew and my basic Nyanja, a language that was also spoken in Malawi.

'Where are you from? Is that your child? You look so young. Is the boy OK? He looks sick. Can I help you with anything?'

As usual I was wary of letting a stranger know that I had fled Rwanda. 'I'm from Kenya,' I said quickly.

'Oh, my cousin studied in Kenya,' said the man, smiling broadly. He was dressed smartly in expensive clothes. It was wonderful to see someone looking so clean and fresh after all the dirty, dusty people I had been travelling with.

We chatted about Kenya for ten minutes or so. He told me his name was Piri and then he said, 'Will you let me buy you lunch?'

In the absence of any alternative plans and a gut feeling that this man would not cause me any harm, I accepted.

'That's great, I'll take you to a nice place.'

He had a very nice blue Mercedes and Jean-Luc and I climbed in and sank into the soft leather seats.

I kept asking myself why this man was doing this for us. I wondered if he was the chauffeur to some rich businessman. Or maybe he had an ulterior motive and planned to rape me. He did not behave like someone's employee, though, and he seemed genuine. Surely if he was rich he would have a driver. Nothing made any sense to me.

'I'm going to treat you to a proper meal,' he declared.

He took me to a big compound that appeared to be the headquarters of some kind of business. I was still wondering if he was the chauffeur. Where's the boss? I asked myself. He spoke to some of the workers in the compound in Chichewa. I could only pick out odd words and had no idea what was going on. Then he jumped back into the car and we drove off.

Suddenly I saw a different part of Lilongwe, with beautiful houses. It looked a bit like home and I started to feel sad. An automatic gate opened and we went down a well-maintained, sweeping driveway to the house.

'Come, let's sit on the balcony, it's cool there. Would you like a drink? Wine?'

'Thank you but I don't drink alcohol.'

'No problem, we have lovely fresh orange juice.'

I gulped the drink greedily, draining my glass in one go. A servant immediately refilled it. Piri spoke to the servant in Swahili and I joined in.

'Oh, you speak Swahili.' He smiled. 'I do a lot of business in Kenya.'

We started talking, and he decided, 'So you are not Rwandise. We have plenty of Rwandise people here. I thought maybe you were one of them.'

My heart started beating very fast. I was terrified of him finding out my true identity and I didn't like the idea of Lilongwe being full of people from my country. I turned away and fixed my gaze on his beautiful gardens stuffed with dazzling blooms.

I had told Piri that I didn't eat meat, and beautiful fresh fish and rice were served to us. He watched me eating and could see from the way I held my knife and fork that I came from a good background. We switched from Swahili to English.

'Oh, you speak English with a French accent.'

There was no possible excuse I could think of to explain away my accent. I broke down in tears.

'I'm sorry I lied. I'm not from Kenya. I know Kenya very well, but I'm from Rwanda.'

'So you are a refugee?'

I looked at him and said nothing.

'Oh, I'm so sorry. I've seen the pictures of the refugee camps on CNN.' He paused, searching around for a way to change the subject. 'How do you find Lilongwe?' he asked at last.

'I don't really know. I've only been here for a couple of days. And with all respect, sir, I need to get back to the place where I'm staying.'

He looked at the address I'd scribbled on a scrap of paper and said nothing. He took us back. He breathed in sharply when he saw the hut that was little more than a hovel that Jean-Luc and I were about to spend the night in.

'How do you live here, Leah?'

'That's life,' I said, trying to smile.

'I can see you again tomorrow, right? You're a very nice person to talk to, very interesting.' He looked as if he didn't want to leave us but at the same time didn't want to be too pushy.

'Sleep well, Leah and Jean-Luc,' he said and walked off thoughtfully.

Early the next morning before he went to work he came back, found the woman who ran our lodgings and asked for me.

We came outside. I had slept very badly and felt grubby after spending a night on the floor.

'Come on, Leah, into the car with your son. I'm going to buy you a good breakfast.'

'No, no, really, you don't have to. Jean-Luc and I can manage.'

'But I want to.' He smiled persuasively. Once again I wondered what his motives were.

He took us to a lovely café in a nicer part of town and we had a fancy English breakfast with bread and porridge.

'Leah, I feel that I want to help you. From talking to you and listening to your French, you're not somebody who should be living in terrible conditions. The place I took you to yesterday is not where I live most of the time. I usually live in Blantyre.' He offered us a place to stay at his home.

'You really don't have to do that, Piri. You're too kind to us.'

'It's nothing. Human beings should always help each other.' He seemed in a hurry to get everything settled. 'I'm leaving town soon so we need to sort this out now. Where's your stuff?'

'I don't have much, just this bag,' I said, gesturing towards my pitifully shabby holdall which contained all our worldly goods. I felt like Cinderella being whisked off to the ball.

We went back to the luxurious compound where we'd eaten the day before. He didn't explain who the house belonged to and I felt it might be rude to ask. He picked up a jeep there and left his Mercedes in the driveway.

'We're going to Blantyre. I'm going to book you into a hotel until I've spoken to my wife and asked her if she can take you in.'

It was the first time he had mentioned that he was married and I felt very reassured by this new piece of information. Surely he wouldn't pounce on me if he already had a wife?

I was beginning to adjust to the luxury in Piri's life, and the hotel was no exception. It was clearly the sort of place that only the rich could afford.

He seemed to know lots of people and introduced me to a smiling British woman called Margaret, who was on holiday. I had never seen a white person lie in the sun to change their skin colour before. It was very confusing to me. She was wearing big sunglasses and her hair was very blond. The idea of being on holiday seemed so distant from everything I had experienced during the last few months and I could no longer remember what it felt like to be travelling from one place to another simply to enjoy a change of scenery or to sit on a beach.

Piri booked us into a room with a lovely bath. It was heaven to have access to such facilities and as usual whenever I found myself near to a source of clean water I flung my dusty clothes on to the floor and dived into the shower, scrubbing myself hard with the fragrant hotel soap.

The next day Piri returned and announced that he was going to take us shopping for new clothes. I only had one change of clothes in my bag and was delighted when he bought me a new skirt and shirt and a tracksuit for Jean-Luc.

'Have you had breakfast?'

He obviously loved Blantyre, with its lively streets, colourful markets and gracious houses, and was keen to show us around. There was another branch of his company here in Blantyre and he showed us his office.

'I'm going to buy you something to eat.' My stomach was rumbling and I knew that Jean-Luc was hungry too. My mouth started to water at the prospect of the delicious food I was sure Piri would provide for us. 'What would you like?'

'I'd love some fish.'

'We can eat fish here at the hotel,' he said.

He led us to a lovely restaurant that was filled with a mix of black and white people. It was a long time since I'd seen such a mixture of races sitting together.

'Leah, my wife is in South Africa at the moment. When she returns next week I'll ask her if you can come and stay with us.'

After lunch Piri said he was going to leave us to rest. 'I'll come and pick you both up for church tomorrow,' he said.

My heart sank. Oh no, he must be one of those born-again Christians, I thought to myself. Maybe that's why Piri is being so kind to us, so that he can get us signed up to his church.

I decided not to protest about the plan. After being betrayed by the nuns at the church we had tried to shelter in in Rwanda, I could no longer look upon these houses of God as safe or sacred places. I tried to keep away from them wherever possible.

My plan was still to get to South Africa with John, but I thought there was no harm in stopping off for a few days to recover from our exhausting journey. Oh well, I have nothing so I don't have much to lose. If he wants me to go to his church in exchange for food and clothes I can handle that, I said to myself.

To Piri I said nothing of the sort. 'Bye. Thanks for looking after us so well, see you tomorrow.'

Piri and his friends were being so kind to me but I felt that nothing inside me was healing. There was a big weeping sore deep inside that refused to go away. Whenever I was alone and Jean-Luc was sleeping I wept for the loss of my family, Christian and my old, lovely life. I managed to put on a brave, optimistic mask most of the time when I was with people but I felt as if I was standing permanently on the edge of an abyss. Ahead of me was nothing but empty fresh air and the only way to go was down into the bottomless blackness.

At Piri's church the service was very similar to the ones I had attended in Zaire as a child; there was no sign of any sinister cult waiting to pounce. At one time I never would have doubted anyone's motives but trusting people no longer came easily to me. All I wanted was to find a place where Jean-Luc and I could be safe enough to stop running, a place where I could work and be independent so that I would never again have to rely on anybody for food or a bed or the clothes on my back. God was praised over and over again during the service but the words had become meaningless to me.

So often in Rwanda I had screamed silently, Where has God gone? I didn't feel that he had returned on my journey through Africa. Yes, we were no longer being pursued by machete-wielding madmen and I was grateful for that, but life, which had always felt so secure and full of certainties, was now a flimsy structure, like a hastily assembled mud hut buckling during the rainy season.

Piri was eager for me to meet his family and friends. Now that I was clean and dressed in nice clothes I think he wanted to show me off to people.

'We're going to go to my friend's house. Just relax. Everyone there will love you and want to talk to you.' I allowed myself to be swept along on the wave of Piri's enthusiasm.

His friends were indeed charming and chatty. They grilled fish and chicken and made mealie meal and green vegetables. The table was piled high with food. Piri simply said that I was travelling with my son, without mentioning that I was a refugee from Rwanda.

There were some girls there of a similar age to me. They were happy and carefree and chattered excitedly about the courses they were doing at university. Suddenly it hit me how abnormal my life had become. If all hell hadn't broken loose in Rwanda, Maman would be looking after Jean-Luc while I studied at university. I realised that I had not only lost the people I loved but also the chance of the sort of future I'd always assumed I would have. As the girls talked on I felt very lost and alone. I had been cheated of the future that had been laid out for me.

After lunch Piri took us back to the hotel. 'I'm going to Lilongwe tomorrow morning for a week or so. Anything you want, just ask for it at Reception. When I return my wife should be back from her trip and we should be able to sort things out,' he said.

We stayed in that hotel for a week, enjoying the luxury and tranquillity. As always when I wasn't on the move, the faces of Christian and my family appeared in my mind. I tried my best to brush these images away. Thinking of the loved ones I had lost gave me an almost physical pain in my heart.

I was bored while I waited for Piri's wife to return and although I tried to avoid seeing the news as much as possible I ended up watching it on the television in the hotel bedroom to pass the time. There were many stories about what was happening in Rwanda and the word 'genocide' was used. I had never heard this word before and had no idea what it meant. The next day I went to the Centre Culturel and looked the word up in the French dictionary. When I saw what the word meant I suddenly felt as if my every vein was filled with lead. I knew that Rwanda had turned into hell but now that the situation had been given this chilling label it seemed even more horrendous. I couldn't eat for the rest of the day; it was as if my brain was burping up images of all the dismembered corpses I had seen. Even Jean-Luc's smiles and attempts to play hide-and-seek failed to cheer me up. I made sure I didn't watch the news again after that.

After a week Piri returned, arriving rather sheepishly at the hotel to report back about his wife's reaction to Jean-Luc and me. He cleared his throat several times.

'Leah, my wife is rather a nervous person. This sounds silly but because you are refugees she is worried that you might be carrying diseases like ebola. I'm going to take you to a guesthouse instead where you will be able to have your independence.'

As soon as I heard the words 'disease' and 'ebola', tears sprang into my eyes. It made me feel that I was less than a human, some kind of creature that needed to be kept at arm's length from civilised company in case I contaminated things.

Piri rested his hand on my arm. 'You mustn't take it personally, Leah; that is just the kind of person my wife is.'

I noticed that he never referred to her by her first name and wondered what their relationship was like.

Piri took us to a three-bedroomed guesthouse that had a maid and a watchman. I felt safe there. He told me that his cousin Janet, who had been studying in Kenya, was going to come and visit me. 'You can chat together about Kenya. I'm sure you will have much to discuss,' he said.

Piri had explained to her what had happened to me in Rwanda. 'I'm so very sorry about all that,' she said, and hugged me. I liked her immediately. She was a lively person, very open and friendly.

Although I hadn't discussed it with Piri, I confided in her that I was hoping to reach South Africa.

'Ahh, my neighbour does regular trips to South Africa by car. Maybe he can help you.'

She started asking me questions about my family. 'You have a beautiful little boy,' she said, tickling Jean-Luc to make him giggle. 'Where is his daddy?'

Once again I took Christian's well-thumbed photo out of my bag.

'That is Christian. He was my childhood sweetheart and Jean-Luc's dad. Sadly he didn't make it. He was flying a plane to the airport just as the President's plane was shot down. Nobody survived that terrible scene at the airport.' I sighed and was about to put the photo away when she said:

'Wait a minute. I'm sure I've seen this guy. I think he's here in Malawi.' She continued staring at Christian's photo. 'Is he Somalian?'

'No, he's not.'

'This guy hangs around a lot with Somalians.'

'Well, you must be confusing him with someone else. Christian is a Rwandan Tutsi just like me. As far as I know he's never been anywhere near Somalia.'

But maybe he was alive. Maybe he'd had a miraculous escape.

Why did so many people say they recognised Christian from the photo?

'Janet, you're the third person who I have showed the photo to who has said that. It would be a miracle if Christian was alive, but I'm terrified of raising my hopes because I've lost so much. If I find out that people have been seeing Christian's double or doubles it will feel like I've lost him all over again. But I would be interested to meet this guy who hangs out with the Somalians. Do you know where I could find him? At least then I'll know one way or the other.'

'I'll ask around. I don't know him but I've seen him. He's very tall and slim and somehow he stands out in the crowd.'

I shivered. That sounded exactly like Christian.

Janet did make some enquiries amongst the Somalians but they said he had moved on and they weren't sure where. I was bitterly disappointed. A tiny part of me began tentatively to believe that he had survived and was looking for me.

Piri returned later on and offered to take me to Centre Culturel Français to borrow some French books to read. He arranged for me to have a library card bearing his surname so that I would appear like a local Malawian. We hadn't discussed it but he seemed to assume that now I had him to look after me I would want to settle permanently in Malawi. He had been extremely kind and generous to me, but I had absolutely no intention of staying very long.

'Piri, whenever I come to a new country I love to try and learn that country's main language. I really want to improve my Chichewa. Instead of French books, could you find some books to improve my Chichewa?'

Piri helped me to find some simple books in Chichewa and dropped Jean-Luc and me back at the guesthouse. I spoke a lot with the old watchman at the guesthouse. He couldn't speak a word of English, so I had no choice but to speak to him in Chichewa.

One morning he thoughtfully brought me breakfast in bed and greeted me in Chichewa. I couldn't believe what I was hearing. In Kinyarwanda it meant crudely, 'How did you fuck?'

I screamed and called the receptionist.

'You people are not nice. I'm going to make a complaint,' I said with tears in my eyes. Piri rushed over and asked what had been going on. I explained to him and he also got very angry. 'Call the person who said that,' Piri shouted.

The watchman came in, hanging his head.

'I didn't know I wasn't supposed to greet her. All I said was Mwasuerabwaji.'

'That's it, he said the same rude words again!' I cried.

Piri started laughing. 'Leah,' he said, 'this man has greeted you in the most polite way. What do these words mean in your language?'

'I can't say it, it's too embarrassing,' I said. But in the end I had to explain what the words meant in Kinyarwanda.

Piri laughed and explained that the words meant something very different in Chichewa. 'You have to learn more Chichewa, Leah, to avoid any more mix-ups like this one,' he said. 'And this man will help you.'

I felt very ashamed that I had misunderstood the watchman and apologised profusely to him.

From that moment on I doubled my efforts to get to grips with the language. I realised that it was a beautiful and very polite language. I started learning Chichewa with the old man. He was a fantastic teacher. The more I understood the language the more I apologised to him.

I decided to broach the delicate matter of a passport with Janet, in the hope that she could gently filter my intentions back to Piri.

'I'd love to get a Malawian passport,' I said to her casually.

'Sounds like a sensible idea. You're as good as a part of the family now, and you can't walk around without ID anyway,' she said.

She mentioned it to Piri, who had no objection. It was agreed that I would use the surname Maluza in my passport application rather than my own Rwandan surname.

'You know I've always wanted to visit South Africa,' I said to Piri.

'Well, you can once you get your passport,' he replied. 'But make sure you don't stay away too long, we'll miss you too much.'

I knew that Piri really wanted me to stay but inside my head the voice screaming *Run, run* was getting louder. I think Piri wanted to keep me in a glass case like a butterfly, but I was suffocating and needed to be free to keep on moving. Also, I knew many African men who had more than one wife and although he never laid a finger on me I began to feel increasingly uneasy about the way he looked at me.

After a couple of weeks my passport came through. I started chatting to a businessman who was staying at the guesthouse who'd mentioned that he travelled regularly by car to South Africa. I pumped him for as much information as possible about the country. The more he spoke of the place, the better it sounded.

'There are many jobs, beautiful streets, freedom from the ugly apartheid system for all our brothers and sisters,' he said. 'If we go in my car we'll reach there the next day.'

He agreed to take me a couple of days later. I got in touch with John and asked if he would accompany me to the border to make sure I got across safely.

'I want to see you continue with your journey, Leah,' he said. 'I know how much it means to you to get to South Africa.'

I'd said nothing to Piri about my plans, for fear that he would try to stop me. His truck left for South Africa every week, carrying building and other home-improvement materials, but he never offered to take me. I had spent two months in Malawi and now it was time to move on.

At the border I held my breath. The immigration official looked at my passport and back at me several times, and then he slowly shook his head.

'No, this passport is not good, you cannot cross today,' he said. 'This passport is no good. I must keep it.' The man took the passport to show the guards and I was too upset to ask what was wrong with it.

'Don't worry, you go,' I said to the businessman. I waved forlornly as he crossed the border without me. At that moment I felt that I was never going to reach a land where I could feel safe.

CHAPTER SEVENTEEN

It was so hot on the border between Malawi and Mozambique that I felt my body would be baked into the ground. Holding Jean-Luc in this heat was horrible: his skin stuck to mine like clammy glue.

I was devastated that my passport hadn't been accepted. Although I knew of the risks, I so badly wanted to get to South Africa that I was willing the border guards to let me pass. Now I would have to resort to finding an illegal way to cross. Although Piri had been extremely kind and generous to me I was determined not to return to him as I knew he would try to make me stay in Malawi.

'Don't worry, Leah, it's not the end of the world. I will come with you, we'll find another way to go. We can take the back way into Mozambique,' said John.

I looked around and could immediately see who the people without papers were. I had become an expert at spotting these people at borders, mainly because I recognised elements of myself in them. The people with passports walked confidently up to the border guards with their heads held high while the rest of us hung our heads and tried to make ourselves look invisible on the sidelines.

If I close my eyes now I can still see the Malawi–Mozambique border as clearly as if I left it yesterday. Many cars were streaming towards it from the Malawi side, while the illegals like me whispered about how we were going to find other ways to cross. I looked gratefully at the nice clothes Piri had bought me to wear. At least I didn't look like a refugee.

I began talking to the huddles of people without papers about their plans. One man said, 'People who don't have a passport cross by that road over to the left, but it's a long and difficult journey.'

I knew that however long and difficult it was going to be I had to find a way to reach Mozambique. I saw a pick-up truck heading in that direction, impulsively flagged it down and asked for a lift. The driver agreed to take us the back way for $50. John, Jean-Luc and I clambered into the truck. I sighed with relief that we were moving again.

As we drove the trees and greenery faded away. For the first time in my life I saw desert. Everything was parched, colourless sand as far as the eye could see. I had grown up surrounded by lush grasses and trees and rich, fertile earth. Green had been the dominant colour in the countries I had passed through since I left Zaire, but now I was in much harsher terrain.

The driver spoke little but said that we would be driving through the night. He stopped at a place where you could buy food and drink and filled his stomach before we set off.

I dozed fitfully throughout the journey. I was so used to sleeping wherever I found myself that I barely noticed the discomfort of the hard plastic seats and the jolts each time we hit a bump in the bad road we were driving along. When the sun started to rise in the sky I rubbed my eyes.

'Did we make it?' I asked.

'Yes, we made it across the border without any problems,' he smiled. 'Welcome to Mozambique. There are buses to Maputo from here but they don't come every day. Maybe you will need to rent a room until the bus comes.'

'Thank you, thank you,' I said as we climbed down from the truck. I was happy to wait for however long it took for the bus to arrive because at least now I knew we were on our way again.

I rented a basic space at the village guesthouse. We were given a mat to sleep on and grilled sweet potatoes to eat. It rained and so we were able to wash using a bucket. I clutched $500 in my pocket that I had saved up from the generous allowance Piri had given me.

It was three days before the bus arrived. John was much better at sitting still and waiting than I was. As I sat on the ground waiting for the bus I reflected on how fast I had had to grow up since 6 April 1994. Although I never would have admitted it at the time, I knew I had been a spoiled little rich girl before, used to things always going my way. But what I'd been through since President Habyarimana's plane was shot down had knocked any vestiges of spoiled behaviour out of me. I felt as if I'd aged at least fifty years in less than one.

When the ramshackle old bus finally arrived it turned out that it wasn't going to Maputo but to a village on the way. The road was impassable because of the rain and the driver said he would have to turn back. There were lots of disappointed people who had to get off the bus.

One man saw how miserable I looked. 'Don't worry, sister, there are some big farms in this area and sometimes tractors pass through. They are better for travelling along bad roads than the buses. Look, a tractor's coming along the road now. Let's see if the driver will let us jump on and pay him some money to take us towards Maputo.'

The driver nodded when the man asked if he would help us on our journey. We paid money and jumped on with three other passengers from the bus. It was painful bumping over the potholes in the tractor but I was grateful to have found a way to continue with our journey. After a while the tractor stopped in a village.

'This is as far as I go,' said the driver. 'Now you must wait for cars to pass. If they are going to Maputo they will give you a lift.'

We spoke to a man who was working in a little garage. 'Ahh, this will not be a good road for you, not many cars pass here. You look hungry; I will try to find some food for you.'

He returned half an hour later with some meat that he cooked for us. I still didn't like to eat meat but I was starving and there didn't seem to be any other food around so I ate what was offered to me. 'Even if you have money, the problem here is finding something to buy with it,' said one of the travellers.

We had no choice but to sleep by the roadside. It was pouring with rain and we all got soaked. The truck or even the bumpy tractor now seemed like luxury hotels in comparison with this. The next morning we found some green bananas to eat. The rain continued to fall.

'The cars will not come while the rain is so bad,' said the man in the garage. He offered us dirty water to drink. Jean-Luc winced and refused to touch it. I had a little cup in my bag and tried to catch the rainwater in it.

We stayed in the abandoned village for about a week. We saw the odd person passing, but there were fewer than twenty people in the village and I couldn't communicate in their local language. There was very little food to eat and at one point the man from the garage brought back a snake. He killed it and skinned it in front of us. I recoiled in horror and held Jean-Luc tightly. There was no way either of us was going to eat that. I had been brought up on Bible stories and as far as I was concerned the snake was the incarnation of evil.

The man with the garage said he had visited Bunia in eastern Zaire so he could speak a bit of Swahili from that area. He was very kind to us and seemed happy to have some company.

In front of the garage was an abandoned brick building. It looked as if there had been some kind of local war there at some point. I did not ask because I didn't want to hear any more sad stories. Instead I asked over and over again, 'Do you think a car will pass soon?' Every day I woke up and the first thing I said was, 'Will it be today that a car passes?'

'Yes, I think so, be patient,' he always replied.

When Jean-Luc slept I cried. I hated being in Mozambique. I felt sure that we were going to be stranded in the middle of nowhere for a very long time. Everything was too hard. This was not my country, my culture or my language. I longed to be back home in Kigali before all the troubles started, curled up on the sofa with Maman, Jean-Luc in my arms and a bowl of my favourite vegetable soup on the table by my side.

There was nothing to do and nowhere to go. All we could do was wait until some sort of vehicle came along the road. Finally a truck appeared in the distance. I became like one of those African village children who cheer every time they see anything on four wheels with an engine.

A lot of people jumped on to the pick-up truck and crowded together in the back: five in our group, and then others from the village who had been waiting somewhere else. Like magic everyone appeared and paid their money to climb aboard the truck. People were trampling over others in their hurry and excitement to get on board.

After travelling for three hours we reached a river. 'This is as far as I can go,' said the driver. 'You have to walk across the shallow part of the river or get someone to carry you.' I was terrified because the water was flowing very fast. I could see how easy it would be to be carried away by the current. I shivered. There was no way back; the only choice was to go forwards and find a way to get across the river.

There were men assembled on the riverbank who had set up a small business carrying people across the river. They were guessing how much people weighed and calculating a rate accordingly. 'The more you weigh, the more you pay,' they explained.

One of the strongest men agreed to carry both Jean-Luc and

me on his back; another took John. All my belongings were kept in one small green bag – a few clothes and a coat for Jean-Luc in case he got cold. I looked at the fast-flowing river and couldn't stop myself from crying out. I was sure that somehow one or both of us was going to drown. I remembered the time I had almost drowned in the lake in Zaire as a child. It had been a terrifying experience. I didn't want to die, and even worse, I didn't want to live and lose Jean-Luc. And I didn't want him to survive if I died.

'I can't, I can't,' I gasped as the man I had paid money to tried to hoist Jean-Luc and me on to his broad back.

He didn't understand what I was saying and didn't sympathise with my obvious distress. He pulled me forwards roughly. I had tied Jean-Luc securely on to my back with some cloth and before I could dither any longer both of us were being carried across the angry, roaring water.

I clamped my eyes tightly shut as I clung to the man's back. A smell of his stale sweat filled my nostrils and spray from the fast-flowing water splashed into my face.

'Please God, let us make it across,' I groaned. Every step the man took felt like an hour. The garage man had reassured me that the men were experts and knew exactly which stones to step on and which to avoid because they were too slippery. We made it across the river and everyone cheered. I was flooded with relief and covered Jean-Luc with kisses. Once again we'd made it. At that moment I knew with enormous certainty that I didn't want to die, that somehow we would make it to South Africa, however hard the journey was.

Once we reached the other side the whole group of us had to walk. We were told by the garage man that we needed to stay in a big group because one of the villages we had to pass through was dangerous. He warned us that they killed people they saw walking at night. It was seven in the evening and it was a completely black African night.

We reached a village and didn't know whether or not it was the one the garage man had spoken of. But we could see no sign of life and thought maybe the place had been abandoned. We were all exhausted and had been walking for more than five hours. There was nowhere to sleep but on the damp, pungent earth in an empty hut. I lay on my back and draped Jean-Luc across my chest to try to protect him from the ground.

We were woken a couple of hours later by angry voices. I didn't understand what was being said as the language was totally unfamiliar to us.

The chief was furious that we had entered without permission. I guessed that we were in the dangerous village. His guards brandished spears and flexed their muscles as they got ready to use them.

Although I couldn't understand a word he was saying, I could see that the chief, who was wearing animal skins, was extremely angry. It sounded as if he was giving orders for us to be killed. I started to shiver uncontrollably. John seemed to be at as much of a loss as I was.

One of the men in our group managed to communicate with the chief and explained our problems to him. I breathed a sigh of relief when I saw his expression change. He became softer and kinder and gestured towards his men to drop their spears.

I had been clutching Jean-Luc tightly to me and I loosened my grip slightly. He asked where we were from and the man who could communicate with the chief translated for us.

'I'm from Rwanda,' I said, hoping that the chief might take pity on Jean-Luc and me because of the ordeal we had fled from. But the name 'Rwanda' clearly meant nothing to him. He looked at me blankly and shrugged. In our school we had a big map of the world, and I knew where all the different countries in Africa and Europe were – but many people had very limited knowledge of other countries and even of other towns and cities in their own country.

Our translator was speaking very fast to him, no doubt wanting to make sure that the chief understood we were friends not foes before his men raised their spears again. It seemed to work because the chief started to smile broadly and woke his wife to cook us some meat, vegetables, maize and traditional juice. We were all hungry and the food tasted wonderful. The chief allowed us to sleep in the hut for the rest of the night and the next day he pointed us in the right direction to get transport to Maputo. We all thanked him very much in his language.

'Thank goodness things didn't turn nasty,' I whispered to Jean-Luc. I had gone into survival mode and didn't think much about how difficult everything was. But I cursed the border guards who wouldn't let me pass through Zambia with my false passport. If I had managed to cross that border I was sure that I would be happily settled in South Africa by now.

After walking for a few hours we reached a big road and sat and waited for the bus to come. Thankfully the rain had stopped. I didn't remember spending very much time waiting around as a child, but now waiting and trudging had become major features in my life. Four hours later the bus arrived and we all climbed aboard eagerly. We reached a town full of shops and cars and people wearing suits and playing music. I thought maybe we had reached Maputo.

'No, no, we're not there yet, but you can take a nice bus to Maputo from here,' said John. 'I am going to go back now. You will be able to manage the rest of the journey from here.'

John had shown me only kindness all the time I had known him. He didn't have much money to throw around but his generosity of spirit was exceptional. He put Jean-Luc and me before himself throughout the journey. He had made sure we found food, sometimes knocking on the doors of people's homes and asking them to cook for us in exchange for money. He was a good minder and fixer.

'Thank you for all you have done for us, John. You are a very good and kind man.'

'It's a pleasure, Leah. Good luck with reaching South Africa.'

He pointed us in the direction of the bus station. Jean-Luc and I hurried there and I bought our tickets.

It took us the whole day to get to Maputo. I was sitting next to an older woman on the bus. We chatted for a while and I could see that her legs were giving her a lot of trouble, swelling up very badly as a result of sitting still in one place for too long. I gave her my seat so that she could put her feet up because I could see that she was in a lot of pain.

Jean-Luc was a wonderful baby. I held him in my arms and we perched in the aisle throughout the journey.

'You've got a lovely boy there,' she kept on saying. He had got used to sitting still for long periods and he barely murmured the whole day.

We arrived in Maputo at around six in the evening. The capital city looked very pretty with all the lights twinkling away. It was nice and clean and I picked out a lot of Angolans and Zairians. I also noticed that there were a lot of mixed-race, light-skinned women walking around. It seemed to be a very cosmopolitan, contented and well-ordered city. The Portuguese had built lots of tall, imposing buildings.

I had only picked up a few words of Portuguese on my travels but somehow managed to communicate with the old lady. She looked at me sympathetically when I told her I'd fled Rwanda.

'Terrible times, terrible times,' she said, shaking her head. 'Do you have a place to sleep tonight? You're a refugee passing through, I imagine you don't know too many people in Maputo.'

I shook my head. 'No, I don't know anybody here, I'm on my way to South Africa.'

'My daughter is coming to meet me off the bus. I'm sure she would be happy for you and your baby to stay overnight with us.'

When her daughter arrived at the bus station the old lady told her how kind I had been to her. The daughter immediately picked up my bag.

'Thank you for allowing my mother to rest her poor swollen legs on the journey,' she said. 'That's very kind of you. You must stay with us tonight.'

She spoke a little French and Portuguese and we managed to understand each other.

'Thank you, that's very kind of you.'

Her mother explained to her that I had fled Rwanda.

'It must have been terrible for you,' she kept saying. 'How you got out with a baby to look after, I really don't know.'

She took us to her home, which was modern and comfortable. It was on the seventh floor of a very tall block of flats. I had never seen such a tall building before. We showered gratefully and she gave us a place to sleep. The food was different from our food but at that moment I was happy to eat anything. She made mealie meal and fish for us cooked in their own traditional way.

'Is it possible for my son to have porridge or some mashed potato which I can mix with milk? Jean-Luc will be so happy to eat that.'

'Of course,' said the daughter.

I hadn't slept in a bed for a while and that night Jean-Luc and I slept wonderfully well.

One thing I didn't like about Maputo was the mosquitoes, which behaved worse than the mosquitoes I had known and swatted in Rwanda and Zaire. In Maputo the insects bit by day or by night, any time, anywhere.

The daughter urged me to leave Jean-Luc with her for a little while. 'Why not go out and have a look around Maputo? It must be exhausting for you to have to look after your little boy all the time with no one to help you.' She had two beautiful girls aged four and six and she said they could all play together.

That's impossible, I said to myself. Inside my head I was still right in the middle of a war zone. The idea of parting from Jean-Luc for even a few minutes was unthinkable.

'Thank you, you are too kind to me. But I must keep Jean-Luc with me. I need to cling on to whatever I have left and all I have left is my son. He's part of me and I can't leave him behind even for a second.'

'No problem, Leah, I understand.' She put her arm around me and gave me a hug. 'There's no need for you to explain to me how much your child means to you.'

The market was lively and bustling. I had passed through many different countries but always the markets were the same. Sometimes the mangoes had a different blush to their skin or the bananas were a deeper shade of green or the potatoes were dusted with a different kind of earth, but always there were women in brightly coloured clothes which blended well with the produce they were selling, sitting, laughing, singing and coaxing customers to buy the riches they had plucked from the soil and the trees.

It was easy for me to spot the Zairians. I wanted to ask their advice about the best way to travel to South Africa. They were nice and welcoming to me.

One of the Zairian men, called Shei, was particularly friendly towards me. 'You must come and stay with me and my girlfriend,' he offered generously. 'But do you have papers? It's important to have some kind of passport here or the police will harass you badly.'

I shook my head. 'I don't have my Zairian passport any more. I lost it somewhere on the journey.' I kept trying to tell him that I didn't want papers because I didn't want to stay.

'Even if you're here for a short time you need papers.' He offered to take me to the embassy. 'We'll say you've lost your papers. Where are you from originally?'

'I'm from eastern Zaire but I speak good Lingala. I think it's important to speak a few languages from home.'

Shei took me to the Zairian Embassy and I got some new papers – a piece of paper giving me freedom to move around in Mozambique and saying I had lost my passport from Zaire.

Shei said he would ask his girlfriend if it was OK for us to go and stay with her. She agreed but her place was so small that Shei stayed at her place and let Jean-Luc and me stay in his home.

It felt so good to be able to communicate with people in my own language, without having to struggle with a few newly learned words in a strange tongue. Shei's girlfriend was extremely nice. She taught me some words of Portuguese and cooked delicious food for us.

Once again I was extremely grateful for the kindness of these strangers. I gave Shei $50 for all his and his girlfriend's help.

'Shei, I need to find a way to get to South Africa. I cannot settle in Maputo.'

'There's a Zairian woman called Sarah who lives near by who often goes to Durban. I'll ask her when she's next going and I'm sure she'll agree to take you with her,' he said.

Sarah traded goods between Maputo and Durban, buying and selling in both places. She was from Mubumbashi in Zaire.

'I've brought one of our sisters to see you,' said Shei.

'Oh my God, she's beautiful. Where are you from? Sit down and let me give you some food,' said Sarah. She was warm and friendly and I liked her straight away.

Sarah cooked Zairian food, smoked meat and cassava leaves and pap. To my horror she added caterpillars to the mix. 'I hope you like this traditional delicacy,' she said.

I shuddered and managed to avoid swallowing any of the furry creatures. We sat down and talked and laughed.

She told me some of her life story, that she had been thrown out of the family home by her stepmother when she was just ten and had to fend for herself. She had ended up in prostitution for a while but now was doing very well as a businesswoman trading clothes and jewellery in the two countries. My spirits lifted that a woman who had had so much pain and trouble in her life could overcome obstacles and do well.

'I'm going to Durban next week,' she said casually.

Shei asked, 'Please can you take Leah and her son with you? She doesn't like Mozambique, she wants to get to South Africa.'

'I'll take her, but the road is very tough. Leah, I hope you won't be too fragile.'

'Thank you, Sarah. I've travelled on some very tough roads since I left Goma. Don't worry about me, I think I can make it.'

'OK, good. I can see that you're tough underneath those delicate features. We'll go together next Thursday.'

I clapped my hands together in delight. 'That's good. Maybe we will be in South Africa by next weekend!'

Sarah spent the evening telling me wonderful stories about South Africa. She had lots of fancy Western clothes that she said she had bought cheaply at markets there.

'It's a wonderful place, Leah. It's not like Maputo, where the police stop you all the time. We can all walk free there; the police don't stop foreigners in the street unless they have committed a crime. The roads are good. There are big shopping malls there, there's a great one called the Wheel. Zaire is too far behind. In South Africa they have shopping complexes with cinemas and restaurants.'

I had no idea what a mall was.

'South Africa is just like Europe. They have lovely beaches, but black and white people do not sit together on those beaches.'

I couldn't understand how that sort of thing could happen when Mandela was in power.

She explained that it was risky to travel from Mozambique into KwaZulu-Natal because there were many soldiers in that area. 'This is a place where many people try to cross the border illegally, both South Africans and people from Mozambique. There is a lot of trade between the two countries, and people like me, even though we have our papers we don't want to cross the border at the official place because then we will have to pay taxes on our earnings. So instead we creep across this part of the border. There are many police patrolling to try to catch us so we have to make a run for it when they're out of sight.'

She warned me that I would not be welcomed by Zulus because I was not a traditional Zulu, I was light-skinned and did not speak the language. (I later discovered that a lot of it is based on Swahili with slang thrown in.)

'It's very, very cold in KwaZulu-Natal, but in Durban it's very hot. You will need to buy a big jumper for our journey, with T-shirts underneath for Durban,' she said.

The following Thursday I arrived at Sarah's place as arranged. The week I had been waiting had felt like a year and I could hardly contain my excitement. Finally we were on our way.

'We'll be leaving at midnight.'

'Why midnight?' I asked.

'There are pick-up trucks that take people to the border and they travel through the night. It will cost us fifty dollars.'

It wasn't difficult to hitch a ride in one of the many trucks passing through. We travelled through the night, passing through many villages. Many of the people using this route were traders who wanted to travel the back way into South Africa to avoid paying tax on their goods.

We were dropped off in an army area in the middle of the bush. Sarah explained that it was a sort of no man's land right on the border. There were many people who had been waiting a week to cross. People from the border villages were selling tea to fortify us for this stage of our journey. Sarah knew everybody very well and laughed and joked with all her friends. She was so laid-back, I couldn't imagine her ever getting agitated about anything.

A group of people smugglers from KwaZulu-Natal were lounging around in their open-air 'office'. I had to pay them $50 to cross the border. They gave us a ticket and told us we had to wait until the army had finished patrolling the area and then run as fast as we could when they gave the sign. This was a lawless area, a place where there was a lot of money to be made out of desperate migrants like us, but what choice did we have?

I felt my chest tighten as I glimpsed some of the soldiers patrolling. I hadn't seen soldiers with guns since I'd fled Rwanda, and didn't like to be reminded of the things I'd escaped from. The soldiers on patrol were passing every two hours with their dogs. I felt very scared when they approached.

'You cannot cross today,' said one of the smugglers from KwaZulu-Natal. The patrols are coming too often. It is not safe.'

People weren't really sleeping in case others stole their money, but they chatted and made jokes to help the velvet-dark night pass more quickly.

I sat on the cold ground and said little. I was glad of the jumper that Sarah had told me to buy and tried to protect Jean-Luc as best I could from the cold night air.

At around six in the morning the smugglers returned.

'Now, now, now,' they half whispered, half shouted.

CHAPTER EIGHTEEN

Everyone moved fast. My heart bounced against the wall of my chest.

There was a fence on the border. The smugglers had cut a hole in it which they'd covered over with leaves and grass to disguise it. We crouched to squeeze through. It was early evening and the air had grown very chilly. I clung tightly to Jean-Luc.

Once we were safely across the border we jumped into one of the minibuses the smugglers had waiting with another thirteen or fourteen people.

We were lucky because we could cross in the easiest way. People who did not have money had to pass through the forest and climb a mountain. That was a very hard journey and many people died *en route*.

I couldn't believe we had finally made it.

'We're here, Jean-Luc, we're finally here,' I kept saying to him over and over again jubilantly. I had dreamed of this moment for so long and now I wanted to savour it. I was absolutely exhausted, though, and the tiredness blunted my emotions. I realised that every fibre of my body had been tense for months. Now at last I could relax and stop running.

I hadn't thought of what I would do when we finally arrived.

Tomorrow I will work out a plan, I told myself sleepily. If only my family and Christian had been with me, life would have been perfect once again.

Eventually we reached a town, where we could see people and cars. The smuggler who was driving our minibus told us to rest at his home overnight. I hoped he would give us a bed for the night. It had been a while since I'd slept in one.

'Tomorrow we will continue on our journey to Durban,' he said.

People in the streets were speaking by clicking their tongues, and their language sounded very strange and unfamiliar to me. Later when I learned to speak it I realised that if you subtracted the clicking and worked out what the slang meant you could decipher the Swahili parts quite easily.

The houses there were beautifully built. First we passed through a shanty town with corrugated-iron huts crammed together, but now we had reached a nicer area. All the houses had fancy cars parked outside them.

'Take a shower, have some food and then sleep,' said the smuggler. He brought us some chicken and chips and then he went off.

I slept better that night than I had done for months. No nightmares, no dreams, just a deep, black sleep.

The next morning we rose early to complete the final leg of our journey. People smugglers are viewed as mean and greedy, but many are genuinely keen to help desperate people to cross borders from an unsafe place to a safe one. This man was very kind to us. Without various kinds of smugglers to move us through the continent I'm not sure that Jean-Luc and I would have survived. In my experience they had been mainly decent human beings. They charged us money but they looked after us well.

I wonder what my parents would have thought if they could have seen me travelling through Africa in this way. They wouldn't have approved of me getting involved with anything illegal, but I'm sure they would have understood that I had no choice.

The smuggler was playing lively music very loudly but it was hard to hear it properly because all the other drivers were playing loud music in their cars too. Everyone had their windows wound down and nobody seemed to mind that their own music was being overpowered by other people's. It was a kind of orchestra of car radios.

I hadn't been able to see too much when we had arrived on South African soil, but now I could see the country in all its glory. Everywhere I looked I could see beautiful parks and gardens where people could walk. South Africa looked nothing like any other country I had passed through. The buildings were big and tall and sturdy. I saw a beautiful library and many shops. I marvelled at the way the roads were built. Most of our journey had been on terrible roads with a few good stretches in between, but here the roads were perfect, just like the ones in Hollywood movies. I found it hard to believe that I was still in Africa.

In the villages we passed through there were women walking around with their breasts uncovered. Back home in Rwanda and Zaire women had not exposed themselves like that. I felt I shouldn't be looking at them and hurriedly turned away. Then I saw a farmer using a machete in a field on his crops. Before I could control myself I had cried out and was overwhelmed by the urge to run away. To this day I have been unable to be anywhere near a machete.

When we reached Durban there were lots of wealthy Indian people walking around. The place seemed like paradise to me and reminded me of pictures I'd seen of New York. The streets were very clean and the buildings very tall. Sarah pointed out the mall to me and at last I understood what she was talking about. It was a huge, covered shopping area that looked as if it was too big to walk through in a day.

I felt as if I had arrived in paradise and for the first time in months I felt safe.

Sarah said she would introduce me to some Zairian people. I was hopeful that they would help me find work. We paid R5 to sleep in a communal hall in an area called Montrose, and used our clothes as bedding. Sarah bought me two blankets. This was not the kind of accommodation I had dreamed of, but it would have to do for the moment.

'Let's rest here now, Leah – you must be exhausted from the journey – and then we'll go to the afternoon market.'

I lay down with Jean-Luc and both of us fell asleep straight away. A few hours later I woke up refreshed. We took a shower and changed our clothes. I felt very scruffy – the clothes that Piri had bought for me had started to wear out and I didn't have the money to replace them.

Sarah took me to a street market where people were selling jewellery and other items from Zaire. She wanted to introduce me to my own people.

They called me 'our sister' and welcomed me warmly.

I had Jean-Luc in my arms and whispered to him, 'I think everything is going to turn out fine for us here.'

The Zairians had big hearts and gave me food. One couple who knew Sarah gave me some advice: 'Leah, you must get papers before you do anything else. It will make life here much easier for you. Just tell them the truth about what happened to you in Rwanda,' they urged.

They told me where to go and the following morning I went to Immigration. Shaking and trembling, I told them about some of the things that had happened to me in Rwanda.

The South African government gave people like me papers but no help with food or accommodation. I did not come across many other Rwandise but I saw a lot of Burundians.

Once I had papers I tried to find work to support myself and Jean-Luc. In all the other countries I had just been passing through and had never considered settling for long enough to get a job. I chatted to the Zairians about the kind of things they did to make money.

'Things are tough here, Leah. There is not much work around for black people, South African or not. We have to take whatever we can get. We cut hair or clean houses. Sometimes the Indian people give us some work.'

I nodded. 'I'm happy to do anything to earn some money.'

I had learned about apartheid at school but I didn't know the whole story. It shocked me to see that everything nice belonged to whites and not to blacks, although we were in Africa, not Europe. In Zaire there were rich black people and rich white people and as I grew up in the post-colonial era I had never felt that the whites were in charge of us. It made me both frightened and angry to see black people as second-class citizens in their own country, especially after the overthrow of apartheid.

Sarah tried to explain the situation to me. 'Sometimes Zulus come into the city from the townships and march to demand their rights. They walk around in big groups carrying their traditional weapons.' I didn't like the sound of anybody carrying weapons and immediately thought of the Interahamwe.

'What are townships?' I asked. I had never heard that word before. I was horrified when she explained the meaning to me.

A couple of days later I saw a group of Zulus marching through the streets of Durban. I tried so hard to block out what had happened in Rwanda but seeing these groups marching with spears brought everything flooding back. The police stood on the sidelines. Sometimes they brought tanks of water and discharged high-pressure water jets on to the demonstrators to disperse them. I could feel the anger of the Zulus and understood that they wanted justice, but every time I looked at the spears, visions of flesh being pierced and blood filling the streets rushed into my mind.

A few days after we arrived I woke up to brilliant sunshine streaming through our windows. I showered, washed Jean-Luc and decided it was a perfect day for exploring.

Further down our road there was a shop selling old goods. I thought that if the things were old and second-hand they would be cheap enough for me to afford, but I didn't realise that some old things could be extremely expensive. There were no antiques shops in Zaire or Rwanda so I didn't know what that word, hanging on a sign outside the shop, meant.

I was dressed in a traditional pink wrapper dress and for the first time in weeks had made an effort with my appearance. Inside the shop a tall, slim, white woman was working. I could see by the kind of clothes and jewellery she was wearing that she was very wealthy.

She looked startled when she saw me walk into the shop, holding tightly to Jean-Luc's hand.

'Oh my God, you look beautiful!' she said.

'Thank you,' I replied.

'And your little boy too, absolutely adorable.' She looked at me intently. 'You're not South African, are you?' she asked.

'No, I'm not. How did you know?'

'Firstly because you don't look South African. I can see you're a foreigner. And secondly because you have walked calmly into my shop and are considering buying something. No black South African would dare to do that.'

I shrugged. 'I don't like the way people set so much store by skin colour. Where I come from I know very well what happens when people start to hate each other for stupid reasons. It does-n't matter to me whether someone is blue, pink or yellow. What's important is if they have a good heart.'

'Yes, in an ideal world everybody would think like that, but we know we have a way to go before we reach that point,' she replied.

She was very chatty and without intending to I ended up

telling her where I was from and some brief details about what had happened to me.

'Oh dear, you've had a tough time. And what a journey you've had. Where are you living?'

'In Montrose.'

I explained that I was sharing a room with good people from other countries – Angola, Mozambique and Burundi. We laid out mattresses on the floor at night and all slept in one room. Looking at this elegant, affluent white woman I couldn't imagine that she had ever had to spend a night like that.

'Are you looking for anything in particular?' she asked.

'A cheap cooker, some plates, a pot and a mattress,' I said. 'Just some basic things we need to live. I arrived here with nothing.'

The woman seemed kind and interested. She told me that her name was Beverley.

'I'm not sure you're in the right place for those kinds of basic items. You might be better off going to the market, where you could pick things up cheaply. We specialise in antiques here. They're old, well-made things and are very expensive.'

I looked around at all the beautiful things in her shop. Some of them reminded me of the elegant, hand-carved furniture Maman and Papa had at home. I was overwhelmed with longing to be at home, curled up in Maman's arms, surrounded by all the lovely things we owned in our old life. Suddenly emboldened, I blurted out, 'Could you give me a job here?'

'Oh, no offence, but I can't,' she replied. 'Apartheid may be over but I'm afraid its rules remain. It would really be frowned upon if I employed a black African. But I might be able to help you with some of the things you need. Give me your address and I can deliver a few things to you that we can't sell in the shop.'

I gave her our address but wasn't really expecting this wealthy, polished white woman to venture into a run-down black neighbourhood.

But the following day she arrived on the doorstep. I could see that she was shocked at the sight of so many people living crowded together in a small space but she said nothing and gingerly sipped at a cup of tea I made for her.

'Now I can see how much space you have I'll get one of my staff to deliver some things to you tomorrow,' she said.

'Thank you so much, that's very kind of you.'

The next day she had her people deliver a beautiful pale green sofa that converted into a bed, along with sheets, pillows, a little stove and plates. She also sent an electric kettle, something I had never seen before because at home we always boiled water on top of the stove.

I gasped in amazement. I hardly knew this woman and yet she had turned into a fairy godmother. I hurried down to her shop and pushed open the door breathlessly.

'Beverley, what you've done for me is amazing. I have everything I need to live now. How can I thank you? Please let me pay you something.'

'Don't be silly, I don't want payment. These were just things that were lying around that I couldn't use.'

I began to visit her regularly with Jean-Luc. She was very easy to talk to and it was so nice to be able to have normal conversations about the weather, clothes and how Jean-Luc was getting on. I decided to stop speaking French to him because it was too confusing for him to hear too many languages at once. I spoke only English and he picked it up very quickly.

Beverley liked to hear me speaking English with a French accent, using French words where I didn't know the English. It was a novelty for her.

It was very exciting for me to have my own cups, spoons and plates. I hadn't been able to go to a cupboard and take out my own plates and cutlery for a long time. I had never realised how sweet normal life could be. Maman had never used tinned food, always preferring fresh. But tinned food was cheap here and I started cooking beans and mixing them with sardines. South Africa makes the best fish and chips in the world and I grew to love this dish.

I was taking things step by step. I still didn't trust the world. With the Zulus marching I knew that things could change very quickly. I remembered how the Interahamwe had marched before the genocide began and how we had tried our best to ignore them – with disastrous consequences.

Now that we were in the country I hoped we could settle in, I tried to create a Leah who was strong enough to take care of Jean-Luc; but I was terrified that if I probed too deeply into the terrible things that happened in Rwanda I would crumble into a pile of dust. But as long as I managed to keep the terrible thoughts about my family and Christian and the events I had witnessed in Rwanda out of my mind I felt better than I had for a long time – more relaxed and settled. Planning where to run to next had become a way of life and it was wonderful not to be thinking in that way any more.

It was easier said than done, though, not to think about the people I loved and had lost. I ached for my family and for Christian. Waves of emptiness swept over me. Every time Jean-Luc learned a new word or said something funny I wished I had someone close to me to share it with. I continued popping in to see Beverley but I was very lonely. Now that I had an address at last I decided to write to my family at our home in Kigali, just in case anyone was still there. I wrote a simple letter to say that I was safe and well and living in South Africa and included my address. I heard nothing. I hadn't expected to, but none the less I was bitterly disappointed.

I began looking around for a church to attend. I hadn't thought much about faith while I was moving from country to country. All I knew was that God had deserted us all in Rwanda.

I had been a good Catholic and although I was angry with God for causing so many people so much pain I never stopped believing.

As I wandered around looking for a church I saw a very smartly dressed Zulu man in a suit. He looks like somebody who'd know where I could find a church, I thought to myself.

'Excuse me,' I said politely, walking towards him. 'Could you tell me where I can find a church?'

What happened next took my breath away. I had no idea what I'd said wrong but it was as if I'd punched him on the nose. I didn't understand what he was saying but a torrent of abuse came out of his mouth. He whistled and suddenly a large group of Zulus appeared, dressed in T-shirts and jeans. I started to run, still having no clue what I had done wrong.

'If you can't speak Zulu, get lost,' he snarled.

'So you *can* speak English,' I said in amazement.

The Zulus gathered around me, singing, '*Kwere kwere*,' which I later discovered is an insulting Zulu word for a foreigner. My head was spinning. These people really think I'm different from them just because I don't speak their language, I thought. But I can't speak Zulu and I'm not a South African. Tears sprang into my eyes. I was both terrified and baffled. I had spoken in many different languages on my journey and as far as I was concerned language was simply a way to communicate. I had spoken to this man in English, a language we both understood, in order to get my question about a church across. What on earth was going on here?

'You are *kwere kwere*.'

I started edging away but the group followed me. I broke into a run and eventually managed to shake them off. I don't think I'd ever run so fast in my life. I was close to Beverley's shop and ran inside panting.

'Hide me please, Beverley, hide me!' I cried.

'Leah, what on earth is wrong?' she asked.

I explained to her what had happened.

'I just don't know what crime I committed by speaking English to this smartly dressed businessman,' I said.

'For you to be speaking English as a black person is an insult to them,' Beverley explained. 'English is the language of their oppressors.'

Now that Beverley had explained it all to me I understood why I had upset them, but still I struggled to grasp the logic of the whole thing.

'All I wanted to do was find where the nearest church was,' I said.

'I'll pick you up next Sunday and I'll take you to a good church where nobody is going to talk about your skin colour,' Beverley promised. 'The way you look you wouldn't survive in any of the churches round here. You don't speak Zulu and you're different from local people.'

'I don't want to go to church any more.'

'Well, just try this one before you make your final decision. A delightful husband-and-wife team of English missionaries run this place and, believe me, they don't judge anyone.'

In all the other countries I'd passed through black people had been happy to speak English with me. But here people were angry. I didn't want to be around this anger in case it infected me. I already had more than enough anger inside me.

I saw so much pain in the eyes of black South Africans. I didn't want Jean-Luc to grow up in an environment of aggression and hatred. The whole thing confused me. Blacks who hated blacks with different shaped noses or who spoke different languages, whites who hated blacks, blacks who hated whites. As far as I could see all of these hatreds were entirely avoidable. I wanted to protect Jean-Luc from all of this.

I had been so inspired by Mandela's speech in Zaire, proclaiming that blacks and whites were equal, but this was not what I found in post-apartheid South Africa. Dreams and truth were two very different things.

Maybe it's just not possible for humans to love each other, I thought.

'OK, Beverley, I'll give your wonderful church a chance. I don't really understand how things work here. Maybe the church will help to explain it all to me.'

CHAPTER NINETEEN

I don't know if I what happened next can be attributed to God. Maybe I just got lucky, but the day I walked into that church my life changed.

The church was about forty-five minutes' drive from Montrose, a quiet, low-key building in a well-maintained white neighbourhood. There I found Zambians, Burundians and people from Mozambique as well as Zulus from the closest township and white people, all singing their hearts out together. Seeing so many people sitting together in harmony made my spirits soar. It was explained to me later that they were singing English hymns.

A good-looking white man with grey hair was standing at the front of the church. I guessed he was in his early sixties. He was dressed in a smart British suit. I sat down with Beverley and at the end of the service she introduced me to this man, whose name was Pastor Levi, and his wife, Aunty Mary. Aunty Mary looked very beautiful to me: she had snow-white hair and was dressed in a brightly coloured, elegant dress. I immediately felt their warmth and openness and responded to it.

Everything about this couple was open and honest and kind. When all hell broke loose in Rwanda something in my soul had iced over. They were the first people who managed to penetrate this iciness buried deep inside. Without being pushy or intrusive they warmed up my soul.

After church they welcomed everybody who wanted to come to their home for dinner. Without realising it I was looking for a replacement family, and almost immediately Pastor Levi and Aunty Mary filled that big, black hole for me. I felt their love whenever I spent time with them. In so many ways they reminded me of my parents. They filled my emptiness and made me feel safe.

I started going to church every Sunday. Beverley only came that first time, but I continued going. I just wanted to be wherever they were and do whatever they were doing. Their mission was to mix black and white people together into one blended humanity.

Looking back, I don't think I was searching for God when I was asking around for a church. But I hoped that inside such a place I would find people who had soft, kind hearts because those were the people I wanted to surround myself with. I began to count down the days until each following Sunday, when I could see Pastor Levi and Aunty Mary.

Although I felt more secure once I started attending church, there were still things about life in South Africa that made me feel very uneasy. The aggression of the Zulus when they staged their protests along the road I was living on set my teeth on edge. I shook visibly every time they passed.

Pastor Levi was worried about me staying in a volatile neighbourhood like Montrose. At all hours of the day and night there was singing, shouting and clattering. I craved a place of peace and quiet where I could rebuild myself and learn to trust the world again.

Pastor Levi knew that I had no means of supporting myself and Jean-Luc and started to pay my rent. Knowing that I was no longer in danger of being evicted because I couldn't pay my rent made a big difference to me.

I started cooking and selling food from my flat to migrant workers from the Great Lakes region – Rwandans, Burundians and Zairians. I didn't earn much but it was enough to provide the basics for Jean-Luc and me.

I became friendly with a Xhosa woman from Montrose whom everyone nicknamed 'Tomato' because she was round. I also became close to some Zulu women, who taught me their language. In my culture a woman is someone you have to protect and be gentle and respectful towards, but I could see that Zulu women were not treated that way. The men were rough and aggressive towards them and some of the Zulu women turned to foreign men, who treated them better.

Sometimes when Zulu men I knew saw me in the street they shouted to me to go over to where they were standing. 'No, no, no,' I remonstrated with them. 'You come over here if you want to speak to me, and please talk in a polite way.'

I had several conversations with South African women and all of them admitted that they didn't like the way the men treated them. We decided to form a women's group with the objective of making the men respect us more. When we were together we had the courage to challenge men who treated us like second-class citizens. Christian had never treated me that way, and Papa had never treated Maman that way. I didn't like it and didn't see why we should have to put up with it.

One Sunday at church I saw a man holding a bible, but not actually looking at it. I watched his fingers moving swiftly over raised dots on the page. I had no idea what he was doing. Pastor Levi introduced us and told me his name was Pastor Graham and that he was visiting from Australia. He reminded me of a blond-haired, green-eyed Sylvester Stallone. He was dressed very smartly.

I asked him jokingly whether he was Rambo. 'You look like Sylvester Stallone,' I blurted out.

'Have you seen him? I never have, so I don't know whether or not you're right about that. I'll have to find out who this Rambo is.'

'How come you don't watch TV?'

He chuckled. 'Because, my dear, I'm blind.'

'What is "blind"? I need the dictionary.'

Then he answered in French. '*Je suis aveugle.*'

'You can't be, because your eyes are open. You dress well, you know when I stand up and what I'm doing.'

He explained that he'd been blind since childhood and had attended a school for the blind. I clapped my hand over my mouth, realising that I had said something stupid and insensitive, telling him he looked like Rambo. But Pastor Graham just laughed.

He sometimes preached at the church and when he did I could see he was touching his Braille bible to remind himself of key passages.

I continued to bask in Pastor Levi and Aunty Mary's love. They did so much to help put me back together again. I never thought anyone would love me as much as my parents did, but I think this couple truly did.

Thanks to Aunty Mary I developed a taste for British food. Aunty Mary made proper British Sunday lunches – roast beef, roast potatoes and Yorkshire puddings. I had never tasted these savoury puddings before and grew to love them. The lunches were full of laughter and jokes. I told Pastor Levi I couldn't eat meat but I managed to eat chicken and loved the vegetables. Pastor Levi always had a large fund of stories to tell about his travels around the world but he never preached or made laboured points about God. He was so normal and ordinary.

Pastor Levi started to pick us up on Sundays to bring us to church and then dropped us back home later on. 'This area is too rough for you and Jean-Luc, Leah,' he kept saying, shaking his head.

A few weeks later he found us a place to stay with some white church members, not far from his own home. They treated us as part of the family and we had our own room in the pool house, which was next to their beautiful home. They were shocked to see that I could make nice European food; it didn't fit in with their image of an African at all.

I wasn't allowed to walk alone in the neighbourhood in case I was attacked by racist whites. The family had two dogs, which I adored; I took them for walks but rarely ventured out apart from that.

I dressed like a European woman so some people thought I was African-American rather than an African. I wanted to be around quiet, gentle people and did not return to Montrose, so I lost touch with Sarah.

I felt perfectly contented living in my little bubble. Jean-Luc and I had a comfortable roof over our heads, nice clothes to put on our backs and enough food to eat. And most of all we felt loved by those around us. I hoped that this situation would continue for ever. By day I focused my thoughts on the here and now, but as soon as I fell asleep the terrible dreams came – Christian, my parents, my sisters and brothers all swam before my eyes. Sometimes they were alive, sometimes dead. Their souls were haunting me. I often woke up screaming. In these terrible dreams I was always running. I still have these nightmares today.

One day Pastor Levi came round to see me and dropped a bombshell.

'Leah, I want you to move from Durban to Cape Town. It will be a safer place for you. We are coming to say goodbye to you. Our mission is finished and we are going back home.'

I was devastated. 'No, Pastor Levi, You and Aunty Mary and everyone from the church have changed my life so much. Please say it isn't true.'

'I'm sorry, Leah, it is true, but you'll be fine. Sometime you will come to England and see us there.'

Pastor Levi and Aunty Mary were my surrogate parents, my

crutch, my protectors and my providers. I couldn't imagine how I would ever be able to survive without them. They introduced me to a new couple called the Greens, Australian missionaries based in Cape Town. They too were warm and lovely people. Thoughtfully Pastor Levi wanted to integrate me with the new people in the new place before he left.

Without Pastor Levi and Aunty Mary round the corner I felt very insecure, so with a heavy heart I packed up our few belongings once again. Jean-Luc had been given a few jumpers from church members and a few other things had been donated to us. Everything we had fitted into two bags. I hadn't felt like a refugee for a while but now I felt like one again. Pastor Levi told me that I shouldn't mind being a refugee because I was a victim of terrible circumstances and I hadn't chosen to be dependent on others, but my views remained the same. I felt that I was an intruder into other people's lives, somebody uninvited and often unloved. Many people want refugees to go away and stop disturbing them without understanding why we cannot go back to where we came from.

'Come, Jean-Luc, it's time for us to get on the bus again,' I said wearily.

CHAPTER TWENTY

The Green family came to pick us up from the bus station in Cape Town. I was happy that we had already met once and didn't feel like strangers to each other. They already knew a lot about us from Pastor Levi and Aunty Mary.

I was immediately struck by their kindness. From the first moment, the family included me in everything.

Pastor Levy and Aunty Mary came to Cape Town to say goodbye to me a few weeks later. I cried my eyes out but I loved Cape Town and already felt settled there with the Greens.

'Leah, we will be back to visit and you must come and see us in England. This is only a temporary goodbye. Don't be so sad.'

'I'll miss you both so much. It is impossible for you both to know how much you have helped me,' I said, clinging to both of them.

But, as Pastor Levi had promised, life did go on without him and Aunty Mary and I managed to enjoy it.

We went to church on Sundays but I still felt no connection with God. I felt angry because the things being preached in the Bible were not what most human beings were doing. I continued going, though, because everybody I lived with was going. It was a habit and a routine for me rather than a spiritual encounter.

I kept waiting and hoping that one day God would touch my heart.

A few months later the Greens told me that their mission too was finished. They found a lovely white couple from their church called Doreen and Alan to take us in.

I became very close to Doreen. She was in her fifties, had never had children of her own and doted on Jean-Luc.

They lived in Fish Hoek, a very white, affluent area. The only other black people I saw were servants. The residents gave me strange looks because they could see I didn't look or behave like black South Africans. I wasn't afraid to walk into white shops and buy things and I certainly didn't consider myself to be inferior to the whites of Fish Hoek. Sometimes they crossed the street to avoid me, and a few made complaints to Doreen and Alan and said that I should leave the neighbourhood.

October 31, 1996, was Jean-Luc's third birthday. It was hard to believe I'd been in South Africa for more than a year. We went to the home of the new minister at the church, Pastor Norman, to celebrate. Everyone made a big fuss of Jean-Luc and presented him with a lovely birthday cake with three fat candles for him to blow out.

I wished that Christian, Maman and Papa could have been with me to celebrate the occasion, but I smiled brightly and pretended everything was fine. Jean-Luc was very excited by the whole thing and raced around the room with some of his little friends from church.

I had managed to get a job at a fish restaurant used by whites. Doreen looked after Jean-Luc while I was at work. I wasn't allowed to be seen at the front of the restaurant because of the colour of my skin and instead was banished to the kitchen. I was fuming about this, but what choice did I have? It had been very hard to get any job at all and I needed to find a way to support myself and Jean-Luc.

Maman had taught me well how to cook and I showed the

chefs how to prepare different kinds of food that they weren't familiar with – chicken curry, dishes flavoured with coconut, Spanish omelettes. The white customers loved the food but they might have choked on it if they had known that black hands prepared it.

One evening a rich white woman came into the restaurant, caught a glimpse of me in the kitchen and asked me to cook a meal for her pet chihuahua. 'Tell her to bring the plate of food out into the front of the restaurant. Otherwise we're walking out of here now,' she said haughtily.

My boss offered to bring the food out herself. When the woman insisted that I had to bring the food my boss said, 'Leah, just go and give her the plate of food that she wants. In this business the customer is always right.'

Tears of anger and frustration sprang into my eyes. What I wanted to do was take the plate of food and throw it in this horrible woman's face. Instead I obediently brought a plate of the finest chicken pâté for her dog.

'Feed the dog while I eat my meal,' she said imperiously. I shifted uncomfortably from one foot to the other. It was 11 p.m. I knew that before I could go home I had to clean up the kitchen and then I had a long walk back to Doreen's place. This loud, racist woman couldn't have made her demands at a worse time.

I muttered in French, 'You must be seriously mad in your head.'

'What?' she said.

The final threads of my patience snapped. 'You heard me. I may be forced to cook for you but I'm better than you. I come from a good family and I should not have to do this.' I felt both humiliated and angry that this awful woman felt it was her right to treat me like a piece of dirt.

'How dare you speak to me like that? You clearly don't know your place. I shall certainly not be coming here again.' She stood up, puffing and panting in outrage at my boldness, grabbed her dog and stormed out of the restaurant.

My boss saw it all. She shook her head sadly and said, 'Leah. I know this woman is horrible but I'm afraid you won't be able to work here any more. What you said to that woman is going to cause me terrible problems. I know that apartheid is officially over but a black person cannot talk like that to a white person and get away with it. Not in this neighbourhood, at least.'

I went home devastated. How was I going to pay my rent? I had been so delighted to get a job: at long last I wasn't a charity case. I was able to buy fresh food in the market and eat the kinds of things I had eaten at home with Maman and the rest of the family. I loved feeling independent.

A few people from church had been in the restaurant when the row happened. They applauded me for having the guts to tell this woman off in French. One of the congregants, a man called Mr Price who was a friend of Pastor Norman, witnessed the whole episode. He was a Dutchman who could also speak French, and the next day he called me and said he hadn't realised I spoke French fluently.

'It's the language I grew up speaking,' I replied.

'My son works in the tourist information office and they really need French speakers. I'll set up a meeting for you.'

My heart leapt. Maybe my outburst would end up doing me a favour.

He fixed up a meeting for a couple of days later and offered to drive me into Cape Town. I realised that I had never actually been to the town centre. It was beautiful, with wide, spacious streets, manicured trees and lots of big, well-built buildings. The city was surrounded by a shimmering ocean and unlike in Fish Hoek there were plenty of black people here. The mood was happy and there was much more harmony between different races than I'd seen elsewhere in South Africa.

I was delighted when Mr Price's son hired me on the spot. In Tourist Information there was just one black woman working there, and a coloured security guard. All the other staff were white. Vicki, the black woman, was very beautiful and she was delighted to see another black person.

'I can't believe how many different languages you speak, Leah, you're just the kind of person we need here,' she said warmly. I settled in fast and loved my work. It was certainly better than feeding a spoiled chihuahua chicken pâté at the behest of its racist owner. It was great to be speaking French again and I loved chatting to the tourists who came into the office. Because I was so busy I had little time to think about the past. Doreen agreed to continue looking after Jean-Luc.

Vicki had suffered a lot under apartheid. She told me that her parents had been killed by white people who came to the township.

'I think your country is a very violent place,' I said.

'It is and it isn't,' said Vicki.

I kept asking her to take me to the township where she lived and she kept refusing, saying, 'You couldn't survive in the township, Leah. It's very tough.' But eventually she agreed to take me.

I could smell the poverty and suffering as we approached the township. People sat outside flimsy shelters made of discarded pieces of metal and wood. Hopelessness hung in the air. People sat on boxes outside their homes, drinking and smoking. Many looked sick. Both children and adults looked listless. Everybody seemed to have given up on life. There was something in these people that I recognised in myself. All of them looked traumatised.

I hadn't seen proper South African earth until now because I had been living in suburban or city areas with good, paved roads. Now I saw the earth and was startled by how red it looked.

Vicki hurried me past this area. She lived in a beautiful house in a part of the township inhabited by people who had good jobs in the city centre. I started chatting to Vicki's friends and my spirits lifted when I saw how strong the community spirit was. Unlike the first people I had seen in the township, Vicki's friends laughed and joked and exhaled optimism.

'Why do the other people in the township not try to find jobs in town so that they can get out of poverty?' I asked naïvely. 'Now that apartheid is finished and Mandela is in charge, they have as much right as white people to be in the town. If you live in fear you die in fear.'

'It's easier said than done,' replied Vicki. 'Not everyone is like you, Leah. People have been through terrible things during apartheid: they've lost loved ones, been injured by the police. It's not always so easy to just jump up and change because we have a new government.'

Vicki told me that sometimes white tourists visited to see what a genuine township looked like, but they didn't leave their cars. It was as if they were viewing wild animals on safari.

A few weeks later some people from the township decided to come to town and protest about their lack of access to the beaches where the white people lazed. I cheered when they arrived. Vicki told me that they didn't usually venture into town because they were scared of whites.

Life for Jean-Luc and me had settled into a comfortable pattern. I loved my work, Jean-Luc was well settled at nursery and we enjoyed happy times at the beach together and outings to cafés and parks with Vicki. I still took out Christian's picture regularly and showed it to Jean-Luc.

'Here is Papa,' I said, smiling. It was almost three years since I'd last seen him and my family. The pain of losing them all remained with me, but it was becoming duller. I was starting to adjust to life alone.

One morning in the office I started taking details from a French tourist who wanted to book a trip to Table Mountain. When he handed me his credit card to pay for the trip and I saw his name, I gasped. It was Philippe, my childhood pen friend! We had exchanged photos as children but I would never have recognised him without seeing his name. We had become close through our letter-writing and I had written to him once from Kenya to tell him that I was alive and running.

'Philippe, it's Bébé Leah,' I gasped.

He started screaming: 'Bébé Leah, I thought you were dead because I never heard from you after the letter you sent me from Kenya.' He picked me up and spun me around. 'I'm so happy to see you.'

He was white and very handsome with nice blue eyes. And he looked as if he was very wealthy.

'Let's catch up as soon as you've finished work,' said Philippe. 'I can't believe that I've found you in Cape Town, of all places. The world is small, Leah, that's all I can say.'

In the evening he wanted to take me to the cinema and was horrified to find that a black and a white person were not allowed to go to such places together. He also held my hand on the way to the train station, not knowing that blacks and whites weren't supposed to do this. Black people started shouting insults at us. They were disgusted that I was doing something like that with a white man.

I could see that Philippe found these attitudes disturbing. 'It's not like that in Paris, Leah.'

'Well, I'm afraid it is like that here, Philippe. You just have to get used to it.'

Philippe was on holiday for two weeks. It was wonderful for me to be with someone I could open up to. I had always told him lots about my life. We had written to each other for five years and in that time had got to know a lot about each other even though until now we had never met.

'Christian is dead, he couldn't make it out,' I said to him with tears in my eyes.

'What?' he said. 'Are you certain about that? If you made it out, maybe Christian made it out too.'

'I'm certain, Philippe. In Kenya the Red Cross had lists of missing people. I put my family's names on the list but I was too scared to put my own name up in case someone found me and killed me. I never found any of my family's names on the list, nor Christian's. I wrote a letter addressed to my family home when I reached South Africa but I never got a response.'

'Leah, you could be wrong about that. Were you there when Christian died? Did you see him get killed?'

'No, but I know for sure that he's dead because he was at the airport when the fighting started.'

'Leah, I think you could be mistaken. I thought you were dead too, but here you are.'

'Can we change the subject? I don't like talking about this.'

'Of course, forgive me. It's none of my business.'

I spent as much time as I could with Philippe during his holiday and was sad when it was time for him to return to Paris. I hugged him as he left and we promised to keep in touch.

'I can't believe that we found each other in the middle of Cape Town,' I laughed.

I had no idea that I was about to have another reunion that would change everything.

CHAPTER TWENTY-ONE

One lunchtime Vicki and I went together to buy fish and chips from a popular local café. There were always long queues outside and I noticed that a tall black man who looked as if he was Rwandise was staring at me. There was something about the way he was looking at me that made me shiver although it was a hot day.

'Bébé Leah!' he called out, and greeted me in Kinyarwanda. I froze to the spot and said nothing. I was terrified that this man had deliberately tracked me down somehow and now wanted to destroy my fragile happiness and sense of security. Maybe he even wanted to kill me.

'Let's go, let's go,' I said urgently to Vicki.

'What about our fish?'

'I don't care about the fish any more, I'm going,' I said, running off.

Vicki stayed in the queue and bought lunch for both of us. Back at the office she said, 'What was that all about?'

'They're here, they're here.'

'Who's here? What on earth are you talking about, Leah?'

I hadn't stopped to consider whether this man was a Hutu or Tutsi. All I knew was that I wasn't happy to be around Rwandise people.

'I'm sure this man wants to harm me. I tell you, Vicki, I'm not safe around Rwandise people.'

'He was asking me a lot of questions. He gave me his number and asked me to give it to you,' said Vicki.

I threw it in the bin.

Three days later he was waiting outside my office. I wanted to run off again.

'Bébé Leah, wait, please just listen to me for a minute.'

I knew that for someone to call me Bébé Leah he must have known me in Rwanda even though I didn't recognise him.

'Just listen to the man,' Vicki said impatiently.

'You need to hear what I'm about to say. I know you, Bébé Leah. You are Christian's wife.'

'So? What if I am?'

'And I'm so very happy to see you because Christian is in Durban!'

'Please don't tell me lies, I know Christian is dead. He died at the airport. Nobody could have survived what happened there. Anyway, who are you? '

'I'm Christian's friend. Here's my card.'

'Let's run, let's go,' I said to Vicki. 'Maybe this guy has been sent by the Hutus.'

I had developed an almost pathological fear of anyone from Rwanda, and decided that the only way I could stay safe was by keeping well away from people from my country. Because my family were all dead I had no need or reason to ever mix with Rwandise people again. Who knew when the Interahamwe might rise up again and finish off those of us they missed last time?

He started appearing regularly outside my office and talking to Vicki. His name was Antoine.

'Tell Bébé Leah I'm not a bad guy. I just want to see her and Christian happy,' he said.

Vicki tried to persuade me to talk to him.

'If he thinks he knows my husband, why can't he give me some proof of that?' I demanded. But a small part of me wondered whether what this man was saying could actually be the truth. He seemed like a very serious man but rationally I knew that Christian could not have survived and the last thing I wanted to do was build up my hopes only for them to be cruelly dashed.

The man disappeared for a month and I started wondering where he was. I even felt slightly disappointed that I no longer saw him hanging around outside my office telling me that Christian was alive, although I told myself that he was no longer hanging around because Christian wasn't really in Durban.

Then he returned and saw Vicki in the street. He asked her for a picture of me to show to Christian.

A few weeks later I was on my way to the office when I saw him again.

'Oh hello,' I said. 'You disappeared for a while. I guess you lost Christian's ghost.'

He laughed. 'He's not a ghost, he's for real. I want you to look at this picture. If you tell me this is not your husband I'll never bother you again.'

I looked at the picture and burst into tears. He showed me a picture of a slim young man with a long, long beard. Christian had never had a beard but I knew immediately that it was him. This poor man had not been lying to me over all these months. My beloved was still on this earth. I started screaming and sobbing, then I hugged him.

'I'm so sorry I didn't believe you, but I was so sure Christian was dead. I thought you were torturing me by pretending he was alive.' I began to rain questions down on him. There was a loud buzzing noise in my head. I couldn't think clearly. Joy was drowning out my thoughts.

'Where is he living? What's he doing? How quickly can I see him?'

Vicki and I had had a picture of both of us taken in the office.

It was the only one I had to hand. Vicki ran into the office to get it.

'Please take this to Christian immediately.'

'I will bring Christian to you as soon as he can get the money together to pay for the bus,' he said, and then he walked off quickly down the street, beaming to himself.

I was reeling. How could Christian be alive? It was impossible to have survived at the airport. So many people had told me that everyone who was there when the plane exploded was killed. Although I had seen Christian's picture, doubt started to creep back into my mind. Maybe it was his double I'd been looking at a photo of.

A few days later I walked out of my office and there was a tall, slim, bearded man, smiling broadly.

'Christian!' I screamed. I flung my arms around him and covered him with kisses.

'Bébé, Bébé, Bébé, I was so sure that you were dead,' he said, in between sobs of emotion.

'Is it really true *you're* not dead, Christian? I was so certain that you were.'

We kept on touching each other's faces to prove that the other one was real flesh and blood.

Antoine told me later that when he showed Christian the picture of me with Vicki it was the first time that he had seen him smile, then he had laughed and cried and screamed all at the same time.

People stopped in the street to look at what all the commotion was about. Everybody who witnessed our reunion was crying, even the office security guard.

My boss was overjoyed for me. He came out into the street to witness our reunion. 'Take some time off, Leah, you have a lot of celebrating to do,' he said, hugging me.

We were both dazed. If you think somebody is dead and then you find them alive, seeing them again has a strange quality about it, almost as if you're meeting them in the next world rather than this one.

We kept saying over and over again, 'I can't believe you're here.'

'How did you get out of Kigali Airport alive, Christian? I thought everybody was killed.'

'I never left Changugu, so I never arrived at the airport. The flight was delayed because of an engine problem. That problem certainly saved my life.'

Our words tumbled over each other feverishly in our rush to fill in almost three years of gaps.

He had waited in Changugu to see if we headed there, but he lost hope when there was no sign of us. He hid there for a week, witnessing many terrible killings but after that had managed to get a flight to Nairobi with the UN.

He explained how he had travelled through Africa from Kenya, finally reaching Durban. My mouth fell open. We had been in almost all the same countries at almost the same time and yet we had never bumped into each other. All those people who told me they had seen Christian when I had showed them his photo had been telling the truth.

'Oh, I was this side,' I said.

'Oh I was there, but I never went to that side,' Christian replied.

'Why did you leave Tanzania then? If you'd only waited another month I would certainly have bumped into you in the street!'

Eventually through tears of joy and sadness we managed to more or less piece together each other's journeys down the continent's south-eastern flank.

Christian was anxious to see Jean-Luc as soon as possible.

'He's started nursery now. Let's go there right away.'

Hand in hand like two innocent children, we ran off down the street together.

Jean-Luc was playing in the sand with the other children. He looked up and waved with no idea of who the strange man by my side was.

'Jean-Luc, your *papa* is back. He got lost for a long time but now he has found us again.'

Christian picked Jean-Luc up and cuddled him. Jean-Luc pulled on his long beard and giggled. He was taking the whole thing in his stride, as if it was the most normal thing in the world to have his absent father suddenly reappear in his life.

Within a few days he had accepted Christian and seemed to have forgotten that he had ever been away. I think the fact that I had kept on showing Jean-Luc Christian's photo and saying the word 'Papa' over and over again made Christian's sudden reappearance less surprising.

Christian was absolutely overjoyed to see Jean-Luc but was sad that he had missed out on so much of his life.

'You've done a great job with him, Bébé. How you managed to carry him out of all the hell in Rwanda I'll never know. I don't think I would have been able to run with a child. It's a miracle that we all made it out and that we've found each other. Now life is good.'

I told Christian that three people had said they recognised him when I showed them his photo but had said he was a Somalian called Yusuf.

'Yes, I changed my name and said I was from a different country so that I could protect myself,' he said. 'I thought it was too dangerous to be a Rwandise Tutsi on the run.'

I should have been less sceptical when people said they knew him and should have considered that maybe Christian had changed his name and origins. After all, I too had pretended on some parts of my journey that I was not a Rwandise Tutsi. Why on earth hadn't it occurred to me that he would do the same? I think I was so scared of the pain and disappointment I would feel if Christian turned out to be someone else that I had stopped being logical about the whole thing. Keeping safe mattered more to me than anything else on my hazardous journey. I didn't like taking risks and had focused all my energy on protecting Jean-Luc and myself from emotional and physical harm.

Christian explained that he had also looked at the Red Cross names in Nairobi but had not seen mine or my family's – because he had arrived in Nairobi before I did.

In Durban he had managed to find a job working for an Indian ice-cream-van company. Then Antoine had told him, 'Leah is working in a posh office.'

'Oh, that's my Leah, she only does things like that, no cleaning jobs for her,' he'd replied.

After our initial frenzied catch-up on the events in our lives since we'd been forcibly separated, neither of us wanted to refer to these matters again. It was too painful for both of us to talk about our own horrible experiences and to hear about the other's suffering. Instead we tried to focus on positive things, to think only of the present and the future and to count our blessings.

'We've been given a second chance of happiness,' I said.

During the first few days of our reunion we continued hugging and touching each other every minute, just to confirm to ourselves that the other one hadn't vanished back into another world.

Christian bought Jean-Luc a football and started taking him to the park and the swimming pool. Before long it felt as if he and Jean-Luc had never been apart. We were a proper family at last.

Jean-Luc had settled into nursery well but I was still anxious about leaving him with anyone. The nursery was close to my work so I knew that he was never far from me, but it was very difficult for me to trust others with his care. Jean-Luc was the most precious person in my life and I fussed endlessly over him, cuddled and coddled him.

When I thought Christian was dead I had often said to Jean-Luc, 'Your *papa* has gone very, very far away.' 'To heaven,' I had added under my breath. At nursery he could see that the other children had fathers and he was happy and relieved that at last he had one too.

Christian was working night shifts and he picked Jean-Luc up from nursery. I was so used to making all the decisions relating to Jean-Luc by myself that I had forgotten how nice it was to be able to share the responsibility with someone else. With Christian by my side I had the courage to start making enquiries about my family. Although I was sure they were all dead, the fact that Christian had turned up alive and well gave me a glimmer of hope that maybe some of the others had survived too. Before, it seemed too difficult and painful to try to search for my family. I was also terrified of facing the misery of getting absolute confirmation that they were dead without having any shoulder to cry on if I heard bad news. But now I felt strong enough to ask any new people from Rwanda who arrived in Cape Town if they had any news of my family. I received no new information but thank goodness I was no longer alone when people said, 'Sorry, I know nothing about what happened to your family.'

Christian and I had both grown up a lot and the people we were in Kigali had gone for ever. Before the genocide we were two young people in love with lots of dreams. Even though I'd got pregnant very young I still led a cosseted and sheltered life after Jean-Luc's birth, thanks to the love and stability provided by my family. But now we had been robbed of the innocence we shared in Kigali. Now we understood how cruel the world could be. Sometimes we smiled together but underneath both of us could taste the fear and horror we had experienced.

I tried to force myself not to, but even with Christian by my side I was living in fear. I felt that everything was very flimsy and fragile. Before I had never thought about whether or not my neighbour might turn against me. After what I'd been through it was very hard to let go and to trust. Who do you trust when you have seen men who you have known for many years as good husbands and fathers killing their wives?

Christian and I praised our good fortune in finding each other daily, and our lives together were happy. But things could never be the same again after what we'd both been through. Before, the two of us had been a perfect whole, like a delicate Chinese vase. The genocide had smashed us apart and now we were glued back together. Not quite as good as new.

CHAPTER TWENTY-TWO

Christian got a job in Cape Town, working as an engineer. He was welcomed with open arms by my friends, and Pastor Norman threw a party for him – a characteristically kind and thoughtful gesture. I was so happy to be surrounded by people I loved and who loved me, and I was convinced that now our little family was complete again everything was going to work out fine.

But I never got used to the insults hurled at black people by whites. I wasn't prepared to tolerate the use of any derogatory words about black people and I became determined to stand up to my tormentors. The more the whites didn't want me to go to a particular restaurant, the more I vowed that I would go there.

Things became increasingly uncomfortable for us in Fish Hoek so we decided to try to find somewhere to live in the centre of Cape Town, which was a much more mixed area. It was just about acceptable for me to be living in a white suburb with a white family, but for Christian, Jean-Luc and I to set up home there by ourselves was a completely different matter.

I phoned up to go and see one apartment in the centre of Cape Town which was within our price range and sounded nice, but when we met the white owner at the address he said baldly, 'You can't live here because you're black.'

'What do you mean?' I said angrily. 'Apartheid in South Africa is finished. Please show me a rulebook which says we cannot live in this apartment block. Is there something wrong with our money?'

'I don't have to show you any rulebook,' said the owner. 'The apartment is mine and I decide who lives there and who doesn't.'

I was about to start shouting when Christian intervened and said quietly, 'Leave it, Leah, we'll find somewhere else to live.'

We did manage to find another apartment to live in, in a mixed block which was clean and had good security. But our race battles continued – with both whites and blacks. We couldn't get a job above a Zulu or a Xhosa, and as foreigners we couldn't get into the good universities. It was difficult for a black person to stand up and say, 'I want to study to be a doctor.'

Avoiding problems because my skin was the wrong colour or because I'd been born into the wrong tribe or country was like trying to avoid getting your feet wet when you go in the sea. It bothered me that Jean-Luc was growing up in an atmosphere of race discrimination.

All of this made me feel unsafe and unsettled and once again I began to think about running to somewhere safer. This was a beautiful country but it was full of injustice. I felt despised by both black and white South Africans. Sometimes if we went to a white restaurant for a meal they refused to serve us. Black and white people didn't sit together on the trains. I realised that the apparatus and mindset of apartheid could not be dismantled overnight, but I felt change was coming way too slowly.

As the months passed more Burundians, Rwandise and Zairians arrived in Cape Town. Their presence made me feel nervous. Feeling unsafe once again made me despair. I had been so sure that South Africa would be a country where I could settle and thrive. Gradually it dawned on me that I wasn't going to feel safe anywhere in Africa. In fact even the word 'Africa' was beginning to make me feel uneasy. The only people I felt truly protected and at ease with were Pastor Levi, Aunty Mary and their English church friends. If all English people were like them, then maybe England was the place where we could finally be happy and put down roots. Christian and I talked and talked about what we should do and eventually agreed that we should save hard to pay for flights to the UK for us all.

Through Vicki I had made some friends in some of the townships, and one of them helped me to get a passport using my real first name and a South African surname. This person also got me a birth certificate.

I talked to as many of my church friends as I could about England, and they tried their best to explain to me how things worked over there.

'It's very different from Africa, especially the weather!' they warned.

Life in South Africa had been relatively calm, but what happened next made me speed up my plans to leave the country.

I had made friends with a woman called Brigitte, and one evening the two of us decided to go out together to a karaoke bar for an hour or two. As we stepped out of the club at about 9 p.m. both of us were grabbed from behind. I couldn't see what was happening to Brigitte because I was bundled into a car boot. I was sure I saw the glint of a gun as the lid slammed shut and I was encased in total darkness, forced to curl up into a tight foetal position because of the lack of space. I could see nothing but blackness but the boot stank of stale bodies and cigarettes. I found out later that Brigitte had been released almost immediately because they realised they'd got the wrong woman.

'Let me out, let me out,' I screamed pointlessly. I was absolutely terrified, but during the genocide I had been blessed with presence of mind in a crisis; I prayed that the calm logic that had helped to save my life on more than one occasion would not desert me now.

I'm going to talk my way out of this one, I said to myself. I didn't survive the genocide with Jean-Luc, get through the long and difficult journey from Rwanda to South Africa and find the husband I thought was dead just so that a bunch of gangsters can blow my brains out.

After about half an hour the car stopped and I was pulled roughly out of the boot by a group of men. I listened to the languages they were speaking and guessed that they were South African and Tanzanian. My heart was pounding and my limbs had turned to lead, no words came out of my mouth. So much for talking my way out of this one.

I couldn't see very much but it looked as if I had been brought to a remote area of farmland. I felt the cold metal of a gun held against the back of my head.

'Where's the money?' they kept snarling. A group of them started punching and kicking me. Pain was everywhere, every inch of me hurting as the blows rained down, and my head was spinning too fast to think clearly.

I was aware that one of the men was looking hard at me. He hadn't joined in with the kicks and punches. I was sure I saw him wincing when they beat me across the face with the back of a gun.

'What if it's not her?' he said in Swahili. 'You might be mixing her up with someone else.'

I prayed that he'd be able to convince his accomplices that they'd got the wrong woman.

'What is your address?' he asked me. The punches stopped to let me answer.

I told him the truth, hoping that they'd realise they'd mixed me up with the person they were after. 'I live with my husband and young son,' I croaked breathlessly. 'We don't have money, we haven't taken anybody else's money. We're just ordinary people trying to get by.'

'You're lying,' snarled one of the other men who had been

leading the kicks and punches. He had a cruel, scarred face. 'We know you've taken a suitcase of money from that ship that docked in Cape Town. If you don't give us the money we'll kill your son,' he threatened.

'What ship? What suitcase of money? Believe me, I don't know what you're talking about.'

'We're talking about thirty thousand dollars that you've taken. This is serious,' said one of the other gang members.

Christian and I hadn't put our savings in the bank because we no longer trusted them. Despite making lots of phone calls we had never managed to get our money back from the bank in Rwanda. We had $3,000 saved in the flat to buy our tickets to England.

'She doesn't want to give us the money. Just go and kill her son,' said the man with the scars.

I was weak from all the beatings, but somehow I found the energy to stand up.

'You can never, ever kill my son. And if you kill me I'll come back to haunt you for ever.' I bitterly regretted giving my address. 'Look, I swear to you that you've got the wrong person. I know nothing about the money you're talking about. But please, please, I beg you, do not kill my son. He is the only flesh and blood I have left in the world. My husband and I have three thousand dollars' savings. We were planning to use it to fly to England and start a new life there, but take it, take all of it. Take all our furniture, the food in our fridge, take everything you want but spare my son and my husband.'

The man who had first questioned whether I was the woman they were after said to the others, 'I think she's innocent.' Then he told me to get into the car, thankfully not the boot this time, and drove me wordlessly back to my building. I could barely sit on the seat because my body was so sore. Relief that I had avoided a bullet in the back of the head had turned my limbs to jelly. When my gangster driver saw our modest apartment block he realised that we were ordinary people.

'So you were telling the truth all along.'

'Yes, I told you what savings we have. Just take what you want. All I want is to get back to my husband and son in one piece. That is much more important to me than any money.'

I opened the front door of our apartment, stumbling past Christian, who gasped, open-mouthed. I took our hard-earned savings out of a drawer and handed them to the man. He looked at my bruised swollen face, then at Christian and our humble apartment, and handed half of the money back to me.

'You were lucky, they could have killed you, even though you were the wrong one,' he said. Then he was gone.

Christian bathed my wounds for me.

'Don't ask,' I groaned. 'I just cheated death again.'

I had been doing so well. Moving forwards with Christian and Jean-Luc, learning to trust again and trying to put the past behind me. But this attack was a huge setback for me. It would take us months to save up the $1,500 we had just lost to pay for Christian and Jean-Luc's tickets, but my instinct was to get out of South Africa immediately.

'I'm really, really scared,' I sobbed to Christian. 'I need to leave now. What if someone else mistakes me for a criminal and puts a bullet through my head? I think South Africa has become an unlucky country for me. If I get a job in England and you carry on working hard here, in a month or two we might have saved up enough for your fare and Jean-Luc's, and then we can be together again.'

Christian understood how panicked I was feeling and agreed to let me go first.

'I've never been parted from Jean-Luc before, but I'm doing this for all of us and we'll be together again soon,' I said. My spirits were lifting at the prospect of leaving a place where I felt in danger.

'OK, Leah, go if you must. You know I will take good care of Jean-Luc. Let's hope we can get the lost money together quickly so we can all be together again very soon.'

'We'll get through this, Christian. Pastor Levi and Aunty Mary will help us settle in England. They will look after us and help us find work. They've told me that their country is a beautiful and peaceful place. I think that at long last we will be safe there.'

The next day I booked my flight.

CHAPTER TWENTY-THREE

At the airport I clung to Christian and Jean-Luc. Because of our enforced separation when the genocide struck I was used to not having Christian permanently by my side. But Jean-Luc was a different matter. I had only ever been parted from him for hours at a time and the thought of leaving him for a couple of months or maybe more broke my heart. He looked at me with his big, dark eyes and clamped his little arms around my neck.

'Mummy, don't go, don't go,' he cried.

'Jean-Luc darling, it won't be for long. Mummy hasn't got enough money for your flight at the moment and I don't know what I will find in England. I hope it will be a nice place for us to move to. It's where Pastor Levi and Aunty Mary live. It's better that you stay here with Daddy and continue going to nursery with all your friends until things have been sorted out. But I promise you we'll be together again very soon.'

I unpeeled Jean-Luc's fingers from my neck and hurried through to the departure lounge. Suddenly I wondered what on earth I was doing. My entire experience of Europe was a few childhood trips to Belgium. It was one thing travelling through Africa, where there were many familiar things in all the countries

I passed through, quite another to arrive with nothing in a brand-new country on a brand-new continent. All I knew of England was that people ate roast meat and Yorkshire pudding like Aunty Mary had made.

I had arranged to call Noli, the cousin of my South African friend Brigitte, as soon as I reached the airport. She had moved to London and seemed to be very happy there. I couldn't wait to visit Pastor Levi and Aunty Mary in Swansea. Once I see them again I know I'll feel safe, I said to myself.

I was wearing a formal purple suit and matching jewellery. My parents had always drummed it into me that you had to dress smartly for Europe, and just in case they were checking up on me from the next world I didn't want to let them down.

It was October 1997. More than three years had passed since I had fled Rwanda. I had travelled through many countries and hadn't felt ready to put down roots in any of them. Maybe England would put an end to my wanderings for good?

When the plane landed and I walked into Heathrow Airport an official asked me where I was from and then took me aside. 'Have you swallowed anything?' he asked. I didn't know what he was talking about.

'Well, I had my meal on the plane and quite a few glasses of juice,' I said innocently. I was so naïve that I knew nothing about drug mules, much less that I was suspected of being one.

'Are you claiming asylum?' the official asked me.

I didn't know what 'asylum' was.

'Where are you from? What have you come to England for? And who do you know here?'

I told him I was from South Africa, thinking it was too dangerous to tell him I had fled Rwanda in case he tried to send me back there. I had only two UK phone numbers, Pastor Levi's and Noli's. I handed over the two phone numbers to the official and he called Pastor Levi, who immediately explained that I had fled the genocide in Rwanda.

'If you're South African we will send you back home, but if you're Rwandan we understand your case. Why didn't you say you're from Rwanda?'

'Because I'm scared you'll send me back, and I can't put my feet back in that country any more. It is too dangerous for me.'

'All you need to do is tell us the truth,' replied the official.

I looked around the airport. It was dirty, the queues were long and the white people looked grey. I had expected England to be some sort of paradise and felt deflated.

I was told to go and sit with a group of people who were also claiming asylum – Indians, Somalians and Nigerians. We were offered drinks and sandwiches but I refused the food. I felt too nervous to eat. I hadn't expected to be held at the airport. I said nothing to the others because I didn't want to be asked about my own situation.

We were X-rayed and weren't allowed to go to the toilet alone. I didn't understand about this, but later I realised it was because they were suspicious that we might have swallowed drugs. Some of the people I was sitting with were taken away by the police.

Heathrow was swarming with people. I didn't think I'd ever seen so many people all moving around in one space since I'd crossed the border into Goma after I escaped from the genocide. Only this time most of the faces were white, with just a few black- and brown-skinned people amongst them. Everybody looked affluent and well dressed, everyone was hurrying and nobody smiled.

I was in the airport from 6 a.m. until 9 p.m. and felt completely exhausted. I wondered if I had made a terrible mistake and should have stayed in South Africa. The officials insisted that I had to claim asylum at the airport even though I didn't understand why I needed to do this. Hearing the officials use the word 'refugee' brought all my memories of the genocide flooding back. I dreaded people saying, *Where are you from? Oh, Rwanda, isn't that the country where you all started killing each other even though*

you are one people, speaking one language? I felt ashamed of my
nation and hoped I wouldn't have to answer any questions like
that in England.

In the evening the officials brought us chicken and chips but
it looked as if someone else had eaten from the plate first and
then given us the leftovers, so I didn't touch it.

Eventually they gave me a piece of paper that I barely looked
at. All I wanted to do was get out of the airport. I had told the
immigration people that I was planning to stay with Noli for a
while and they made a note of her address.

'We'll write to you in about a month about your asylum claim.
Let us know if you change your address.'

I phoned Noli from the airport and she told me how to get
to her house on the tube. I had no idea what the 'tube' was and
she explained that it was a fast train that travelled underneath
the earth to avoid London's terrible traffic. I couldn't imagine
what this would be like and felt nervous of stepping on to such
a train.

I clung on to the rail for dear life, not knowing which way the
busy train might throw me. Eventually I found my way to Noli's
flat. As soon as I walked through the door I collapsed in an
exhausted heap on her sofa. It had been a very long day.

Noli greeted me warmly. 'Welcome to London, Leah. I hope
you've brought warm clothes with you. It's going to turn very
cold in the next few weeks.'

Noli told me that I could stay with her for as long as I needed
to. I explained that I had been told to claim asylum at the airport
but didn't really understand what was going on. She said she
would ask around and find me a good immigration solicitor. I
had no idea why I would need a solicitor but she assured me that
without one I wouldn't win my case.

The first thing I noticed about London was how many people ate
as they walked down the street. I wasn't used to that and when

we were growing up our parents had expressly forbidden us to do such a thing. 'Bébé, it is very bad manners to eat and walk,' Maman had said to me. 'That is why we have a table and chairs in our house, so that you can sit and eat nicely.'

As I sat on the bus I was amazed by how big and organised everything was. Well-built roads, lots of traffic, big red buses with an upstairs and a downstairs and lots of big, old buildings that looked strong enough to withstand an earthquake or even the volcano that sometimes erupted in Goma.

The shops were very big too, with fancy displays in the windows and signs made of flashing lights. I hadn't seen shops like this in Africa, not even in Cape Town.

A couple of weeks after I arrived in England Noli offered to take me to church. The sun was shining strongly through the window and the sky was the same dazzling shade of blue as in Africa. Until now every day in England had been full of rain and grey skies and I hadn't realised that there was also nice weather like in Africa.

'You'll need a coat, Leah, it's cold.'

'No, I'll be fine,' I said. 'The sun is strong today.'

'That sun is deceptive, it's cold outside,' replied Noli.

After church Noli said she wanted to go to a place called Harlesden where we could buy African foods. I was starting to shiver, although the sun was still shining. I didn't understand how sun and coldness could happen at the same time; I had never seen anything like that in Africa. By the time we got home my lips and hands had frozen. I had never felt cold like this back home and didn't realise that hands could turn such a strange colour in the cold. I looked and felt terrible. Noli went to an off-licence and bought me a little bottle of brandy to revive me. I was wearing gold earrings and she had to remove them for me because the metal was giving me ice burns in my earlobes. My hands were so cold they had lost all sensation because I had no gloves. I had only just discovered the existence of gloves – there had not been much need for them anywhere in Africa.

It was a painful way to learn about the British weather, but after that I was always prepared. I never left home without umbrella, jacket, scarf and gloves.

It was unbearable to be separated from Jean-Luc. He sent me pictures in the post all the time and I called and spoke to him and Christian every day.

Jean-Luc chattered away about what he had been doing at nursery and seemed to be surviving well without me.

One of the first things I did was go to Swansea to visit Aunty Mary and Pastor Levi. I regarded them as my surrogate parents. They met me off the bus and we hugged and hugged. Seeing them again made me feel very warm and safe inside. Jean-Luc's photos were in their living room, alongside those of their own grandchildren. I felt very blessed to have them in my life.

London was full of people of all races but in Swansea I only saw white people. I didn't mind being the only black person there, though. I felt very at home with the two of them. They knew how to make me feel loved and secure without stifling me.

'Leah, have a good look at Swansea and see if you think it's a place you, Christian and Jean-Luc could settle in,' said Pastor Levi. 'It might not be right for you, but if it is of course you're welcome to stay with us for as long as you need to.'

'Thank you, Pastor Levi, you are always so good and kind to me,' I said, giving him a hug. I stayed with them for a few weeks but ultimately decided that Swansea was too quiet for me. I looked for work but there were few jobs available. I decided to go back to London and try to find work there. Noli had told me that I could stay with her until I got myself sorted out and she assured me that there were plenty of jobs around.

'Leah, you know that we will always be here for you,' said

Pastor Levi. 'We're so happy to see you here. I'm sure you'll settle in in a jiffy.'

Gradually I started to adjust to life in London. Although people had many more material comforts than most people in Africa, nobody smiled here. Back home so many people smiled and said hello, even to strangers. But the longer I spent here the more London changed in my eyes. Never before had I seen people from so many different parts of the world all living alongside each other without fighting or arguing. It seemed that people of the whole world were in London. My dream of all different kinds of people getting along together was actually true. Of course things weren't perfect here, but I began to feel that London was a very special place. And I felt safe here too. Christian was saving up as much money as he could so that he and Jean-Luc could come and join me.

Noli was very kind and hospitable to me but she hadn't given me a key and I felt too embarrassed to ask for one. If I ever had to go out for an appointment I stayed out until she came back from work. Sometimes when I was waiting for Noli to come home I sat in the Underground at Hyde Park Corner station, next to the buskers where it was warm. It was very strange for me to see white people begging, but I quickly became friends with some of them. Beggars don't judge you. One man told me he used to be an accountant but his wife kicked him out because he got depressed and turned to alcohol. Then he lost everything. I saw the way he and his friends shared beer and cigarettes. They knew how to share and they helped each other out. I hadn't seen too many English people doing this.

Noli found me a lawyer who agreed to represent me in my asylum claim. She was a lovely woman called Helen, who told me that my case had a good chance of success.

I went back to Noli's place after the appointment with her but Noli was late home that day and I had no alternative but to sit outside on the steps and wait for her. It was another very cold day and I soon felt too cold to move. A neighbour I had never spoken to saw me sitting outside on the steps, blowing on my hands and shivering.

'Come on inside,' said the neighbour, who was Italian. 'If you sit there any longer you'll become a block of ice and we'll have to scrape you off that step.' He led me inside and gently put me on the couch, wrapped me in a blanket and gave me some coffee with whisky in it to warm me up.

Even though my parents were coffee farmers I had never actually tasted coffee before. As children we had not been allowed to have it because it was a drink for grown-ups.

When Noli came back she was mortified that she hadn't thought to give me a key.

'Noli, I need to find a job so that I can pay my own way and send money home to Christian and Jean-Luc for their air tickets.'

'You know how to put make-up on very well, don't you? Your English is OK, you speak French and you know about perfume. I know of an agency that might be able to get you a job on a perfume counter in a big store,' said Noli.

She sent me to a place called Visage Personnel which supplied staff to work on beauty counters in big stores. I got a job on one of the perfume counters in Selfridges and felt like a child in a sweet shop, surrounded by so many luxurious cosmetics, the kind of thing I hadn't seen since my modelling days. I loved advising the wealthy customers about perfume and make-up. It was so very different from my life in the last few years, and that did me good.

Helen was truly wonderful. I trusted her and confided in her. She knew all the right places to call for me to get help. A couple of months after I arrived in the UK she called me: 'Leah, congratulations. You can stay in the UK for ever: you've been given indefinite leave to remain. That's because the government recognises that you were persecuted in Rwanda during the genocide and that it isn't safe for you to return.'

I immediately called Christian. He screamed down the phone. 'That's fantastic! Now we can be together again.'

CHAPTER TWENTY-FOUR

I threw myself into a frenzy of work in the hope of getting the money together for flights for Christian and Jean-Luc as quickly as possible. Early in the mornings I worked as a cleaner at Merrill Lynch. I returned home at 7 a.m., had a quick shower, then went off to Selfridges. Then I raced home to look after a friend's daughter until her partner came home at 9 p.m. Each night I slumped into bed and fell into an exhausted, dreamless sleep, desperately trying to use every second of free time to rest before the same pattern repeated itself the following day.

When Christian and I had saved up enough money between us for one flight Jean-Luc came over, chaperoned on the flight, by an air hostess. I just couldn't bear to be parted from him any longer. He was almost four and we had been separated for four months. Throughout that time I'd felt as if I had a big, draughty hole in my body because my son wasn't by my side. The night before he was due to arrive I tossed and turned the whole night. I was beside myself with excitement but also felt very nervous. What if he had forgotten me, or had changed too much?

My fears were groundless. At the airport my beautiful little boy walked calmly through with the air hostess and screamed,

'Mummy!' as soon as he saw me, throwing himself joyfully into my arms. I showered him with kisses.

'This is England, Jean-Luc. I hope you're going to like it,' I said to him as I sat him on my knee on the bus. 'The sun doesn't shine as much as in South Africa but it's very nice here; they have lots of good schools for you and nice green parks for you to play in.'

Noli fell in love with Jean-Luc immediately and he quickly looked upon her as part of the family.

Two months after that, Christian came. Back at the airport once again, I waited for him and rejoiced that our little family was about to be reunited.

We were given a space in a reception centre for a few months and were then moved to a council flat in Newington Green, a grimy and polluted part of London that hummed with traffic day and night.

But we were happy to have our own little place, a two-bedroomed flat with our own kitchen and bathroom. Jean-Luc settled in well. English was the language he spoke in South Africa so he had no problem making friends with other children in the neighbourhood.

One sunny morning he said he wanted to go and ride his bike on the ground floor. I went down with him and he pedalled around the forecourt of the flats happily. I had bought him some lollipops the day before as a treat and he begged me to go and get him one from the kitchen. I calculated that I could race up the stairs, grab the lollipop and be back down again in just a couple of minutes.

'OK, Jean-Luc, I'll get you the lollipop, but don't move from here. I'll be back very fast.'

As I ran back down the stairs I heard Jean-Luc screaming and thought he must have fallen off his little bike. To my horror I saw that he was surrounded by older, white boys, who were punching him. Blood was pouring from his nose and mouth.

'What are you doing to an innocent child?' I screamed at them. They ran off before I could get a good look at their faces. We called the police and Jean-Luc had to spend the night in hospital. I was terrified and refused to go back to that area. Eventually the council rehoused us.

Jean-Luc made a quick recovery from his injuries but the whole incident had devastated me. I had taken my eyes off my child for just a couple of minutes and he was beaten up. The sight of so much blood reminded me of the genocide. My fragile healing process had been smashed to pieces. I had never seen a child beating another child up in Africa, and once again I had the familiar urge to pack up and leave the place where I no longer felt safe.

I hated people I didn't know and became over-protective of everyone I loved. When I laughed or smiled there was no genuine emotion underneath, just a dark, gaping emptiness. The trust in human beings that I had started to build up evaporated. I became depressed, and was overwhelmed with the guilt of surviving the genocide.

Christian and I didn't talk about it because we avoided all conversations that might lead back to the genocide, focusing only on the present and the future. I noticed that as time went by he was getting quieter and more uncomfortable about talking about anything connected with our past.

And so I talked to myself. Why had I survived when members of my family and other people I loved had perished? What was the point of going on when life was full of pain and struggle? I had no answers. It didn't occur to me to seek medical help because I didn't trust doctors. I even doubted Christian. Before the genocide we had been together every day and knew everything there was to know about each other, but I had no real idea what had happened to him during our time apart, and that lost time created a space between us. The only person I completely trusted was Jean-Luc. I knew every crease in his skin and every thought in his head. He was part of me, my only flesh and blood left in the world, and I knew with a certainty that I didn't have about others that he would not let me down.

Christian encouraged me to go to the gym to vent my frustrations. On one level it worked: while I lifted weights or jogged my mind was blissfully empty. But the aching emptiness never left me. I didn't want to be in the world any longer; but I knew I couldn't leave it because of my responsibilities to Jean-Luc. I wondered if the reason I had survived was just so that I could suffer more.

I started to go to college in Finsbury Park to improve my English. In Rwanda I had dreamed of becoming a doctor but now that dream seemed impossible to achieve. More than ever, though, I wanted to look after people, to fix things for them, and I started thinking about becoming a nurse.

Jean-Luc started primary school and while he was there I went to school too. Christian was studying computers and engineering at college. I didn't want to return to any of the things that had made me happy in Rwanda in case they were snatched away from me again, so it never occurred to me to do any modelling.

Even though I had a roof over my head, a warm jacket to wear and I could afford bread, I was still plagued by the past. I kept saying to myself, Maybe I should have died. Why did I survive?

My legs started to swell up and were covered in red blotches that looked like cherry tomatoes. My doctor said that sometimes depression and post-traumatic stress showed themselves with physical symptoms like that.

I missed Maman and the rest of my family every single day. I grieved for Papa and hoped he'd been killed instantly and hadn't suffered too much. How did Maman and my sisters and brothers die? I wondered if they had all been slaughtered with machetes. Just thinking about what might have happened to them but not knowing for sure meant that I couldn't lay their ghosts to rest. Their spirits travelled restlessly with me wherever I went.

A friend called Janet helped to heal me. When she offered me reiki at the end of 2005, I thought it was voodoo and didn't want to try it.

'No, no, it's not voodoo, it's a Japanese treatment,' she laughed.

She worked on my body for three months. 'No need to talk, just feel my energy running through you,' she soothed.

With reiki the heat comes through the healer's hands into your body. Some people say that treatments like that have no effect, but all I know is that it transformed me.

'There's a lot of work to do, things that need releasing in you,' she said.

I felt like I was a piece of cloth and could bend in any direction she guided me into. She worked on all different parts of me. Before I started the treatment I felt that I was carrying a brick on my chest. After the first session the brick was still there, but it had lifted a few centimetres.

As the treatment relaxed me I knew I needed to find out what to do with this life I had. I could have stayed in Mille Collines and awaited my fate but I chose to leave and escape the back way. Now I realised that that was the direction my spirit had always leaned in. I did not only do this once, I did it many times. I didn't die because I challenged those who wanted to kill me. I fought for my life over and over again when it was about to be snatched away from me, but now that I wasn't in danger I didn't know how to live.

I wasn't the only survivor of the genocide who was suffering. Christian and I became friendly with other Tutsi exiles in the area and we got together every Friday evening. We became each other's surrogate families. We drank and partied and never talked about our pain. It was not a good strategy for everyone, however. One woman in our little group lost her mind and ended up in a psychiatric hospital. I prayed that that wouldn't happen to me. It made me more determined to find a way to move forwards.

'I don't believe in God any more,' I confided in Janet at the end of one reiki session. 'I tried to reconnect with Him but it didn't work. Rwanda was a very religious country but it didn't stop us from killing each other.'

She nodded and offered no opinion on the matter. She was a Buddhist and she taught me how to chant. I found it a very soothing thing to do. I envied the sense of inner peace that she had and wanted some of it for myself. Through Buddhism I began to understand more about my inner life and that the reason I had survived was to give something to others.

I had never thought of my life in terms of a mission before. But knew that I could reach out to people easily. Instinctively I could feel their pain because I knew exactly what pain felt like.

CHAPTER TWENTY-FIVE

My lawyer Helen and I kept in touch after I got my leave to remain in the UK.

'Don't give up on finding your family, Leah,' she urged me. 'I have heard of so many cases where people thought their relatives were dead and then they found them alive and well. People told you that your father had been killed but nobody you know has confirmed that other members of your family have died. I think you should go on searching for them, really I do.'

I shrugged. 'Helen, I cannot live with false hope. I have suffered enough torture. I need to get on with my life as best I can and I must come to terms with my loss.'

In 1998 she persuaded me to put my name and some of the family's names on the Red Cross family-tracing list. I agreed, although I thought it a pointless exercise. 'Helen, I put their names on the Red Cross list when we were in Nairobi; I heard nothing. I wrote a letter to my family's home in Kigali when I reached South Africa; I heard nothing. Christian and I made many enquiries amongst Rwandans in South Africa about both our families, but again we got no news. I really don't think there's much point putting their names on the Red Cross list again, but if it will make you happy . . .'

I heard nothing and assumed that my worst fears were correct and every single member of my family had perished in the genocide. I devoted a huge amount of energy to pushing all thoughts of them out of my mind. I have to focus on our future, I kept telling myself. But it didn't stop the nightmares. When I slept the faces of my beloved family still crept inside my head and refused to budge. 'You can't run away from the past, Leah,' they cried out to me.

At the end of 2001 I got a phone call out of the blue from Helen. She was so excited, she could hardly get the words out. 'Leah, we have to celebrate. I've got the champagne all ready.'

'Don't tell me you're having another baby,' I said.

'I'm not pregnant again, Leah, but really you need to come to my office right now, this minute. Drop whatever you're doing.'

'You sound a bit serious. OK, I'm on my way.'

'Hurry, hurry. I don't want to tell you over the phone, because you'll scream when I tell you and I want to see you scream.'

Obediently I jumped on the bus, baffled at what Helen could have to tell me that was so desperately urgent. Various scenarios ran through my head. Maybe she had heard of a wealthy Rwandise who wanted to employ me.

I arrived at her office and she ushered me inside quickly.

'Here, look at this,' she said triumphantly, handing me a yellow piece of paper. Then I screamed and collapsed sobbing on the floor.

'Maman, Maman!'

It was a full five minutes before I could speak again. Helen put her arms around me and let me cry as much as I wanted. I kept staring at the piece of paper that had Maman's name on it and an address in Kampala.

'Helen, it can't be true that she's alive, that she survived,' I said eventually.

'Leah, it's absolutely true. I told you you shouldn't give up. You see, the Red Cross list worked. Apparently your mother and some of your sisters and brothers settled in Kampala. Your mother was having problems with her eyes and went to a charity that could help. Somehow the charity's computer was linked to the Red Cross database and when your mother gave her name, your name flashed up as a relative searching for her. They told me her reaction was similar to yours when they told her her daughter was alive and well and living in London!' She wiped away my tears. 'I love it when I can give my clients good news,' she grinned. 'Your mum doesn't have a phone but I have a number for her friend and neighbour, a woman called Faith. I can call her now if you like, so that you can confirm everything.'

So I spoke to Faith, who told me she was going to run to Maman's house right now so that we could speak to each other.

'Call me back in a few minutes,' she said excitedly, caught up in the drama of the whole event.

I could hardly breathe. Once again I had that buzzing sound of joy inside my head that I'd experienced when Christian and I were reunited.

We waited for a few minutes. I paced Helen's office, hardly able to contain myself. I wanted to run into the street, yelling to the whole world, 'Maman is alive and for all these years I thought she was dead. Life is full of miracles.'

After five minutes I called Faith back and the familiar voice I loved so much but thought I would never hear again said agitatedly, '*Allo?*'

'Maman, is it really you?' I cried.

'Bébé, Bébé, I thought you died at Josephine's place. I can't believe this.'

Maman and I both collapsed into hysterical tears of joy and it was several minutes before either of us could speak.

'Maman, don't say anything now. I'm going to rush off to the travel agent to buy a ticket to Kampala. This time tomorrow we'll be together. I have so much I want to say to you.'

'OK, Bébé, I'm here, I'm waiting to take you in my arms, my precious daughter.'

Then my brain started spinning. 'I need to get to Kampala tonight. I have to get my ticket and my visa. I've been without Maman for so long, I can't wait another minute,' I said to Helen.

'Of course,' she nodded. 'You better get a move on, then, if you want to be in Kampala by tomorrow night.'

'Thank you, thank you, thank you, Helen, you were right all along,' I said.

I hugged her tightly and ran out of her office. Suddenly I had a lot to do.

I floated out of the offices at London Bridge with the widest smile on my face and called out to complete strangers, 'Hello, hello, isn't it a wonderful day?' as I crossed the bridge. They probably thought I was completely mad.

I had a credit card but had never used it because I didn't like the idea of being in debt. I raced to the travel agent's and handed my card over eagerly. I wasn't even interested in hearing the price of the ticket. Nothing else mattered now except for being reunited with my family.

All I could think about was getting to Kampala. I rushed over to the Ugandan Embassy, explained what had happened and begged them to give me a visa so that I could get on the flight the following day. They said it would not be possible to get the visa now.

'Please, just do anything you can, bend the rules, give me that piece of paper. My plane leaves tomorrow morning.'

Miraculously the rules were bent and I left the embassy thirty minutes later clutching my precious visa.

I raced home and told Christian and Jean-Luc that Maman was back from the dead. I did not sleep that night, tossing and turning and imagining being in the arms of my beautiful *maman*. She would make everything all right again, she always did.

I was agitated when I stepped on to the plane. I wished I could have been the pilot so I could have driven it twice as fast. I felt as if I was trying to push the plane forwards with the sheer strength of my will. I told some of the air hostesses about my news. They were all thrilled for me and cried. 'You're an angel who deserves some happiness, and that's why you've found your mum,' one of them said.

I passed hurriedly through Customs at Entebbe. The brother of a Ugandan friend of mine in London had agreed to come and pick me up from the airport and take me to Maman's house, about forty minutes' drive away.

I was shocked when I saw the house; although it was in a secure compound it looked rundown and shabby. This was not the kind of place Maman was used to.

And then I saw her – sitting fanning herself on the balcony. I felt as if my heart stopped, then it bounded out of my chest because I was bursting with so much joy.

I kissed her again and again, but it was hard to believe that she was Maman – she looked more like my grandmother. My joy was clouded by my anxiety at how much my superhero Maman had faded. I'd imagined that she would still be the beautiful, capable, powerful, youthful woman I left behind in Kigali. Instead I found this diminished, old, half-blind woman who had Maman's voice but no longer looked like her. It was almost eight years since I'd seen her, a third of my life. How could I have spent eight years without her when she had been alive all along? I felt cheated of time I could never get back.

The last time I had seen her she was standing in her clean, spacious kitchen, telling me to give Jean-Luc some porridge when we got home, hours before all hell broke loose in Kigali. It was that image of Maman that I carried around inside my head throughout the genocide. Now she had white hair and was not taking such good care of herself. She had always worn expensive perfume but I couldn't smell it now. She had grown very skinny and frail. Before she had been such a strong, broad woman.

'Maman, you've grown old,' I said, before I could stop the words falling from my mouth.

'It's life, Leah, that is what has made me old,' she said, laughing and crying at the same time. 'I can't believe you're back from the dead, my precious Bébé.' She kept on pinching my cheeks so hard I thought she might pull the flesh away from the bones. She couldn't believe it was really me and had to make sure I was a living human and not a ghost.

I couldn't stop kissing her on her eyes, her hands, her feet, and she did the same to me. Jean-Claude, Henri and Alice, and Brigitte's daughters Vicki and Alida, gathered around me excitedly, and we all hugged and kissed each other over and over again.

'Where is Micheline?'

Maman shook her head, devastation passing over her radiant face like a black cloud.

'And Christine?'

Again Maman shook her head.

'And Pauline and little Sans Souci?'

Tears started to fall from Maman's eyes.

'All gone, Leah, all killed right at the start of the genocide. Hutu neighbours came to our house and slaughtered them before my eyes. You can't imagine how it was to witness my children's murders and to be able to do nothing, nothing.'

I felt as if I was going to be sick as the enormity of the loss hit me. After all the years spent wondering, now I knew for sure who was alive and who was dead. I cried with Maman for the loss of my beloved siblings, but also for Maman. Now that I was a mother I could imagine the enormity of the pain of losing a child.

'What about Timotei?' I asked, hoping for some better news. He had been at university in Kinshasa when the genocide started.

'We've had no news of him, we can only think that he died too. Many Tutsis were arrested in Kinshasa during the genocide. The government in Zaire supported the Hutus and saw the Tutsis as the cause of all the trouble,' said Maman through her tears. 'Life, Bébé, is very cruel.'

In fact Timotei had survived, although we didn't discover that until much later. He had been arrested in Kinshasa, was later released and finally made his way back to Kigali in 2004, appearing on the doorstep of my uncle's home. Another miracle that filled our family with joy and rubbed out a little bit more of our pain and loss.

That night Maman and I slept in the same bed, our arms wrapped around each other like two lovers in the first flush of passion. 'Now that I have seen you, Bébé, there is nothing else I want in this life' was the last thing she said to me before she finally dropped off to sleep that night.

I had arrived at Maman's house in the dark, and the next day, as the sun beat down, I was shocked by how scruffy the place was. There was no clean water and they had to fetch dirty water from the river. Inside Maman had made the place as clean as she could, but it was infested with mosquitoes. I wanted to get everybody out of there as quickly as possible and settled into a nicer place.

Maman told me that a family friend called Chris was living near by and seemed to know everything about Kampala. I called him right away and asked him if he knew of any nicer apartments that I could move my family into.

'Bébé, great to hear your voice, I thought you were dead. I'm sure I can find a nice place for your family. I'll make a few calls and come back to you.'

He found a lovely modern, three-bedroomed apartment in a nice neighbourhood, and I moved everybody in the same day.

I was behaving like a maniac because I was so determined to fix Maman and polish her back to the state she was in before. I wanted to treat her to all the luxuries she'd missed out on during the last few years.

'Maman, I'm going to book us into a nice hotel in Kampala for a few days, just you and me, so that we can catch up properly. You look so exhausted, you're in need of some pampering.'

Maman was in a daze and agreed to whatever I suggested. It

was as if she had been sleepwalking through the last few years and finding me had done nothing to rouse her. At the hotel we lounged in the jacuzzi and the sauna, ate delicious food and visited Lake Victoria.

Although so much had changed, in some ways nothing had changed. We picked up the conversation where we had left it that terrible night at Josephine's when the phone line went dead.

'So where did you go from Josephine's?'

I explained briefly. 'And what about you?'

'Oh, we stayed in the house until they came to burn it down, and then we ran.'

In tattered fragments we told each other our terrible stories. It is not in our culture to speak immediately of pain. Such things must come out gradually in their own time.

When I described my journey through Africa she gasped in shock and admiration.

'I can't believe you did all that with Jean-Luc, Leah, and so young too. Well, you always said you wanted to travel and you certainly got your wish!'

Maman didn't leave Rwanda during the genocide and its aftermath so she suffered throughout the whole period. After Papa was killed the family remained terrified in the house. A few weeks later four Hutu neighbours stormed in and killed my three big sisters, Sans Souci and some of the servants. Maman witnessed everything. Somehow she managed to carry on for the sake of the younger children but she was traumatised and became very withdrawn. She thought she was losing her mind and became over-protective of her surviving children, feeling jumpy every time one of them left her side.

The family moved from Kigali to Byimana near Butare, a place she knew as it was where her mother came from originally. She forgot the Western life she had led before and became a simple village woman. She never spoke of the war, she never drove again, she never went back to Kigali. Like me Maman stopped eating meat completely and the family survived on vegetables. There was no lake nearby so it was difficult to eat fish.

Tragedy blighted our family again when my beautiful brother Henri was attacked in 1998 by the Interahamwe. Although the genocide was finished long ago, rogue Interahamwe still lurked in certain areas and attacked Tutsis. They removed my innocent brother's chin and part of his skull after he wandered into a Hutu area. He survived but was disfigured and Maman was not surprisingly retraumatised. She had just about managed to keep going after the genocide despite her terrible memories, but this was too much for her to bear.

That was the day she decided to flee Rwanda. After my brother had been treated for his injuries she rounded the family up and took a bus to Kampala. She decided she didn't want to have anything to do with Rwanda ever again.

My heart felt as if it had snapped into little pieces of agony, hearing Maman recount these events. She saw the horror in my eyes and hugged me tightly.

'Bébé, let's enjoy the moment and try to forget these terrible things for a while. How is Jean-Luc? Does he still like eating porridge?'

'Jean-Luc is a big boy now, he's a proper Londoner, working hard at school.'

'Does he speak good French?' she asked. Maman spoke perfect French and was eager for the rest of us to speak the language well too.

Maman knew that I was in a state of shock. She appeared to be reviving as her maternal instincts pushed some of her pain aside. I climbed on to her lap and she held me like a little baby, kissing me all over.

'You look just like me, *chérie*,' she said.

I was determined to sort out whatever problem she was having with her eyes. Within days I had found a hospital that could perform the required surgery.

'At last I'll be able to see you properly' was the last thing she said before the anaesthetic knocked her out.

The operation was a complete success and she could see perfectly once more. Every single day she thanked me for giving her her sight back.

I was conscious that the relationship between us was shifting and I was becoming her mother. I begged her to come to London so that I could look after her properly. But Maman did not want to come.

'Bébé, my spirit rests in Africa. I think it will be killed if I leave my own land and come to Europe.'

I couldn't bear to be parted from her. On the last night we both cried and cried and didn't sleep the whole night.

'Maman, I promise to return as soon as I have saved up some more money. And next time I will bring Jean-Luc with me.'

Although I didn't want to be parted from Maman I was happy to see she had put on a bit of weight in the two weeks we had been together, and thanks to a session in the hotel beauty salon her skin, hair and nails were restored to their former beauty. But the thought of how much she had suffered during and after the war tore me apart.

'How do you cope, Maman, when you have lived through so much pain?'

'*Chérie*, remember what I told you when you were a little girl, about the bracelet that someone takes from you? You have to behave like you never had it in the first place and quietly adjust your life.'

I left her with a recent photo of Jean-Luc, Christian and me. She clutched it to her chest.

'Come back soon, my darling,' she said. 'This photo will keep me going until the next time.'

I sat on the plane back to London with tears splashing on to my tray of food. But I felt happier than I had felt for a long time. Being with Maman had taken away a lot of the gaping emptiness

I felt inside me. I vowed that I was going to find a way to get her old life back for her. Naïvely, I thought that if I smothered her with enough love and enough money everything would come right again.

CHAPTER TWENTY-SIX

After my reunion with Maman I felt as if I wanted to do something useful with my life, in the hope that it would make her happy. My focus had been on Jean-Luc and Christian, but in 2003 I decided to become a volunteer at the Royal Free hospital in Hampstead. I had been thinking about becoming a nurse for some time but hadn't done anything about it. Suddenly I felt I had a purpose in life, that I could be useful and I could help people. It made me happy to wash old women and put powder on them. Everybody on the wards worked together very well and the cooperative atmosphere lifted my spirits.

I had always loved being in hospitals (when I was not sick), visiting or helping. But when I saw people coming in bleeding from accidents, I turned away. I still found it hard to look at blood, but I had a crazy plan to stop death, an irrational urge to fix everything, not only Maman and my own family, but everyone I came across with problems. Because I knew what it was to suffer I wanted to try to stop others from suffering wherever possible. If you're in a hospital, you shouldn't die, I said to myself. I had seen too much unnatural death in Rwanda to be able to accept natural death through illness and old age.

I went to a local college and after studying for six months got a certificate to be a care assistant. I was allowed to do basic things like giving medication and taking temperatures, but I couldn't give injections. A few months later I embarked on a nursing degree. As I progressed I was allowed to read patients' notes and write down symptoms. I stood with the doctors while they did ward rounds and willed them to cure everybody they saw. I loved my work. At long last I was doing something useful.

Maman was very happy that I was studying to be a nurse. 'I wish you would study more though, Leah, so that you could become a doctor, like you always wanted to be.'

'But Maman, I have to confess that I hate studying. The information just won't stay in my head. I got sick when Donata and Jean-Luc and I were in Kenya and I no longer knew how to read and write. I had to relearn everything, and since then it's never been as easy for me to study as it was when I was a little girl.'

Maman too was making progress. I think when she saw me she woke up and remembered who she had been before. I hope I had reminded her that alongside the pain there were some good things in life, as she had reminded me. She asked me to get her a sewing machine so she could teach women in the villages how to sew. When it came to sewing she had magic fingers and before the genocide she had always done a lot of work with women in the villages, teaching them to read and write, to sew and to keep themselves and their children healthy. Although she had lived a privileged life she understood the ways and thoughts of the women in the villages as well as members of her own family. She was very happy to become a teacher again.

I never completed my nursing degree. I struggled with the work and wasn't able to focus on my studies as well as I should have done. Even if I had gained full qualifications I don't think I would have been able to go into an operating theatre and witness people's stomachs being cut open. I had already seen too much of that.

I was satisfied to perform the small tasks I could handle. For two months I worked in a cancer ward. I adored the children but seeing them so sick and with tubes coming out of them was devastating for me and I got too emotionally involved. I wanted to be God and take the pain away.

Christian became increasingly concerned about me. 'Leah, I think your job is killing you. You're too fragile to be working in a hospital,' he said.

But I didn't want to leave. The patients seemed to like me and it was good to feel needed and useful. I became particularly close to a gentle, beautiful old lady. I used to put make-up on her and cheer her up as she had very few visitors. In her final moments she called out to me, but I wasn't there because I wasn't working that day. I was racked with guilt that I hadn't been with her to hold her hand and whisper soothing words to her at the end, and decided to take a break from nursing.

I'd been thinking for a long time about returning to Rwanda in the hope of laying a few ghosts to rest, and in April 2004, a decade after the genocide, I decided to return to the country I had once loved so much and was now terrified of. Maman agreed to go with me. She hadn't been back since she'd moved the family to Uganda in 1998.

Maman had always yearned to go to Ethiopia and I was determined that she would fulfil her dream. We agreed to travel there after we had spent some time in Rwanda.

I met Maman in Uganda and we flew together to Kigali. I insisted that we fly rather than take the bus because I knew that the bus would pass along many of the roads I had walked with Donata and Jean-Luc to get out of Rwanda in 1994. I couldn't bear to retrace those steps. I was agitated on the plane and clutched her hand tightly, just as I had done when I was a little girl. Now Maman was the stronger one again. I was shaking so much that she had to lay a steadying hand on my knee. She had lived in Rwanda after the genocide, so returning did not hold quite the same dread for her as it did for me. She had her own nightmares about her country, but at least she had seen that after the ravages of the genocide peace had been restored and some semblance of normal life resumed.

It was a huge relief to me that it was night when we landed at Kigali Airport, so that I was not able to see too much of it. One of my uncles, who was in the army, met us off the plane. He was part of the brave new Rwanda, relentlessly looking forward to the future with lots of optimism and no fear. He was determined that we would enjoy ourselves and remember the good times rather than the bad ones during our visit.

Maman and I both wanted to face our demons, and my uncle wanted to help us to lay them to rest. He treated us like royalty, taking us to the best restaurants and hotels. As we walked through the wide, well-maintained streets of Kigali it was almost impossible to imagine that these roads had once been rivers of blood, with body parts piled high and roadblocks manned by machete-wielding maniacs. Everything felt peaceful. Money had been poured into Rwanda by Western donors to repair the battered infrastructure of this small, beautiful country. Kigali was thriving. Rich people were building European-style homes all over the place. My uncle thought that if he drove us through the new Rwanda I would be happy to see so many changes for the better. It was true that I couldn't find the old Rwanda, but it didn't stop the flashbacks.

Maman was holding back her own suffering and concentrating on trying to make me better. We both felt nervous and were unable to share my uncle's enthusiasm about this brave new world. He, however, wanted to relive some of the happy times in the past, to try to prove to us that there was more to Rwanda than memories of the genocide.

'Bébé, I would love to see you play tennis again. Your tennis used to be the talk of the town. I'm sure you haven't lost your talent for the game.'

'But, Uncle, you know my knee isn't good since it was cut in the genocide. It gives me a lot of pain,' I replied.

'My knee isn't good either. Come on. Let's play.'

We were at a nice tennis court and he had brought along two racquets and some brand-new balls.

Half-heartedly I picked up the racquet and started playing with him. I was stiff and rusty but managed a passable game. Maman sat on the sidelines weeping.

'I never thought I'd see you playing again,' she said.

Part of me enjoyed playing again, but I wasn't ready to take such a big step back into the past. My old life flashed in front of me uncomfortably during the game. After half an hour I threw the racquet aside angrily. I was annoyed that I'd allowed myself to be persuaded into a game I didn't want to play.

My uncle bought me a beer. 'Leah, you can still make it,' he said. 'You have to stop being angry about the past.'

'That's easy to say, but not so easy to feel,' I replied.

My uncle kept saying that he wanted to take me back to the Hôtel des Mille Collines. But every time he mentioned the place I shook my head. 'Not today,' I kept saying. The hotel had been restored to its former status as a place for the wealthiest Rwandise and foreigners. As with the tennis, I finally gave in to my very persuasive uncle. He held my hand gently as we approached.

'Why do you not want to be there?' he asked softly. 'After all, it may have saved your life staying there.'

I shrugged. 'Too much pain, too many terrible memories. I know that some of those people I was crammed into the hotel with ended up dying.'

'Leah, it's OK. We'll just go inside for five minutes,' he said.

We went in and he bought me a glass of wine. The place had been redecorated but it didn't look so different from the way I remembered it.

'You don't need to talk about what happened here; we can talk about something else,' my uncle said. Everything that had happened there flashed before my eyes and I wasn't able to talk about anything at all.

That night I had terrible nightmares. These dreams were always more or less the same – bad people were chasing me and I couldn't escape fast enough so in my dreams I sprouted wings.

'She's not ready,' Maman said to my uncle. 'She will break through in her own time.'

'Why did we survive? So that we can suffer more?' I asked Maman. 'All our family can never be together again. We can't have our house, our cars or our cows back.'

'Bébé, don't talk like that. You have a lot of love to give, but first you must learn to love yourself again.' Maman was right about so many things. She could look at my soul and see my inner turmoil without me having to explain anything to her.

'But Maman, I find it so hard to trust people.'

'You have to remember the good people, Leah. Yes, people did terrible things during the genocide, but think also of the good ones. Like Mustapha, the lorry driver you told me about. You have to love everyone, Hutu and Tutsi. God left Rwanda when the genocide happened, but there are still good people here.

'It's easy to think about all the badness, but you have to reverse these negative thoughts and think about all the good people who helped you to survive.'

'I'll try, Maman, really I will. But it isn't easy.'

'I know, Bébé, I know.'

I heard from other Rwandise people that they had gone to see members of the Interahamwe in jail, to look into the eyes of the people who had killed their family members and vent their emotions. Church people had said to me that if I could find it in my heart to forgive the people who had killed members of my family it would help me to heal and move on. I did not particularly want to come face to face with my sisters' and Sans Souci's killers, but I was desperate to heal.

Maman knew the names of all four of the Hutus who had burst into the family home and killed my sisters and some of the servants, so I asked my uncle, who was well connected, to see if he could find these four men.

A lot of Hutus took their own lives after the killing spree and others escaped to different countries. My uncle reported back that he was only able to track down one of the four, who was in prison in Kigali. 'You can visit him any time you like, Bébé,' he said.

Maman didn't want to come with me. She had witnessed human beings she had known as perfectly likeable neighbours turn into beasts and kill some of her children, and the thought of facing any of them was too much for her.

I went to the prison with my uncle. The closer I got to the man who had killed so many members of my family, the more anger boiled inside me. I thought maybe I would jump on him, beat him with my fists, show him that just because he had had power once didn't mean that he had it now. I wanted to scream at him and tell him exactly how much pain his acts of brutality had caused to the rest of the family.

I was expecting to see a member of the Interahamwe like so many I had seen at the roadblocks, hacking limbs off people, eyes blazing with hatred and arrogance.

The man was brought into a bare room furnished only with an old table and a few chairs. He wasn't somebody I had known before the genocide and I froze when I saw him. Maman had told me that he was a well-educated man, a teacher. When he saw me he burst into tears before I could even open my mouth. Maybe when he saw my face he saw instead the faces of my sisters and brother, contorted with agony in the final moments of their lives. He looked nothing like so many of the Interahamwe I had seen during the genocide.

'I'm so sorry, so very, very sorry,' he wept. 'Why are you torturing me by coming here?'

'What do you mean, torturing *you*?' I said sharply. 'We are the ones who were tortured, and continue to be tortured by the terrible things you and the other members of the Interahamwe did.'

I looked into his wild, deranged eyes and could see that his mind was lost. He looked as if he had once been a handsome, strong man but now he was completely broken. As he sat hunched in his crisp, pink prison uniform I could see that he was a dead man living. I tried to imagine his life before, as a good person, a teacher, a helper of people. I could only conclude that some sort of mass spell had been put on people like him.

As he wept and ranted and pleaded for forgiveness something extraordinary happened. My anger evaporated and was replaced by feelings of sorrow, not for myself but for him. He was a small, pathetic, shrivelled creature, a decent human being so over-whelmed with remorse that he could barely drag one foot in front of the other any more.

The atmosphere in the room was so tense it was almost impossible to sit still on my chair and pretend to be composed. My uncle had a glacial look of calm on his face. I wondered what thoughts were rushing through his head.

'They told me if I didn't do it they would kill me,' he whimpered.

'The terrible thing with killing is that once you start it's hard to stop. I was in a trance and it actually felt good at the time to see the blood spurt and have the power over life and death. Things got to the point where I genuinely believed that you were all giant cockroaches. As you know, it is easy to kill cockroaches by stamping on them. But then I woke up and realised what I'd done.'

All I had wanted to do was to see his face. I had no plans to say anything much to him, I just wanted to see how he looked and felt. 'How did you kill my family?' I asked, my voice shaking so much I could barely get the words out.

'I didn't own a gun, so use your imagination how I killed them,' he said grimly. He continued weeping, but at the same time seemed keen to continue talking, to explain and perhaps absolve himself. 'After I did it I became somebody else. I know

I cannot bring your loved ones back, but believe me, I am in hell,' he said.

I could see that he was scared of neither jail nor death; his wish was only to die. It was impossible for him to live with himself any more.

'You know they forced me to kill my wife too. She was a Tutsi. No human can do that, I know that now.' He had forgotten that we were in the room with him and kept repeating over and over again, 'I killed them all. I killed them all.'

I had never seen anybody as tortured as this man who sat before me weeping uncontrollably. I looked at him and realised that a human being cannot do what he did. Something else had taken over, something Christianity would describe as the Devil. Demons can take hold of any one of us so easily, robbing us of our judgement and leaving us as weak and foolish as babies.

'I forgive you,' I said, standing up so that I could leave this small airless room full of death as soon as possible. 'You are a human being but you were not a human being then. I don't hate you for what you did. I hate those who gave the orders, the politicians who organised the genocide. They were not brain-washed the way you and so many others were. They understood exactly what they were doing.

'You know, I never believed all that stuff about hatred between Hutus and Tutsis. I never hated Hutus and I'm sure you never hated Tutsis. You and I are just two ordinary human beings who wished nothing bad to happen to anyone else. Both of us were victims, in different ways, of evil meddlers. Once again I say that I forgive you. Now you must try to make peace with yourself.'

I left the prison sobbing and shaking but at the same time feeling lighter than I had felt for years. I was beginning to make sense of the nature of evil and to understand how it could lodge itself in the souls of good people.

I had suffered great pain during and after the genocide but I knew that my pain would never be as great as his because I had no blood on my hands, and there is no greater pain than never being able to wash away the blood of others, which left an indelible stain inside the minds and bodies of the killers.

Many people came back to Rwanda after the genocide who had lived in exile for years or even decades. These people didn't live through the horror of the genocide and so, while they are appalled by it, they cannot fully understand it. I believe that the Rwandise people who experienced the genocide will never be able to fully move on. What they witnessed will haunt them for the rest of their lives.

That meeting was an important part of a process for me, a process I'm still going through, of trying to trust and to love again.

'That's the first time I have met a dead person who is still breathing and talking,' I said to my uncle as we left the jail.

'Bébé, you did very well in there; you were strong and brave. Now you must put these thoughts to the back of your mind and prepare for your trip to Ethiopia. I'm sure you will have a wonderful time. But before you start packing, you and I will go to a bar and get very drunk. It's time to stop thinking about all this.'

By the time I had downed my third glass of wine I had decided that my uncle was a very wise man.

When we tottered back to his house, Maman had cooked my favourite food of delicately spiced fish and spinach.

I told Maman briefly how the meeting had gone and how, to my amazement, I had ended up feeling sorry for the man who had slaughtered so many people that I loved.

Maman nodded. 'I know you didn't anticipate this, Bébé, but this is how I thought and hoped you would react.' She put her arms around me and hugged me tightly, her eyes moist with pain. She didn't want to know any more details about the man who had killed her children.

We both loved Ethiopia. The capital, Addis Ababa, was busy and lively. Ethiopia is famous for its amazing runners and early in the morning we could see many people sprinting barefoot along the path by the side of one of the main roads. Poverty was everywhere and children with sad, hungry eyes tapped on the windows of our taxi and tried to persuade us to buy the little packets of tissues they were selling.

We saw churches of many different Christian denominations. This seemed to be a country where religion was taken very seriously. But I observed that there were similar problems between Ethiopians and Eritreans as between Hutus and Tutsis.

Maman thrived on the trip. She reminded me of a flower gradually opening its petals towards the sun. I had bought her some new glasses from SpecSavers and she looked fantastic in them. We spoke little about Rwanda, determined to focus on the present and on being together. One thing Maman never discussed with me as long as she lived was the loss of Papa. Theirs had been an exceptional love, a perfect combination of passion, friendship and loyalty, and I think that even the mention of Papa's name was like a knife scraping across her soul, opening up a wound that could never heal.

We bought ourselves traditional white Ethiopian dresses and giggled as we paraded around in them in our hotel bedroom.

Maman was very contented. She loved eating *injera*, the traditional bread which is served with every meal, and seemed to feel at peace there. Ethiopia is famous for its coffee ceremonies and she enjoyed watching the rituals surrounding the drink she knew so well. Seeing Maman happy made my heart burst with joy.

She hadn't lost her love and concern for others. She spent much of our time in Addis visiting poor people. That was how she was when she had a lot of money, but I marvelled that now she was poor she still wanted to do that. 'Whatever you have you must share,' she said. I had lost count of how many times she had said those words to me during my childhood.

We discussed her returning to Zaire. It had changed its name to Democratic Republic of Congo and I wondered if she would be happier there than in Kampala.

'I don't think I could settle back there now, Bébé. So much has changed and it is unwise to try to bring back the past. But I would like to return for a visit. I want to go back to the villages I used to know so well and find out how all the women I used to teach to sew and read are getting on. They were all good, kind, straightforward people and I miss them very much.'

Maman and I had a wonderful time together in Ethiopia, shopping and chatting, relaxing and sightseeing. I felt closer than ever to her and wished that we could find a way to be together permanently. But her heart lay in Africa and mine in Europe. I had been away for a month and had missed Jean-Luc and Christian every minute. The trip had shown me that Rwanda was not a country I could live in again. England was my home and my heart leapt at the thought of going back there and being reunited with my husband and son.

When I landed at Heathrow, I knew I had finally stopped running.

EPILOGUE

Maman returned to eastern Congo at the end of 2004 and spent four months there. Her heart was broken when she saw how much things had changed.

The forests of eastern Congo had become dangerous places, where Interahamwe forced into exile after the genocide had made their homes. Different rebel factions fought with the Interahamwe, and the damage to the local population was huge. Rape was endemic.

Rwanda had managed to purge itself of its troublesome elements and the country was rebuilt in a relatively calm and peaceful atmosphere. But the problems had not been solved, simply hidden from view. Eastern Congo had never known this kind of problem before the genocide occurred, but now the population was exposed to an orgy of suffering.

'Leah, you need to work with these people who are going through such terrible experiences. It will help you to heal and to become strong. What is going on is horrific and few people understand the truth. You have a lot to give and a big heart. You will be able to give love to these people who need it so desperately,' Maman said. 'It's very important that you help Rwandise and Congolese to love each other again. You're in Europe, Leah; you can fix all of this.'

'Maman, I don't want to get involved. I have enough of my own problems to deal with and I don't think I'm strong enough to help these women. My life is in London with my son and my husband.'

'But you have to do something, Leah. You need to fight for peace. Believe me, it will not come by itself.'

She became obsessed with this issue and raised it every time we spoke on the phone.

But I kept pushing her pleas to the back of my mind. Her demand that I should help overwhelmed me and I had no idea how I, one woman living in Europe, could help ease the suffering of thousands in eastern Congo.

In June 2008 Maman became sick. She was diagnosed with heart and liver problems, although the doctors were not precise about exactly what her condition was. They urged me to come and see her as soon as possible:

'Leah, your mother's condition is very serious. I think it will help her to see you.'

Grief-stricken, I hurriedly booked a flight. I wasn't ready to let go of Maman, especially because I had lost so much time with her. I bought my ticket and sat on the plane cursing the fact that it was going so slowly. I thought back to my journey of a few years before; I had wanted the plane to hurry that time too, but for very different reasons. I closed my eyes and focused on Maman, willing her to get better. Suddenly I felt the connection between us cut off, as if someone had snipped the umbilical cord holding us together.

'No, no!' I screamed in the middle of the plane. 'Don't leave me, Maman.'

'What on earth is the matter?' asked one of the air hostesses, hurrying up to me.

'I'm on my way to see my mother who is sick. But I know she has just died. I have an overwhelming sense that she's left the world,' I said between sobs.

'Don't be silly,' said the air hostess kindly. 'I'm sure she isn't dead. Wait until we land and you might find the news is better than you think.'

The journey was interminable. I writhed in my cramped seat, desperate to get back on to solid ground.

A family friend called Elizabeth met me at the airport.

'I know Maman is dead,' I said flatly. I felt as if I had no tears left to cry.

'No, she's just weak,' she replied. But I knew she was dead and that Elizabeth was just trying to spare my feelings.

Alice, Vicki and Jean-Claude were still at the hospital and greeted me, sobbing. 'Maman tried to hang on for you,' said Jean-Claude. 'She turned her head whenever she heard footsteps in the ward, in case it was you.'

'She told us to tell you how much she loved you and that she knew you would be fine,' said Alice.

I felt too numb to think about the enormity of my loss. I couldn't bear to go to the morgue and see her lovely face stiff and dead. Instead I sprang into action.

'Come on, everyone. There's no time to stand around the hospital crying. There's so much work to do organising the funeral.'

I had the rest of my life to cry and grieve for my beloved Maman but now I had to stay calm and controlled to make sure that she had a magnificent funeral, an event where we could show what an incredible and deeply loved woman she was. I felt the same way I had when I was trying to get out of Rwanda, convinced that I had lost everybody I loved. I had tried to push those thoughts out of my head as I went into survival mode; now I was doing the same thing again.

I started running around to find Maman the best coffin and the best dress to be buried in. Still I couldn't look at her face. Apparently when she first died her face was contorted in pain but then her expression changed. People said it was because she knew I'd arrived.

I was so strong for the next ten days. I don't know how I managed it but I think her spirit crept inside me and sustained me.

I had always dreamed I would be able to save up enough money to buy Maman a lovely house, but I never managed it. Instead I was buying her a house to be buried in.

When I was a little girl I had found her wedding dress stored in a suitcase and she said, 'I want to be buried in it.'

'Oh, Maman, you're too big to fit into that now,' I'd replied.

I ordered a dress just like her wedding dress for her to be buried in.

The coffin was in the house for two days but still I could not look at Maman's face. People came to pay their respects and said how beautiful she looked. 'She looks so young, the way she did when she was twenty,' remarked one. Brigitte's children said she looked as if she was sleeping: 'She's been sleeping for a long time, it's time for her to wake up. Why is she sleeping in that box?'

We took her body to Kigali, where many family members were waiting for her. When we arrived there some of our relatives said that her wish had always been to be buried in eastern Congo where she had spent so many years of her life. I know she dreamed of peace between Rwanda and eastern Congo, a return to the way things had been when I was growing up. It was like some sort of pilgrimage, carrying Maman's body from Uganda to Rwanda to Congo, the three countries she had spent most of her life in, a kind of final farewell to the parts of the earth she had lived and breathed in during her fifty-nine years.

When we arrived in Goma I knew exactly where Maman would have wanted to be buried, a simple cemetery where some of her friends and neighbours already lay. I wanted her to be surrounded by people she had been close to in life.

It seemed that the whole of Goma had turned out to pay their respects. The cathedral was full to bursting. We were supposed to bury her at 2 p.m., but by the time people had finished paying tributes it was closer to 5 p.m.

I hadn't realised that she was not only a mother to all the children she carried in her womb, but to so many other people too. I had no idea how well known she was and how much she had done for people. Everyone called her 'the mother of many people' and cried, 'Maman, don't leave us. Who is going to teach us now?' So important was her passing that her death was announced on the local radio. The presenter referred to her as 'a mother of the town'.

At the funeral people talked of how she had funded the building of a community centre in Goma called Foyer Goma. They praised her for the expert way she delivered babies and told of how she taught women many things. Seeing how loved Maman had been by so many people blunted my grief. It was a great comfort to me.

I had converted to Buddhism and regularly chanted the words 'Nam-myoho-renge-kyo'. I had explained to Maman that I chanted that phrase when I was in pain or was feeling disillusioned, and taught her how to say the words. Elizabeth mentioned this phrase at the funeral in Goma. 'Your sister told me that these were the last words your *maman* uttered,' she said. When I heard that I was so happy.

They were about to close the coffin when I called out, 'Wait, wait!'

At last I was ready to look at Maman's face. I ran up to her coffin. She looked beautiful, smiling and at peace. In fact she didn't look dead at all, but just the way she looked when she was having a siesta. I didn't cry when I at last looked at her. I smiled with relief because now I had seen for myself that Maman was at peace.

My plan was to stay in our home in Goma for a while and then return to London. As I sat in the house the day after the funeral, tears rolling down my cheeks, I heard Maman's voice as clearly as if she was sitting by my side.

'It's time to stop moping around, Leah. Who on earth is that going to help? You need to go and do something to help those women now. What are you waiting for?'

The voice shook me out of my stupor. Once again I felt as if the fire of Maman's spirit burned inside me.

'Yes, Maman,' I replied silently. 'Now I know what I must do. I am ready.'

I slept well and rose early, fired with a new sense of purpose.

'I'm going to Bukavu,' I said decisively.

'You can't,' people gasped. 'You have to stay here for ten days to mourn.'

'I would rather go and do what Maman wanted me to, instead of staying in the house and feeling sad,' I replied.

Friends met me off the boat in Bukavu, thinking I had come to mourn Maman.

'I'm not staying. I'm going to Walungu tomorrow. I want to help the women in that area that Maman has been talking to me about for so long.'

I knew how dangerous those areas were because they were infested with rebels and nobody was doing anything to restrain them. But I believed Maman's spirit would guide and protect me.

I rose at 5 a.m. I had hired a car and drove by myself, taking only water with me. In the villages close to the town of Walungu I could see signs of normal life, women carrying heavy bundles of firewood on their heads and their backs and children skipping by their sides. Huge clouds of dust rose up from the pot-holed roads. It was how I imagined driving on the moon would be. Stretching off on both sides of the road was lush green vegetation, bushes and trees and planted crops of cassava.

But before I even reached the hospital I saw horror. Bodies were lying in the street. I thought all that had finished with the genocide and couldn't believe that the same thing was happening again. I found one woman whose stomach had been slashed open, exposing an infected womb.

'I'm going to die,' she moaned.

'No you're not, I'm going to put you in the car and take you to Walungu Hospital.'

The doctor laughed sadly when I arrived. 'How many people are you going to bring here? We can't even cope with the cases who fall through the door.'

I could see so many women lying around needing help and groaning with pain, but there was only one doctor at the hospital. When I asked what had happened the women whispered and croaked that they had been raped in very brutal ways by rebels. I knew that if that number of women reached the hospital, there would be so many more in the villages who were in need of help but who couldn't get to hospital.

I stocked up with supplies of soap and salt, which I stacked into the hired jeep. I had more energy than I had had for a long time. It was as if Maman was with me, giving me the strength to carry on.

I phoned a few old friends and asked them to join me. Four men who had been childhood friends agreed to go back to the villages with me. Now I felt more confident. 'OK, we'll take you but we're not going to go as far into the forests as you want to go because we want to come back alive. This area is very dangerous, Leah. We will call some people who can help and they can advise us which villages are safe to reach and which are not.'

There were many UN trucks in town and I couldn't understand why they did not reach the rural areas.

In African culture a man is stronger than a woman and has to protect his family, so the first thing the rebels were doing was killing the men to leave the women vulnerable. I walked into village after village where there were no men at all left. I was too appalled to speak. The women spoke cautiously to me at first, blaming the Congolese and Rwandan governments for letting the various rebel groups run riot in the area.

Day after day I returned to these villages. I sold my clothes and shoes to buy supplies for the women. I took photos, showed them to the chemist and begged him to donate paracetamol.

I was witnessing things that I hadn't expected to come across again in my lifetime. There were so many echoes of the genocide and I kept saying to myself, It's not true, it can't be happening again. Why do I have to see all this again?

The more villages I visited, the more the scale of the disaster hit me. Thousands of women had suffered the most appalling rapes, rapes with objects that had damaged their wombs beyond repair and left them mutilated for life. Women and girls had had their breasts chopped off, an act of barbarity designed to cause them maximum pain and shame.

They didn't understand what was happening to them and hadn't got to grips with the political and tribal roots of the conflict. All they knew was that their previously peaceful lives were being systematically destroyed. Before they had lived fairly contented lives, growing their crops, raising their children and living with their husbands. They knew little about the Rwandan genocide and didn't understand that they were pawns in a continuing power struggle. But for me it was a kind of *déjà vu*. I could see that just like me these women hoped that they were dreaming this hell.

At first they saw me as a rich, white woman because my skin was lighter than theirs and I came in a jeep. On the fourth day I started crying and said, 'I've been through the same things.' I hadn't been raped, but my body had been cut. I told them about running from men with machetes, about all the killing I had seen, about how my sisters and brother had been slaughtered in front of my mother. 'My lovely *maman* has died. I have only just finished burying her and my heart is grieving but she begged me to help and so I am here.'

When I had finished talking everything changed. The women looked at me as one of them. We all cried together, then we laughed together and talked.

'How come you look so nice, as if you have never had any problems?' asked one.

'I still have scars and I don't think I look so nice inside, but I've got a little boy. He has made me stronger and helped me to repair my life.'

A woman everyone called Madame was amongst the first to open up. She had been raped by soldiers and left for dead.

Suddenly everyone was queuing up to tell their story. My male friends were crying when they heard the women's accounts. 'Excuse us, it's not every man who is like that, you were attacked by animals.' They had never been to the villages before and it gave them another perspective on life. They showed a lot of compassion towards the women.

Over the next few weeks I returned daily. The most horrible stories tumbled out – females as young as one and as old as ninety had been raped. Girls and women were held captive in the forest by one rebel group or another for weeks, months or even years. So many of the women had been infected with HIV as a result of their multiple rapes, but they had no prospect of getting any treatment.

'What have we done to deserve this?' one of them said to me, wringing her hands, her eyes emptied by the terrible trauma she had suffered. I could not give her an answer.

I listened to hundreds of women and girls tell their stories. Although the stories were horrifying I was happy that at last I had found out what Maman had wanted me to do. Now I understood why she had been so insistent that I should help. I believe that Maman wanted me to see how precious my life was and to take nothing for granted. Even now I have times of feeling sorry for myself, but it doesn't last for long. I am at my happiest when I am working with these people. My job as a nurse was preparation for this. I could help the women to dress their wounds and could educate them about their own bodies and about birth control. I found myself talking like Maman. I told them that they were entitled to respect from men.

I decided to try to raise awareness back in London about what was going on. 'I'm going to film you and show your pictures around the world. I'm not rich but the only way I can help you is by exposing what is going on. I don't think the politicians here will act to help you unless a lot of pressure is put on them,' I said.

I sat on the plane home determined to do something. I knew that the films I had in my suitcase could change lives. I was horrified that things like this were still happening in the twenty-first century. While I was enjoying myself in Europe there was so much suffering elsewhere. I could wake up, put the kettle on to make myself a cup of tea, and choose my food. I realised how much I was taking for granted. I had always loved nice possessions but I was happily selling them now to raise money for the women. I could choose which doctor I wanted to see, whereas these women did not have access to any doctor. I hoped that if I brought the testimonies back to the UK, the place I now call my home, I could promote their cause and make a difference. And that doing this could help me move to the next stage of healing from my own pain.

The time spent with the suffering girls and women of eastern Congo was a confirmation of why I had survived. Now I understood why, although I'd had so many brushes with death, I had not died.

The last words I said to the women before I returned to England were 'I promise I will not forsake you. I will find a way to tell the world about your suffering. I will raise money to help you recover from all your pain, and I will be back.'

When I returned to England I passed my footage to the *Guardian* which published an article about the suffering of the women and girls of eastern Congo. I couldn't believe it when they put the story on their front page and made a film using my footage for their website.

After that it felt like the whole world was knocking on my door, asking me to talk about the suffering women of eastern Congo. I was filled with hope because so many people showed that they cared. I realised then that, however many obstacles there were, I had to keep going until the women could rebuild their damaged lives in a safe environment.

Politicians, journalists and human-rights organisations asked me to give talks about the plight of the girls and women. I talked about the links between what had happened in Rwanda in 1994 and what was happening now in eastern Congo and how we all had to stand together to prevent another genocide from taking place. Lots of people promised to do lots of things. No matter what problems we had in the world, people told me that these girls and women were in their prayers and in their thoughts. It felt good to have so much support behind me.

During a trip to see Maman in Uganda a couple of years before she died, I had visited eastern Congo and was appalled by the number of street children, many orphaned by the genocide, with no one to look after them and pay for them to go to school. I set up an organisation called Everything is a Benefit to try to support them. I sent £50 here and £20 there to a friend in eastern Congo and asked her to use it to help the street children. Whenever possible we sent money to pay for some of the children to go to school. After I returned from my 2008 trip I extended the organisation to also support the women and girls caught in the terrible crossfire of the rebels' war.

I found myself in touch with people from all over the world – Afghanistan, Ethiopia, Somalia – asking me for advice about how to deal with war trauma. I would like to help not only the women of eastern Congo but others who have suffered similar traumas. The circumstances are different but the suffering is always the same.

It has been very humbling to see those women dancing for me

in their land. Despite everything they can still feel joy. They have become my new extended family.

Living through the genocide changed me for ever. My carefree innocence and simple trust in other human beings has gone. But I do not hate everybody involved in the killing. I believe that human beings are weak and it is easy to make them follow a siren call if it is packaged in a tempting way. This cannot be said for the architects of the genocide though, educated men who were not brainwashed by radio stations or any of the other tools used. They were the puppet masters who pulled the strings of their foot-soldiers across Rwanda. They knew exactly what they were doing and what the consequences would be. For them I continue to feel the utmost loathing and contempt.

The genocide has left a terrible legacy in me but it also taught me about love. There are a few people to whom I owe so much. Habi, the reluctant member of the Interahamwe, is a true human being with a good heart. He deserves to have a good life. Mustapha the Tanzanian truck driver who helped us so much, Kamal and Piri too. Claire and Sarah, Pastor Levi, Aunty Mary and their friends, all the smugglers. Those people made me who I am today. They have helped me not only to survive but also to move forwards.

Sometimes when I think about the genocide I feel a physical pain in my scars, although they have long since healed. I know it is because the trauma from that terrible time lives inside me still. But I know that I am lucky to have survived and that I can make a contribution.

In the summer of 2009 I returned to eastern Congo. I was optimistic that, after all the media coverage and political concern in the previous few months, things would have changed for the better. But if anything things had got worse. Very few of the women had received any aid or support. Despite the biggest UN peacekeeping force in the world in the area, women and girls were still being raped on a daily basis.

Everyone I had seen a year before was still suffering, still quaking in their worn out flip-flops as they wondered when the rebels would next pay them a visit. What had I achieved by speaking out? The world had tutted and then turned away.

But I am determined to keep on sounding the alarm, and I know that as a survivor of the Rwandan genocide I am well placed to do this work. The region straddling eastern Congo and Rwanda is one of the most beautiful places on earth, with its lush green vegetation, abundant fruits and vegetables and dazzling flowers. But more human blood has sunk into its fertile earth than in almost any other region of the world. There is so much more to do.

I made a promise to those women and girls to help them recover and make them safe. I am determined not to rest until that promise has been fulfilled.